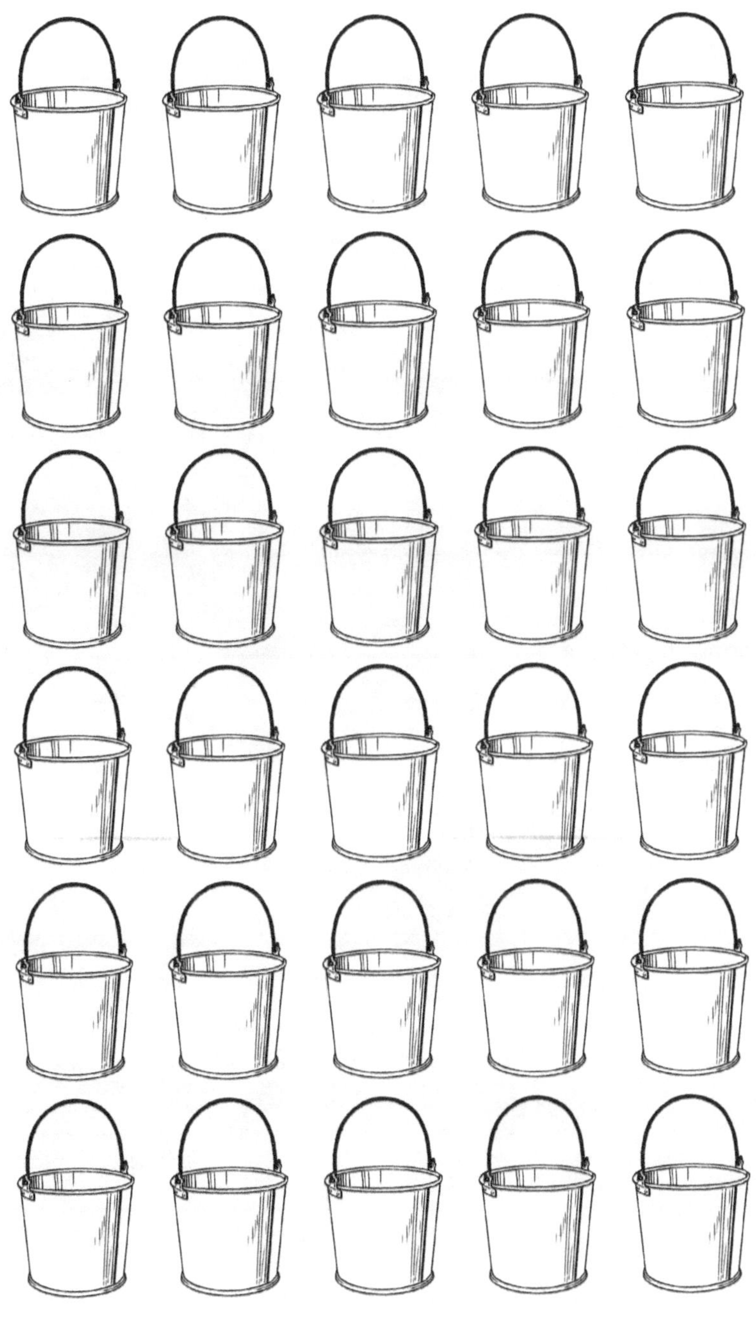

Pure Slush Books

October November December 2014

a Pure Slush compendium

First published January 2015
Edited by Matt Potter

Pure Slush Books
4 Warburton Street
Magill SA 5072
Australia
Email: edpureslush@live.com.au
Website: http://pureslush.webs.com
Visit the Pure Slush Store: http://pureslush.webs.com/store.htm

ISBN: 978-1-925101-48-5

Pure Slush proudly features (both online and in print) writers from all over the English-speaking world. Some speak and write English as their first language, while for others, it's their second or third or even fourth language. Naturally, across all versions of English, there are differences in punctuation and spelling, and even in meaning. These differences are reflected in the stories *Pure Slush* publishes, and it accounts for any differences in punctuation, spelling and meaning found within these pages.

stories by

Guilie Castillo Oriard

Townsend Walker

Derek Osborne

Gloria Garfunkel

John Wentworth Chapin

Lynn Beighley

Andrew Stancek

Rachel Ambrose

Gill Hoffs

Susan Tepper

Jessica McHugh

Shane Simmons

Michelle Elvy

Len Kuntz

Michael Webb

James Claffey

Gwendolyn Joyce Mintz

Stephen V. Ramey

Gay Degani

Sally−Anne Macomber

Mandy Nicol

Margaret Bingel

Darryl Price

Teresa Burns Gunther

Matt Potter

Gary Percesepe

Nathaniel Tower

Kimberlee Smith

Vanessa Weibler Paris

Joanne Jagoda

h. l. nelson

October

Illusions, Lethal Weapons, and a Can of Maggots

by Guilie Castillo Oriard

Wednesday, 1st October 2014

The sunlight, already sharp this early, makes the skin of Pélagie's back glow like honey lit from below. Luis has only minutes before she wakes. She's up every morning at six, no alarm. In a different time zone, would she wake up at six Curaçao time? Or does her body tune into the ebb and flow of day, like a radio? Maybe he'll find out if she comes to visit him in London.

She won't, though. What they have, beautiful – surprisingly, breathtakingly – as it is, is inherently momentary. (And isn't that what adds the edge?) He experiences childish relief every time she agrees to see him. Every kiss, every orgasm, every time he makes her smile; it's all just the unwinding of their clock.

He settles back on the pillow, sideways so that Pélagie's skin fills his view. He doesn't have to spell out the thought to feel the bite of regret: he's going to miss her. Another in the long list of reasons to despise Milena.

"Please don't stare at me." Pélagie's voice, rough with morning gravel, startles him.

"I'm not."

"Is that your hallmark? Staring your lovers awake?" Her foot finds his leg under the bedsheets, but he's faster now; before her toes find purchase, he swings both legs out into the air-conditioned chill and onto the covers.

Even through the Swiss duvet he's been carrying around since his time in Zurich, like some sort of security blanket, he feels a pinch on his calf hard enough he's sure it left a bruise. "Ow!"

"I barely touched you."

"Your feet should be registered as lethal weapons."

He rolls on top of her, pushes his weight into her, and for an instant he's giddy with the illusion of dominance. Illusion, yes. A charade. How can someone so tiny – he can encircle both her wrists with one hand, her feet look like a doll's when she shuffles around in his flip-flops, his shirts reach more than halfway down her thighs – be so strong?

Maybe it's not about strength, but about weakness. His, in fact. Take the sex: he's always watching himself, measuring out passion like a nineteenth-century chemist preparing laudanum tincture. Detachment is power to some; Luis knows better. Confidence breeds fearless love, fearless sex. He's no monument to poise, sexual or otherwise, but he's never been this self-conscious. It's not the slightness of her body; Pélagie's proven, both in and out of bed, to be anything but fragile. The risks of emotional investment feel closer to the mark, but that's stupid. He'll be gone before either of them get a chance to invest anything in anyone.

She lifts her head up from the pillow, reaching for a kiss. He pulls away. "I haven't brushed my teeth yet."

"Eww, morning breath." She grins, and the sunshine glows brighter. "Kiss me anyway."

Instead, he blurts it out. "Will you come visit me in London?"

"You're taking the job?" Her smile broadens. Should she be so happy he's leaving? No attachments, yes, but isn't unbridled joy at his departure carrying it a bit far?

And yet, whether for pride or masochism, or a quaint, uniquely masculine, mix of both, he can't stop himself. To avoid that bright smile while he rips the lid off this can of maggots, he bends to nuzzle her neck. "Will you visit?"

There's a heave from under him and then he's on his back with Pélagie pinning *him* down. "Who cares if I visit? You said London was, I quote, the best opportunity to get your career back on track." She bites his chin. "End quote."

"I care." He grasps her wrists; so slight, like twigs that might snap with one wrong move. Sometimes he wishes she were – no, not fatter, just … heftier. More substance. Like that adage for legal documents, *substance over form*; he loves her body, the grace in the very lack of substance, but the practical aspect of interacting with such a body makes him feel like the proverbial bull in a museum of Ming porcelain.

"Don't." The lightness of her kiss does nothing to soften the admonition. She bounds off the bed, away from him and his grip with nary an effort. "Can I take a quick shower?"

"Go ahead," he says. A shower together isn't on the table. She emphasized *quick*. And there's her refusal to talk visits.

Al is waiting downstairs. Loyal, unconditional Al, who rushes out to his favorite palm tree every morning, no matter how early, to let out a stream of decades–long pent–up pee.

He's going to miss the dog, too.

When Pélagie joins them, wet hair smelling of his shampoo – and what pleasure he derives from these small, small things – he's out on the porch with two mugs of coffee.

"I don't have time," she says, but she picks up a mug anyway. "Got to be at the vet at – damn, now. It's going to be a hell of a day. Six dogs scheduled for sterilization."

He sips at his coffee. "Plans for tonight?"

"Home, with the convalescing. Why?" Her fingernail clicks a Morse code of impatience on the coffee mug.

"There's something I want to ask. It's about Al," he adds, as incentive.

"The traveling stuff? You know I'm more than happy to help with –"

"I can't take him with me. London is – I'll be in a tiny apartment, working sixteen hours a day. It's no life for him. And the weather. He's used to the warmth, the sun ..."

Pélagie's face is blank. If he tapped it with a knuckle, it would most likely sound hollow and dry. Like a wooden mask. And her voice is flatter than the surface of a mirror when she says, "You're going to leave your dog behind."

"I have no choice. And it's the best thing for him. He'd –"

"Please. It's the best thing for *you*. Dogs are forever animals, Luis. They don't understand human circumstances changing. To him, this is abandonment. You rescued him from the street; surely you can see how horrible it is for him to go back to –"

"I'm not sending him back to the street!" Anger sparks to life at the base of his throat. He sits back, crosses a leg, breathes in. "That's why I'm asking you to take him in. He knows you, *I* know you. He couldn't be in better hands."

Pélagie's mug cracks down on the patio table. "I, personally, already have sixteen dogs. As an organization, we have over a hundred and forty dogs looking for a home. How is coming to me better for Al than having his own human?"

"But I can't take him! I didn't know I'd be leaving so soon!"

"You did, though. You were here for only a year or two. Sooner or later, you would've left. And still you took him in."

Luis leans forward. Why is she making this so difficult? "He needed a home, he –"

"He still does! You –" She turns her head away, takes a breath. "I love what I do, you know that. You also know how violently I hate that it's necessary. A perfect world, for me, would be a place where all of us animal rescuers were out of a job. But we're decades – centuries – away from that. Because of people like you. Damn you, Luis. I thought you were different."

He's shocked into silence. Not so much by the insult – he sees her point, of course he does, but his situation is different. She'd understand if she weren't so biased. No, his shock comes from having seen, just before she disappeared into the house, a glistening at the corner of her eye.

He is suspicious of women's tears. They may not be always manipulatively produced, but they always manipulate *him*. He didn't think Pélagie was like that.

I thought you were different, she'd said.

I thought you were different, too.

"I'll take Al." She's standing by the porch doors, dry-eyed, face again a mask.

"Thank you. I know it's –"

"I'll come get him over the weekend. I'll email you."

"Hey, no rush. I'm still here for another month. I'd like –"

"The sooner he begins to adapt to your absence, the better. For him. And it's all about what's best for the dog, right?"

"Come on, Pélagie –"

"Don't. Aside from whatever arrangements we need to discuss for Al, I'd really prefer to avoid all contact."

Al watches her leave from the edge of the porch. Inscrutable.

"Come here, boy."

The dog comes to Luis without hesitation, always eager, always trusting. *You have no clue what's about to happen, do you?* Luis strokes the silky ears.

Al gazes up at him, panting. Is he maybe a bit too close? A tad less relaxed? Is Luis just imagining what he wants to see?

Pélagie says dogs can smell anything. Emotions: fear, anxiety, anger. Intentions. Lies. *What does goodbye smell like, Al?*

La Ronde / Lana and Alexei

by Townsend Walker

Thursday, 2nd October 2014

Lana walks into her brother's office at Morgan Stanley. It's a different–looking Lana from the one Sal knew. Today, she's in a large man–styled shirt of pink silk, a billowing tan scarf, brown leggings and ballet slippers, trailing a long black coat on the floor. Her hair close to her head, a pixie look. "Dorogoy."

Alexei turns away from the three computer monitors he's tracking. "How did you get in here without me being called?"

"What do you want to know – how I did it this time, or how I'll do it the next?"

"Now that you're here, what do you want?"

He's impatient, doesn't want her here; she senses it. But that's not unusual. A little softening up. "Little brother, I've come to see how you are. You are looking well. Pink cheeks, no gray among the blond, only a little sag under those sky blue eyes of yours." She musses his hair and produces a faint smile on his face. "Why do you always think there is something I want from you?"

"Because you do." The promise of a smile disappears.

Lana ignores the reply and looks around the office, a frosted glass and steel box, decorated by someone not–her–brother: Warhol lithos, thin bronze maquettes, blown glass bowls; she walks over to the window. "Nice view." Looking at the Hudson River, she thinks about Sal. *Will his body ever turn up?*

"What's with the new look, Sveta?"

"Keeping in practice. And it's Lana, I keep telling you."

"I'll try to remember."

"What's this new position, Executive Director – Senior Liquidity Sales?"

"It would bore you."

She walks to his desk, leans across it. "Tell me, I might have to bore someone sometime."

"My group sells money market funds, treasuries and commercial paper to banks, hedge funds and universities."

"How do you make money?"

"Many of them trust us to quote a fair price, and we do. We make money when we don't."

"How often *don't* you?"

"You're not here to learn about investments, certainly."

"I need information for a job."

"A Dmitri job?"

She nods.

"Too bad about Dmitri, you know. He wasn't one of the smart ones in the family. Wrong father. Should have stayed in Leningrad." Alexei rolls his chair back and puts his feet up on the desk. A Dmitri job means only one thing in the family.

Lana notices that since she last saw him his shoes are custom, his pants are cashmere, and he's sporting a Patek Philippe. *Must have been a brilliant promotion. Perhaps he won't try to crowd me on this.* "I'm trying to identify a guy at Goldman, supposed to be important."

"Tell me." He twirls a pencil between his fingers and his thin lips spread into a Cheshire cat smile.

I was wrong. He wants a piece of the action. "I'd rather not."

"It's the only way I'm going to give you any information."

Lana strolls from one end of the office to the other, knocks books off the coffee table, swipes at a Giacometti, tumbling it to the floor. She fakes fury. "Do I ask for much? I do not. A little help now and then."

Alexei continues to sit quietly in his chair, a thin smile, as if bemused, seemingly unconcerned about the broken maquette, unnervingly (to her) accustomed to her tantrums. "A small cut of the action would be useful."

A girl (short red skirt, tight white blouse) bounces through the door, doesn't see Lana, goes around to Alexei's side of the desk, leans over him, a near kiss. "A message, lover."

She's eighteen-if-a-day. That look in his eyes, torn between propriety and infatuation.

His eyes flick from the girl, to Lana, and back signaling they're not alone. "Maria, this is my sister, Lana."

She stands up, brushes down her skirt, and smiles (*too broadly?*) at Lana. "Sorry to interrupt the family gathering. I'm out of here." She leaves with a little tail shake at the door, thinking Lana won't see.

"And she is?"

"My assistant, Maria Rodriguez."

"To the subject at hand. With all your money, you want a cut?"

"This business is sunshine and rain. The last guy in this position lasted a year. Plus, I have two kids and a wife ..."

She tosses one of the glass bowls in the air and catches it. "And two mistresses to support, or is it three now?"

"How do you know?"

"I know. How are Sally and the boys?"

Alexei slumps in his chair. "Christ, how did you find out?"

"You're careless, and I keep track of what's going on. Plus, you've never have been able to hide a secret, not even when we were little and played Verish' Ne Verish'."

He opens the bottom drawer of his desk. "Something to drink?"

"Not coffee."

"Vodka?"

"Scotch."

"So what do you want to know?"

Lena tells him about a guy at Goldman, probably a department head, maybe management committee, who has a price on his head. Put there by his wife. He beats her, plays around, sometimes loses the kids (two: boy and girl) when he takes them to the park. She has bits and pieces of a physical description.

"If I look around, what's it worth to you?"

"If you provide a full description, there's 25 in it for you. If you don't, I talk to Sally."

"You wouldn't."

"I would. In the trade, we call it doubling down on the stoolie's incentive."

"Tell me the bits you've heard."

"Prada aviators, tall, overweight, Italian suits." Lana twirls in front of his desk, arms, shirt and scarf filling the air and flings the office door open. "Ta, ta, little brother. You have my number."

Saying Goodbye

by Derek Osborne

Friday, 3rd October 2014

"So, never how we plan, eh old girl?"

A cold northeast wind is blowing, typical for October. *Gadabout* swings at her mooring. The family asked Max not to come out to the boat but they knew when to stop, his mind made up; there are things to do while he still can and this is certainly one. A look from Rebecca was all it took for them to let go, even la senora. Eddie drove him down to the pier, started the outboard, made sure his SAT phone was fully charged.

"I'm just checking," he told Max, seeing the look on his face, but Max didn't complain when he also got into the skiff and started the engine.

"Sorry you're out in the cold this year," he's now telling the boat, "maybe your new owner will get you south."

He has come to say goodbye. Standing in the cockpit, one hand on the wheel, the other grasping the canvas cover along the main boom for balance, he's exhausted just by the climb up the ladder. His strength changes constantly, one moment stable, only to find he cannot stand without help the next. His body is slowly, steadily giving out.

Max has never left anyone, anything, for that matter; he's always seen it through. It's been the hardest part of dealing with to no one in particular, the spaghetti can deaf in the bottom of the dustbin. Come to think of it, he still has his father's wedding suit in the upstairs, all wrapped in nice tissue paper and zipped inside a large plastic suit–carrier to keep the moths off. Wouldn't it give that old hoor, Mary Igoe, and her ilk the shock of their lives to see the Bird at the altar, waiting for the beautiful Melodie?

In the game of love, much like the art of fly–fishing, it's the patient man who gets the prize at the end of the day. The Bird knows his limitations when it comes to certain skills such as playing the fiddle, or singing an old ballad, but there's no better man to wait still as a corpse in the water for the trout to nibble at the fly. He'll set his flies out for Melodie, maybe a nice Copper John, or a Callebaetis Nymph to tantalize her and bring her to shore? Oh, no better man. No better man. The Bird rises out of his chair and shuffles his feet in small circles about the kitchen floor, dreaming of Melodie's warm body in his arms.

In the midst of his daydream, the Bird closes his eyes. Against the lids he traces the red lines filled with blood, a varied roadway of capillaries, blood filled with longing for Melodie, filled with longing for revenge, filled with a hatred for the nuns next door. Brides of Christ. He would make sure to leave all the windows of the upstairs open on his wedding night, so the pitiful creatures in their gunnysack habits would hear the piercing screams of the orgasms as he made love to Melodie over and over again in the darkness.

When he opens his eyes again the Bird is repulsed by his weakness, the sauce stained fingers and the spattered remnants of his meal on the wall. He is embarrassed by his pathetic desire for a woman who clearly has no need for him in her life. He imagines himself as pathetic as a sheep in a grassless meadow. Stupid animals, sheep. Stupid man, the Bird. No. There's to be no wedding. No marriage of true minds. Only the bitter cud of a cuckolded man's revenge. That's how he'll exact his portion from her, slowly, surely, and with the maximum pain to her soul.

The Last One Standing

by Gwendolyn Joyce Mintz

Friday, 17th October 2014

Aaron sends a text to both Phil and Mora. He's willing to meet – thinks they should meet – but whatever, he writes.

He's at Kelly's. If they don't want to meet here, it is Friday night after all, they can go somewhere else.

"Let me know," he says out loud, looking at the phone screen. "Call me. Text."

A male server passing by stops. "Do you need something?"

Aaron shakes his head and the guy moves on.

Aaron sets the phone aside. He lifts the glass of water he ordered when he first came in and takes a sip.

What do you want to do?

Mora had jetted out of the restaurant at the start of last month's meeting without taking a sip.

Aaron had followed her. At her car, watching her struggle to get her key in the lock, he'd reached out to console her but she'd pushed him away.

"You and your club!" she'd spat. Once in her vehicle, she'd sped away, her driving frantic, Aaron fearing for her life.

It's probably too late to rescue her. You shouldn't.

Back in the restaurant, Aaron had returned to his chair. He'd spun the flute slowly on the table and said, "She'd want us to be happy for her."

Phil hadn't replied.

Aaron had glanced over at him.

Phil had raised his good hand and swiped at his eyes with the back of his hand.

"How're you feeling," Aaron had asked.

"Dead," Phil had replied. He'd chuckled. "Crazy, huh? 'Cause that's what we wanted and now it somehow feels all wrong." He'd picked up the champagne flute, however. "I'll be a good sport though. For her." After downing the drink, he'd asked Aaron to take him home.

He's been in hiding ever since.

At least that's what Aaron hopes.

He sighs. He's about to call it a night when there's a text message alert.

I'm outside, it reads.

Aaron stands, digs in his pocket then drops a few bills on the table. He wanders the parking lot until he finds Mora leaning against the door on the driver's side. Her right arm is tight around her waist as she smokes, the cigarette in her left hand.

She turns at the sound of approaching feet then turns away.

Aaron shoves his hands into his front pockets, shuffles.

Mora had called into work as many days as she could without losing her job. If the two of them were scheduled for the same shift, she had avoided him.

"You brought Diane to me," he says.

Mora takes one last drag from the cigarette then drops the butt and scrunches it with the toe of her shoe.

She crosses both arms and sighs.

Aaron wants to console her but he also wants her to toughen up. "Nobody held a gun to her head."

It's a few moments before Mora replies, "She wouldn't have liked that. Too messy."

Aaron's wry smile disappears as quickly as it came. "We continue on," he says.

Mora laughs. "Yep." She fumbles in her jacket pocket for her package of cigarettes. As she works to light another, she says, "One day she was talking about killing herself and I asked what I'd do when she was gone. Diane told me to get my 'Mick' on." She took a deep breath.

She jerks her head toward the restaurant. "Is Phil there?"

Aaron shakes his head. "Haven't seen him since last month's meeting." He runs his foot along the gravel on the lot.

"Well, he was alive on the 23rd, if that's any consolation." Mora blows smoke into the dark night.

"The 23rd?"

"The day of Diane's funeral. He was there."

"You went?"

"Yeah. Screw those rules."

Aaron drops his head. He'd dressed, then had changed his mind –

"You know you will be the last one standing," he says.

Mora nods with a slow, determined motion. "You know when I was a kid, my grandmother used to tease me when I'd play with a jack–in–the–box she had. *You jump even though you've been cranking the thing*, she'd say. Even when I knew it was coming that never stopped me from being surprised."

The Death of Mystery

by Stephen V. Ramey

Saturday, 18th October 2014

12:01 AM

Mystery is dying. Anne told me earlier that we should have her put down before our vet closed for the weekend, but I couldn't do that. I've never connected with an animal the way I connect with this cat. After eighteen years, we know each other's signals. I can walk up to my recliner, point, and she'll move to one side so that I can sit with her. It works the other way too. She'll hop up – usually when I'm busy on the laptop – meow once, and stare at the gap between me and the armrest until I squeeze to one side. Then she'll snuggle in, purring like mad.

God, I love this cat.

She's settled in beside me now, forelegs toward the back of the chair. There's no purring tonight. Her eyes are clear, her breathing steady, but I saw her try to walk earlier, listing to the side, barely coherent. Anne was right. But not about putting Mystery down. Killing Mystery. Never that.

Mystery is different. She always has been. She'll tell me when the time has come.

Eighteen years ago we had just moved to a college town in Indiana. I was managing an office while Anne pursued a graduate degree. It was a trying time for us. We rented a house next to a farm, and an old barn stood at the northeast corner of our property. Mostly it was no problem, but sometimes we'd hear machinery, or smell fertilizer.

One morning, as I was getting into the car for work, I heard a racket I had not heard before. Savage growls, a yowl, and then a steady yapping that would not let up. It was coming from the barn, and that hollow shell amplified everything.

I went to check it out.

12:08

Mystery's sides move out and in, not heaving but breathing steadily. Blink, those golden eyes shutter. She licks her lips.

"I'm here," I whisper, and I stroke her head. She doesn't acknowledge me, but I know that she knows. She could have died while I was on my crazy walkabout, but she waited. She knew I would return.

The yapping did not let up as I reached the front of the barn. I wedged through a gap between the doors. The interior smelled of hay and motor oil. A tractor loomed.

A Rottweiler was snapping on the other side. I leaned down and watched it through the gap below the undercarriage. It lunged, yapped, jumped.

"What's the matter, boy?" I edged around the tractor.

All of a sudden, Mystery rolls onto her back and paws at the air, some sort of seizure. Her tongue lolls, and for a moment I am in the blackest place. My eyes sting. My chest squeezes. *God help her*, I think. I don't believe in gods, but if there is one this is the time to convince me. I don't know what to do.

She rolls back, sighs, and resumes her steady breathing. She blinks. *Is that the best you have? I'm not going to make it easy.* I stroke her head, tell her how proud I am to be her buddy, how lonely it will be without her. Without Mystery. The words echo from places I have hidden from for so long.

A cat's body lay torn across the straw, black intestine, head hanging by a thread, eyes glazed.

"Oh, God." I dropped to my knees. The dog came to me, tail wagging. "No," I said. "Bad ... bad dog." I smelled blood on its breath, fresh–tilled earth, shit.

12:22

I'm suddenly all over myself with grief and second thoughts. "I should have listened to Anne. I'm so sorry, I never meant you to suffer." And Mystery gives me this annoyed look: *Get a grip.* I know it's me attributing emotion, but I can't help that. Out and in, out and in, she breathes.

I counted three kittens, three tiny bodies wadded up like rags against the darker sludge of the mother cat. The dog licked a scratch on its nose and whimpered.

12:44

Another seizure. This one lasts longer. I focus on that pink nose, those round eyes squeezed tight. I wish I could take her place. Powerless, I cup my hand near her face. The thrashing subsides. She steadies, rolls back, breathes. A ragged smile escapes me. *My little engine that could.*

There, huddled on the tractor tire was a kitten, gray fur bristled like a powder puff. I stood, and the dog stretched up beside me onto the top of the tire rim. The cat hissed, but did not recoil. There was no fear in those eyes, no quit. Kill me, but I will not go easily.

12:57

Mystery shifts. I twist to make room until I'm leaning on my side, butt pressed to the opposite armrest. She closes her eyes. I stroke her from her head down to her tail, and she leans into me. Sadness hangs in the air. I want to stop inhaling.

"It's okay," I said. "I'm here to help you, little buddy." I reached for the kitten, and I could feel instinct urging her to flee. Instead, she let me scoop her onto my palm.

The dog jumped. I kicked it hard. It lunged. I kicked again.

1:03

She can't get comfortable. She doesn't seem to be in pain, but won't lie still. "Kitty, kitty," I murmur. "You're the best buddy I ever had, you know that, right?" The sound of my voice calms her. She settles.

"Rory, get over here." The barn door opened wider, and our neighbor stepped through in his Workman jeans and leather boots. "Rory!" The dog dropped down and pattered to its owner.

"That your animal?" He nodded at the mess.

"No," I said. "I heard them fighting."

I can only imagine the terror of witnessing my mother torn to shreds, my brothers and sisters tossed like ragdolls. That memory must have lived inside Mystery all these years, and yet she never shied from people or anything else. Always social, demanding, one of the family from the start.

"Do you want it to be over?" *Aspirin?* I watch her breathe. She won't give up. That's partly why we bonded, me dealing with constant rejection and uncertainty, her always so sure of herself. She won't give up, and I won't give up on her.

"Just as well," the neighbor said. "I don't cotton to barn cats." He nodded at my hands. "That one hurt?"

"I don't think so. It was on the tire."

1:18

A third seizure hits. Sobs wrack my chest, great heaving shudders. Will this never end? Then I think of what the end will mean, and take the wish back.

A sliver of light shines through the curtains. I think of Mystery lounging on the deck, leaving chipmunks – sometimes one a day – on our porch back in Indiana. She always loved to be outside.

Carefully, I scoop her up. Cradling her as gently as I can, I carry her to the sliding glass door, and open it with my elbow. Cold air rushes in. It's chilly tonight; frost by morning.

We sit on a lawn chair, my shoulders hunched against the cold. The night is clear. A crescent moon hangs in the sky.

Mystery stirs. I feel tension draining from her as her eyes shift from the apple tree to the garage to the stars. She's grateful, I think. I hope.

My body shudders through a combination of cold and grief. "I'm with you," I say. "As long as you need me, I'm here." I stroke her head. We watch the moon rise, so slow you cannot see it, so fast it hurts to imagine.

The neighbor gave a low whistle. "That's quite a climb."

"Yeah, I don't know how she made it."

1:43

I'm shivering steadily now. "It's too cold." I stand, holding her close, and step toward the doorway. A whimper from Mystery stops me. I return to the chair and sit.

1:59

I can barely keep my eyes open. "I'm sorry, buddy, but we have to go in." I carry her to the door, wondering if it's the right thing to do. I want her to be warm, but maybe the cool feels good to her fevered senses.

We navigate to the recliner and I sit carefully, Mystery stretched across my stomach. I cover her lower half with a blanket, and kick up the stand. “You and me, buddy,” I say, and I pet her, one long stroke after another along her side. She blinks and focuses on my face.

She sighs and lowers her head onto my chest. *It’s time. I trust you.* And it’s as if a clapper has struck my heart. A feeling reverberates: three parts sadness, a tinge of rage, one part euphoria. In that shining instant, my life comes clear, the struggles, the sadness, sprinkles of joy. What was never enough, suddenly is. Mystery hasn’t given up – she never will – but it’s up to me now. That I deserve her trust after all I have done and not done, makes me happy in a way I have never been.

2:43

I jerk awake. For a second or two, I’m disoriented, but it doesn’t last. Mystery remains stretched over my torso, my hand cupped across her stomach. *Is it over?* I hope so, and then I don’t. Her eyes are fixed on my face. The resistance in her joints tells me she is dead.

When the sobs are done, when my body has finished its convulsing, I curl Mystery into my arm and take her to her favorite box lid in the kitchen. With my bare foot, I nudge it closer to the sliding glass, and lay her inside. I find a towel and drape it over her, leaving her face exposed, eyes open onto the moonlit deck.

She looks at peace.

2:52

I head upstairs. Treads creak beneath my feet. I feel gutted, drained of emotion. I may never smile again.

Anne stands at the rail overlooking the stairs. The whites of her eyes reflect the nightlight.

I nod. "She's gone."

I expect Anne to nod back and return to bed, but she doesn't. She steps onto the stairs. We meet on the landing halfway up.

"I'm sorry," she says. Her cheeks are slick. Whatever passive–aggressive reply I might have said dies in my throat.

"Me too." My arms fold around her. Her cheek settles against my chest. We cry together. Our tears fall.

"It's a mystery," the neighbor said eighteen years ago.

"What is?" I asked.

"Life."

Devil Wind

by Gay Degani

Sunday, 19th October 2014

It happens every October in California, hot Santa Ana winds whip through the Old Road, stripping leaves from oaks, sucking up moisture. The devil stokes his furnace, and heat rises from the ground.

Inside Gus's bungalow, squeals and guffaws blare, his TV on *The View*, but he stares out the window instead, Gracie on his lap, his mind wandering from his aching hip to the naked branches outside, to his son's homelessness and back to the throb in his hip. He didn't break it in the fall he took a couple of months before, but climbing up from the creek is painful, his walks with the dog now confined to sidewalks. The air–conditioner drones on.

Next door, Ian is sprawled on his bathroom floor, having spent most of the previous night with old high school friends – drugs and drinking or just drinking, he won't remember – in a state of semi–consciousness, feeling useless. He sees the word, each individual letter, as if stamped on the back of his bathroom door. He sees no other door.

Across the courtyard, Mrs. Renke's bungalow is coffin–dry, empty five months now, her belongings collected by son and granddaughter, the left–overs donated to the Salvation Army. The few boxes stacked in the dining area belong to Jamie for when she returns with her two small children. Sybil won't rebuild their bungalow crushed by the old oak in January so they will have Mrs. Renke's.

Sybil scuffs through her own cottage, muttering, "I don't feel like myself. I don't know what's wrong with me." She shakes her head as she moves through her darkened living room into the brightness of the kitchen. She blinks and turns back into the shadows. She feels old, older than she's ever felt before. She stops at the window and stares into the courtyard. It's too much. Too much.

Back to the bedroom, she sprawls across the bed. So tired.

A knock on the front door rouses her. She hadn't realized she'd fallen asleep. The knock comes again. Louder. "Sybil?"

It's Gus and Gracie.

She doesn't want to talk to Gus, but the landlady part of her – what if it's a gas leak? – forces herself up and pads to the front, retying the sash of her silky robe. The outdoor heat hits her when she opens the door, the wind quiet for the moment. The bitter scent of smoke drifts in. Must be a fire in the hills nearby.

He droops on the porch, sweat trickling down his face, his little dog in his arms. "You okay?" he asks, poking his wrinkled face toward Sybil, squinting, his breathing hard.

"What can I do for you, Gus?" She holds onto the door, tries to keep annoyance out of her voice.

"Mars could fix your sprinklers. He could use the work."

She eyes the old man. Knows the two of them don't get along. "Where's he staying?"

Gus's sigh is deep. "Don't know. Maybe down at Union Station. That Rita kicked him out after what he did to her son. He says he's working when he can, but I don't know."

Wearily she steps away from the door and says, "Come in, Gus. I'll make us some ice tea."

"I don't like ice tea much."

"Come in anyway." This time she lets herself sound impatient. She watches him shuffle in and doesn't mean to, but slams the door. "That's okay with you if he's living at a shelter?"

"He's done it before."

"Yet you're over here finding him work."

"Work's one thing. Charity's another," the old man's voice rises. "I don't want him living with me."

"Sit down, Gus. You're scaring your dog." This isn't true, but it has the right effect on Gus. The old man puts the dog on the couch and lowers himself down next to her.

The lethargy she's felt all day dissipates a little as Sybil opens the shades. She glances through the glass into the courtyard and sees that the sprinklers must not be working. Odd she hasn't noticed. Ever since the young girl on her horse found the body down by the creek, Sybil has felt unsettled. For the girl, of course, only fifteen, struggling to control the animal after he caught the scent of death and when she finally reined him in and looked back, she saw the body.

"I just don't know, Sybil. Just don't know anymore."

She swipes her daily paper off an armchair and sits down, puts her feet up on the footrest. "Why couldn't he live with you? You have two bedrooms over there."

"He's a grown man."

"So what?"

"The police think he killed that woman."

"No they don't. If they did, he'd be in jail and not out on the streets."

"He's been in jail before."

"For murder?"

"No, nothing like that."

"Having him stay with you would help out with the rent. Mars can pay his share with work, and you can pay half of what you do now." Sybil could offer Mars the empty bungalow, but then, he's not her responsibility. And besides, it's for Jamie and the kids when they come back.

"No. I've earned my peace."

Sybil shakes her head. If she'd had children ... but she doesn't let herself consider that thought. She presses her fingers to her forehead and rubs hard. They sit in silence until she asks, "Have you seen the husband around, the doctor?"

"Yeah. He seems to be getting along. You saw he's selling the house?"

"Ian told me. Didn't give the listing to him or his mother, though. Rita blames Ian for not jumping on it right away."

Gracie leaps down and begins to sniff the carpet. Sybil smiles. She should have gotten herself a dog a long time ago or at least a cat. She'd had the jay though, the blue jay who sat on the railing of her porch every day for what, years it seemed. She misses the bird. She frowns and looks up at Gus, saying briskly, "How about some ice water? For you and the dog?"

"Water's good," he says.

When Sybil returns from the kitchen, she carries a tall glass and a small plastic bowl. Man and dog drink gratefully.

"It was a nice funeral," she says, sitting again in the arm chair. "You should've gone with me. For the husband's sake. His name was Sam, right? Hers, Charmaine."

"I don't like funerals and I barely knew those people."

"But they're neighbors. I'm not sure he'll ever recover."

"He'll be fine. We all get fine after a while."

"But she was murdered." Sybil hesitates, then whispers, "You don't think he did it?"

Gus shrugs. "Who knows anymore?"

The words resonate, who knows. Indeed. At first when she'd heard there was a body in the Arroyo, she thought of Jamie who'd disappeared the night of the big wind storm in January. She's always feared something had happened to her. But this is different. Sybil has told herself Jamie is safe, but no word has come to her from the woman, none at all in the last nine months, and she can't shake her sense of foreboding. They hadn't been close, really, though Sybil babysat the kids, yet she felt – still feels – something like motherliness toward the young woman with the abusive husband. She'd run away, of course, taking advantage of the chaos caused by the storm to cover her trail. Sybil shouldn't have expected her to keep in touch. And yes, she has to admit to herself, she'd felt relief it was Charmaine Martin, not Jamie, who'd been found murdered down by the creek.

Gus and Sybil sit for a while longer, not talking, the heavy day pressing down.

Finally Sybil leans toward Gus. "How do you reach Mars? Does he have a phone?"

"He comes for Mac–and–cheese every once in a while."

Sybil bites her tongue. If she had the energy, she'd take the old fart by the shoulders and tell him to take care of his son. Instead, she says, "Tell him I need him to do some more work when he comes."

"If he shows up."

She shakes her head.

Then Gracie barks.

Sybil stands up and hurries to the window, peeks out. A man and a woman stride through the courtyard toward her bungalow. They're almost to the porch before she recognizes them as the two detectives who had spoken to her about Charmaine's disappearance. She'd mentioned Jamie to them, told them how she too had disappeared. She reaches for the door handle, so near to the air conditioner, it's icy cold.

Swapsies

by Sally–Anne Macomber

Monday, 20th October 2014

To: Milton Flaxmill, Red Cow Publishing
From: Trudy Polaris
Date: October 20, 2014 10:28 a.m.
Re: A Cheery Tune

Milton! Milton! Milton!

Remember me, the woman who sent you *Nuclear Fission in The Pyrénées*?

Have you heard anything more about my nomination for The Nobel Prize for *Nuclear Fission in The Pyrénéees*? The Nobel Committee has been surprisingly silent this year, so the Nobel–snoops are saying, and given the sad lack of communication here in the Tyrol – I mean, to find out I'd been nominated to be nominated, I was forced to use tin cans with some string tied between them, for God's sake! – I was just wondering if you'd heard the magic words *Nuclear Fission in The Pyrénéeas* mentioned in a warm and glowing way recently?

And that designer dress for the award–bestowing ceremony in Oslo in early December isn't getting made any quicker while I wait!

On a different note from *Nuclear Fission in The Pyrénéyas*, the Sanchez Brothers, Guillermo and Geronimo, are sitting in the kitchen of our Tyrolean hideaway, going over the projected numbers with my husband for the made–for–TV adaptation they are planning of my musical *!Sillas¡ !Sillas¡ !Sillas¡* (which is *Chairs! Chairs! Chairs!* in español). The Sangrias (as I like to call them, though I also call them Señor Jim and Señor Jerry when they're not looking) heard about *Nuclear Fission in The Pyrénayas* through the award–season grapevine and their ears pricked up. Cut to a few days later and they heard on the musical theatre grapevine about *Sillas¡ !Sillas¡ !Sillas¡* (which is *Chairs! Chairs! Chairs!* in español) and they got even more excited and caught the next plane here to the Tyrol (from Miami, direct! So it's probably possible to do the same from Boston, Milton) to negotiate with me personally.

Maybe they can bring *Nuclear Fission in The Pyrélayas* to the small screen too because they are the top telenovela producers on Miami Beach. And the Sangrias are talking big smackers!

So obviously, my writer's fee for *Nuclear Fission in The Pyralayas* will need to be discussed anew.

Nuclear Fission in The Pymalayas

I will be involved in casting *Sillas¡ !Sillas¡ !Sillas¡* (which is *Chairs! Chairs! Chairs!* in español) and I am having written into the contract that *Nuclear Fission in The Pimalayas* will be mentioned in any press that is done for the production. So it's all very exciting!

So just how is the editing going on *Nuclear Fission in The Himalayas*?

See you on the red carpet!

Trudy

To: Leonard Strauss Jr., Red Cow Publishing
From: Trudy Polaris
Date: October 20, 2014 10:36 a.m.
Re: Please pay Milton a visit

Dear Herr Strauss Jr.,

Even though I have still not heard from you, could you do a favour for me? Could you go upstairs and check on Milton Flaxmill?

I just sent him an email. I am desperate to change the title and setting of my book to *Nuclear Fission in The Himalayas* before they give me my Nobel Prize, so the rhythm of the language in the email is designed to lull him into a stupor and make him adore the name and setting change.

It's a complex process and too difficult to describe in an email – perhaps I could describe it when you next visit Frau Erdbeeren here in Tirol? – but I just need to know if it has worked. A good sign would be his eyes are popping out of his head, he's staring into space, and his chin is wet with saliva.

Frau Trudi von Polarissen, Nobel nominee nominee

To: 'Boy' Polaris
From: Trudy Polaris
Date: September 20, 2014 11:48 p.m.
Re: Re: starving

The best way to boil an egg is in water. It's sceince!

Stop being so demanding!

Mother

Revelation
by Mandy Nicol

Tuesday, 21st October 2014

For the first time in years the family is together, sitting around the dining table drinking coffee. Though Anthony calls his *a cup of Joe.*

Anthony's home from New York.

Celeste picked him up from the airport and drove him here on Sunday night. I'd forgotten how tall he is, and how his hair is as red as mine. Celeste hasn't been red–haired since she was sixteen. She's currently a brunette. Last time I saw her it was honey blonde, or eggplant. One or the other.

Anthony's been zonked out with jetlag until this morning, snoring loud enough to be heard in every room of the house. He's now wide awake and ready to announce his grand plan.

Normally Celeste would have scooted back to Melbourne as soon as her car was unpacked. She must be desperate to find out what he's up to. Either that or they're in cahoots. They did have three hours alone together in the car. I look sideways at her but she's not wearing that smug I–have–a–secret smirk of hers.

But Mum is wearing a smirk. And her good black dress, the linen one I made for her with the scooped neck and long sleeves. She looks a bit like the Mona Lisa except her hair is grey and she has a Pomeranian on her lap. But Mum's smirking because she's glad Anthony's home, not because she knows anything about his plans.

Peregrine likes Anthony. He's lying on the floor beside his chair, watching him and wagging his tail. Traitor.

Anthony taps on the screen of his mobile phone then pushes it to the middle of the table. "There you go," he says with a flourish of his right hand.

We all lean forward.

There's a photo of a tree.

We look at Anthony.

"It's an olive tree," he says.

"You want to grow olive trees?" asks Mum.

"You want to be a farmer?" I ask.

"You came back from America for that?" asks Celeste.

"Yes, I want to grow olive trees. But not just olive trees, look …" He swipes at the phone again and again. "… Oats, barley, lentils, eggs, prime lambs. Diversity, that's the key, that and biodynamic farming. I want to change the way this farm works. And I want to run it myself."

He leans back in his chair, crosses his arms and beams at us.

"Are you sure about this?" asks Mum. "You hated anything to do with the farm when you were a boy. Dad had to haul you out by your ears when he needed help with the fencing."

Celeste snorts.

I snort.

Mum gazes at Anthony, eyes wide, waiting for an answer.

"Yeah well that was then, I feel different now." There's an echo of teenage Anthony in his voice. He tilts his head and juts his chin. "I need to do something that … something that actually *means* something." He looks around the table at each of us. "I've done my research and this can work. Really work."

He points a finger at me. "Nadia, you're a part of this. You can look after the free range chooks and do the office work. You know, the mundane day to day stuff, you'll be good at that."

I glare at him. "What about my sewing?"

"God, you won't need to do that, not when this takes off."

"But I like sewing."

"Well, you can fit it in somehow, I suppose, if you like it."

"Gee, thanks."

He ignores the sarcasm, if he noticed, and turns to Celeste. "Now you," he says. "You're a problem. I can't see how to get you involved unless you and Scott want to relocate."

Celeste stops scowling to say, "For fuck's sake Anthony – sorry Mum – of course we're not moving up here. And where's the money coming from to set this up? You can't be that rich. Are you having some sort of breakdown?"

Mum gasps.

I smile.

Anthony shakes his head. "Ok, ok, I know this is out of the blue. I'll give you time to think it over, let it sink in for a bit. We'll talk again after lunch. By the way, what is for lunch? I'm starving."

The three of them turn their eyes on me.

I shrug my shoulders.

"I have no idea," I say.

Max is smiling. Andi notices.

"What are you smiling at?"

She'll be fine, Andi. You can go be with her if you want. I'll just lie here and listen.

"How is everyone?" Pam says, entering the room. She was upstairs taking a nap. She sees the kids have all gathered in the hall, struggling to get a view.

"Get them out!" la senora snaps. "Anja, have you called the doctor?"

"They're getting him," she hears Anja yell from in the kitchen.

Rebecca looks over at Max. A rare flood of sunlight filters in through the French doors that line the harbor side of the house. The room is radiant. They have set Max up in what was the living room. Rebecca is still on the porch. They're getting her settled onto the bed. She glances over at Andi and then back to Max. Andi presses her hands together by the side of her head. He's sleeping. Rebecca smiles at the curious children. They'll remember this day. Right then the first of the contractions come.

"Whoa!" Rebecca says, catching her breath.

"You are already dilating. This child is in a hurry," la senora says. "Anja, where is that doctor?"

"He's on his way," comes the voice again.

"Aye, cunjo," Rebecca groans when the next contraction comes.

You'll be fine, Becca, you'll be fine. Won't she, Mags? Why don't you go over and take a peek? We're old pros at this, aren't we? Kind of glad I'm not over there. Remember Mike and Marsha when Sam was born? She jacked him right off the floor and screamed, 'You did this to me!' Don't think I've ever laughed so hard in my life. Yeah, I remember you didn't share my humor. But Becca's strong, she'll be fine, won't she? Why don't you take a look?

"Dad, are you trying to say something? It's Andi, I'm right here."

She's been watching his face, lips parting as if to speak, then going back to that same hint of a smile. He seems peaceful enough. Through the doors leading out to the porch, across the gray empty harbor, she can see the flashing red lights of the ambulance winding its way through the village. They've all been so helpful, everyone, people showing up with covered dishes, even Betty, the neighbor, who is probably a billionaire from selling balloons and party favors out of her fifteen hundred stores, who's been coming once a week to disinfect the kitchen and rooms where Rebecca and Max sleep … everyone. "I started out cleaning floors," she said that first day. "I still clean my own house." *Gadabout* sits at her mooring, alone, the docks dismantled, only the orange Coast Guard cutter across the way for company, her bow facing the house as if she, too, is waiting. A potential buyer is supposed to come out this Friday. They haven't told Max.

Breathe Becca, breathe into it. Bend to it. How's she doin' Mags? Talk to her. Go and whisper, tell her I'm still here, tell her I'm not leaving, not yet.

Max can hear the siren coming down the road. His old friend, Tommy, has entered the room. He's standing now at the foot of the bed. "Tom," Max whispers. Andi leans down.

"What did you say?"

"Tommy's here."

Max struggles to open his eyes.

"Tom? You mean Uncle Tommy?"

"What's he saying?" Rebecca calls from the other room. She can see Andi leaning over the bed.

"I'm not sure. I think he's hallucinating."

Tommy's here, Andi, he's right there at the foot of the bed. Your Mom is here too. Tell her Mags, tell her you're here.

"Daddy, Tommy's not here."

But he is, hun.

The doctor walks in with a nurse, two paramedics stand out in the hall. Rebecca likes him, he looks like a doctor, small and thin, balding on top, wire rim glasses, nice Jewish face. "Who called Central Casting?" she says as he enters. It's been their little joke.

"Oh, I forgot my cap," the nurse says. She is also straight out of Central Casting.

"We're laughing," the doctor says, "we're laughing. This is a good thing." He walks over to check on Max. "How's the big guy?"

"He's pretty out of it."

The doctor lifts one of Max's eyelids, takes his pulse, placing a hand gently on his forehead. He's learned long ago not to show his thoughts, but he's grown close to this little group, this mix of old and new. Andi is searching the doctor's face. He pushes his glasses back up his nose. "You stay close, Andi, I've got to be with Rebecca. Hold his hand. Let him know you're here." The others are watching, listening. For a moment the room grows quiet. The children can sense it, the older hushing the little ones. They crowd at the portico straining to see. "So, this one is in a hurry," the doctor says, pulling Rebecca's sheet to the foot of the bed. "Children in the kitchen." This over his shoulder. They scamper. Doctors mean business.

"Shouldn't we take her to the clinic?" la senora says.

He looks about the room, the long wall of delicate doors, white linen drapes touching the gray slate floor, *Gadabout* standing close by. "No, she's a little early but last week everything looked fine." He's moving his stethoscope over Rebecca's belly. "I've got the bus right outside." He takes a quick glance toward the other room, then speaks directly to la senora. "This is a good place."

Thanks, Doc.

"OK, folks, let's clear the room. Rebecca, you're already dilating. It all looks good. Let's get this baby born."

Go for it, Becca, bring him now. We've already talked about this. I'm sorry I won't be here, I'm sorry I won't be able to help you through all those times when you'll need me. Find a good man. I mean that. When Maggie told me to find a good woman I never thought it could happen and then, there you were …

Max can hear the sounds of labor. He should be used to them now, but he's not.

I'm still with you on everything we spoke of. I just thought by now I'd have figured it out. I thought at least I'd be able to leave you with some final wisdom. Isn't that what's supposed to happen? Maybe that's it, the grand illusion, there is no answer, only the wonder and majesty. Maybe that's what Gadabout was trying to show me, no home to come back to, only the journey, the joy of the journey.

He hears the doctor coaching, Anja's words of encouragement.

You have been my greatest joy. That night we drove home from the restaurant … sitting on my lap all the way … That's not a betrayal, Mags, it was just that I knew by then every moment was borrowed, every moment, even when we fought I cherished you. Every second with you, Becca.

The sounds are growing distant. His old friend, Tommy, stands by the foot of the bed, his hand outstretched. The room has filled with light.

Not yet, Tom, not yet.

Rebecca's cries sound stronger.

I've tried to tell you all the stories, all the important ones, ask the others, I'm sure there're a few I've forgotten. Tell them to Max. Get him into a boat, sooner than later. A boat is a great way to build confidence … Don't cry … I can hear your cries … It's beautiful, Becca, it's beautiful … and I am not frightened of dying. Fitting, don't you think? I've had such a good life. Maggie and Tommy are here. They're here to help. They're here … they're all here …

"Push Rebecca!"

"Daddy, he's coming!"

"Push Rebecca. One more time."

Is that him?

"Max, we have a son!"

The others are silent. Newborn cries pierce the light.

"Daddy? Daddy don't go …"

"Max?" Rebecca calls.

Andi is lifting her father's hand to kiss.

"Max?"

The baby's cries fill the room. The doctor is placing him onto her chest. Andi looks over, smiling through tears.

"Oh Max."

Into the light, and into the light.

An Early Thanksgiving

by Gloria Garfunkel

Tuesday, 4th November 2014

I started to wonder how to get through Thanksgiving. We decided to celebrate it unconventionally early, yesterday, with just part of the family. I was in an OK mood but didn't want to go anywhere and stayed glued to the TV watching *Law and Order: Special Victims Unit*. I love Detective Munch. He's my kind of cynical, paranoid Jew obsessed with conspiracies. I had my sister's family over for a low-key vegetarian feast she cooked for me. I can't stand to kill a bird for a Holiday.

We were just sitting down to eat. Phone rings.

"Your father died in a car accident. One car," said my brother-in-law Mitch, blanching. "The funeral is tomorrow."

I'm not surprised. This is one of his many one-car crashes. He's been in and out of psych units with Bipolar 1 my whole life and has made various suicide attempts. If Chloe and I had kids together, they wouldn't have a fighting chance.

Chloe has stayed up with me all night and into the morning, baking me brownies and brewing me tea. I'm in numb mode. I don't feel a thing. It's like he wasn't my father at all, even though we talked to each other about how work is going on the phone every Sunday afternoon. He lived in New Jersey and I'm in Massachusetts. I have all these flashes in my mind of what he looked like at different ages and bipolar moods, from violence to hilarity.

Jade

by John Wentworth Chapin

Wednesday, 5th November 2014

When Charles gets back to work, there's only a pair of older women shopping in Eastern Antiques. His father, Chuck, is there, unpacking a shipment, and Deonna is nowhere to be seen. The two men nod at each other, more like co-workers than estranged father and son. Dealing with shipments and new merchandise is generally Charles' job, but he hates it, so he settles himself behind the cash register. Chuck crashed on Charles' couch for about four days after he arrived out of the blue, and then moved on to Deonna's place. Charles is both mortified at the whole situation and a little impressed that his father can weasel his way into situations like this so well. Problem: If he's living with her sleeping with her, what's to say that Deonna doesn't decide that it's not worth it to pay Charles anymore when she can have Chuck for free – and out the door goes Charles? He hasn't had the heart to tell Deonna about his father's no-good-ness. It's embarrassing to tell people that your father stole from you, and there's a certain amount of the-apple-doesn't-fall-too-far-from-the-tree that Charles worries about. If his father is a lout, doesn't that sort of imply that he's a lout, too – or at least put people on wary notice? If they know about his father, it seems to Charles he'll have to work extra hard to distance himself from the bad. Easier to keep it quiet.

"I'm thinking of moving," Charles announces to Chuck. In a big, antiqued mirror with flecks of algal green, he watches Chuck work, unpacking trinkets.

"Where?" Chuck asks.

"Not sure," Charles answers, shrugging.

"Moving is a pain in the ass," Chuck says.

"Nothing keeping me here," Charles replies.

Chuck squints at his son with one eye. "You can move around all you like, and there's nothing wrong with it. But leaving isn't going to do you an ounce of good if the problem's not where you live but who you are."

"Thanks, Chuck. Good to know."

"I hate that sarcastic shit. Say what you mean. The whole goddamned world is sarcastic nowadays. It's weak."

Charles says, "Thank you for telling me I'm damaged and weak." He glances at the two women shopping; his father strikes him as grubby and low–class.

"You're being sarcastic."

"I don't know how to be anything else, Chuck."

Chuck is silent, and Charles spies him lifting a cat figurine and peering into it. Then Chuck steals a sideways glance at Charles, unaware that Charles is watching him in the mirror. He fishes a small plastic bag from up inside the cat and tucks it quickly into his back left pocket, eyes darting back to Charles.

Ah. And there we have it, Charles thinks.

"Well, sarcasm isn't good for you. But move if you want. It's no skin off my nose. Hey, where do think Dee wants this?" Chuck indicates to Charles the dark green porcelain cat in his hand, and then he walks all the way across the store to Charles and hands it to him. "This one looks like it's worth something," he says. "Probably should go someplace special."

Charles looks at the cat carelessly, trying not to seem too interested in it, casually rolling it over and noting that the inside is hollow and empty. He holds it up to the light. "There's nothing special about it," he says.

"Dee!" Chuck calls.

Deonna appears moments later in the doorway to the back office, her crazy hair pulled down in wisps around her face. "What?"

"I'm helping Charles unpack," Chuck says. "Where would you want that green cat?"

Charles feels the room roll away from him, like he's on the deck of a pitching yawl in a storm.

Dee is irritated by the question. "Lord, Charles, help your old man out. That goes with all the other cats." Then she stops. She wrinkles her brow and steals a glance at the two women shoppers making their way to the exit.

"Goodbye, ladies. C'mon back soon now," Deonna says.

She looks back at Charles, her eyes ablaze. She strides across the store to Charles' perch behind the register, and she takes the cat from him. She turns her back to Charles. Charles watches two things in the mirror: Deonna reaching into the cat with two fingers and Chuck watching Deonna.

Deonna stands upright and walks the cat to a glass shelf, where she sets it next to the other green porcelain cats and frogs.

"I want to see you in the back, Charles," she says, voice brittle. She disappears through the doorway into the office. Charles follows her, watching Chuck watch it all.

In the office, Deonna whips around to face him, inches from his face. She lays her hand out expectantly, her jaw set tight and grim.

Charles looks at her hand and looks at her.

"What?" he says, stupidly.

"Fork it over," she demands.

"Fork what over?" Charles asks.

The expectant hand shoots out and slaps him, hard, on the cheek. It makes a louder sound than he would have expected. She's wearing heavy rings that hurt his jaw.

"What the fuck!" Charles exclaims, his hand coming up too late to defend himself.

Deonna hisses, "Don't fuck with me. Give me the bag."

"I don't have any bag," Charles says. "Go ask your boyfriend."

Deonna moves to slap him again, but Charles grabs her wrist before she can hit him.

"It's pretty goddamned low to blame your own father for your own shitty behavior," she says. "Now hand it over." She tries to pull her arm from his grasp, but Charles holds her firmly.

"I don't have anything," Charles says. "I don't even know what you're talking about."

"Let go of me," she says, trying to pull away.

Charles clamps her wrist more firmly. Suddenly, her other hand shoots out at him in a fist, and Charles raises his other arm to ward off her blow. A sharp pain bursts from his forearm, and he hears a brittle snap. She has stabbed him with a pencil. An inch of broken pencil protrudes from his arm in a growing circle of blood.

She yells at him, screaming and cussing while she beats at him with her free hand. He's warding off the blows with his bleeding arm. Then Charles feels himself pushed sideways, two hands clamped on his bleeding arm. He sprawls sideways and lets go of Deonna's arm as he tries to stop from falling. He crashes against the tall antique green filing cabinet where Deonna keeps all her invoices. He catches himself on her desk with a flailing hand and turns to see his father and Deonna both glowering at him.

"Give it to me, you little fucking faggot," Deonna hisses.

Charles looks to his father to see his reaction, but the man has an incredible poker face. Either that, or he feels nothing.

"Give you what?" Charles asks. He has a piece of paper stuck to the blood on his forearm, and he notices that the pencil nub is still stuck into him, the rest of the pencil dangling by a splinter.

She scowls. "You know what I mean."

Charles gingerly picks at the pencil nub and pulls it straight out of his arm; it was sticking in a good half–inch. Blood gurgles into the hole, almost dark green in the weird fluorescent light.

"Why don't you call the cops if you think I'm stealing from you," Charles says. He flicks the bloodied pencil piece at her and she recoils.

"Honey, I've got your number," Deonna says. "You call the cops and they're likely to find all sorts of things on you you don't want them to find."

"I didn't say I was going to call the cops. You have no idea what you're talking about," Charles says. "First of all, whatever was in that cat is in Chuck's back left pocket."

Chuck actually looks genuinely surprised. "What? Don't drag me into this," Chuck says. She looks at Chuck for approval and he shrugs. She swipes a couple of fingers into his back left pocket. Nothing.

"You're a real asshole, you know that?" Deonna says.

"What do you mean that the cops're likely to find all sorts of things?" Charles asks, replaying what she just said over. He doesn't like the sound of it.

Deonna smiles. "You have a brown suede jacket in your apartment. The inside chest pocket has a baggie with a tiny little smear of something almost black. You want the cops to find that?"

Charles' jaw drops. "You planted something on me? Why the fuck would you do that?"

"Honey, I planted several things. That's just one. Let's just say you probably don't want any police dogs sniffing around you or your clothes or your car. I call it insurance."

Charles says, "I don't have whatever you think I have. I quit and I'm leaving."

"Say goodbye to your last paycheck," Deonna says.

Charles doesn't answer. He leaves his father and Deonna together, walking toward the front door of the store. He looks at the mirror as he leaves. He realizes that he saw Chuck tuck the baggie into his mirror image pocket. It's in the other pocket.

Charles shrugs and walks out of the front door of Eastern Antiques.

Pale

by Lynn Beighley

Thursday, 6th November 2014

If this was a movie, I'd be complaining about my bridesmaid dress. You'd see me in it, and you'd think, "Hey, she looks kind of hot even if the color is <whatever>." But this is real life. So it should be vile.

And yet, when you see me on the latest episode of YOU TELL ME, the reality show, you'll notice that the color and the dress is perfect. Fits me, and my recently personal–trainerized body, perfectly. The color, ivory, suits my slightly tan skin. My red hair, in extravagant ringlets that cascade over my pale shoulders, well, blah blah blah. It all works. And it damn well better.

I've sold myself out completely. This wedding, my participation in it, pays for my dad's medical crap, the current festivities, and quite a few of my unpaid utility bills. Oh, and much more has been promised if I play along.

So I do. I walk my dad's intended up the aisle. Or rather she drags me along. I am trying (HEY TV PEOPLE, I'M TRYING) to smile and appear happy to be here.

And in front of me, there's Bill Plover. Bill Plover, the rhinoceros of a man who made me a reality show villain when I turned down his wooing on camera. The same Bill who visited my dad every day in the hospital. The Bill who is my dad's best man. Thing is, when I see him, I smile. Because, well, he's okay. In spite of the reality show that pushed him in to asking me out, and proposing, in spite of all of this, I ...

I like Bill. But look, I don't love him. Don't even think this.

If we were, improbably, to enter into a romantic relationship, there'd be a headline. Something like:

"MAN STABBED WITH MANY TOOTHPICKS."

"LOCAL PROGRAMMER FOUND MURDERED WITH HIS OWN FAVORITE ACTION FIGURES."

"REALITY STAR SLAUGHTERED WITH IPAD SHARDS."

Oh, the possibilities are endless. Fortunately, we remain just friends. He looks at me in ways that make me think he wants more, and I glare at him in ways that tell him to fuck off. Nicely. And he does.

But I am not calm when I spot him up the aisle, waiting. Here's the thing: Dad's wedding has been paid for by TV people. And they paid for it so they could film the drama between Bill and me. So I suspect something will happen. A big obnoxious TV thing.

So far, though, nothing. I walk what's–her–name, my dad's new wife, the taxidermist, up the aisle as her maid of honor. Okay.

I step back as I was instructed. The religious ooga booga guy does his thing. And nothing weird happens. America, you fickle viewing audience, you are being kind to me.

So then Dad and the short perky woman kiss.

And then

then

MUSIC. Like someone turned on the Andrea Boccelli. A curvaceous Jessica Rabbit type bursting with twenty–something hawtness steps out in a wedding dress.

I don't know who she is. But she's dressed like a bride, and she's standing next to Bill in front of the preacher.

Okay, it's a double wedding. Bill is marrying this cartoon of a woman. My mouth is open and many happy little gnats are playing chicken with my tonsils. The TV people are getting their money's worth.

I catch myself, just before the big "man and wife" kiss, and close my mouth. I put on whatever semblance of a smile I can.

Hey America, You Tell Me, are you happy? Am I?

A few minutes later, I wander off in search of the open bar.

The Hall of the Mountain King

by Andrew Stancek

Friday, 7th November 2014

Doctor Bilak bounces into the experimentation lab with a smile for the cameras, tosses back his blond mane. "Today is breakthrough time. Results. I guarantee it. I've prepared additional tools. We are about to fly." His steps are lithe, feet crackle with electricity. The general's team and the government grey suits are still watching, third day of the proceedings, from the glassed–in observation deck above. While Bilak is the last resort, the urgency and hope remain high. They tap their fingers and stare while Colonel Brusk reminds them to erase from their collective consciousness yesterday's unfortunate accident.

"Adam's mother had a heart valve prolapse," Brusk says. "A healthy woman of her age should have absorbed much greater voltage. Collateral damage, that's all. Adam watching her convulsions and cardiac arrest might have induced his cooperation. It could have been fortuitous, but unfortunately our subject remains obstinate. In Bolivia, captured *cocaleros* are routinely made to watch the rapes of their mothers during interrogation. And Stalin of course. No need to belabour the point. Accidents happen and Congressional medals would have been awarded if as a result Crowboy had revealed his secret. We'll leave it now to good Doctor Bilak and his specialization."

Bilak floats in the limelight, gloats in the attention. After a career shrouded in obscurity, labouring without recognition in spite of spectacular results, he feels on the verge of receiving his due. His comments are more for his legacy than for the spectators.

"Professor Holzlohner in Dachau performed crucial studies with ice water. His subjects expired after five hours. Such a result would be counterproductive to our research and accordingly this specimen is being removed from the tank after a mere three hours." Bilak watches a burly assistant hoist the grey child's body by the shoulders, then another lifts the legs, and places it on the table. He paces, right hand moves to a nonexistent cigarette in his mouth; he looks up, grimaces, then modulates his voice into paternal concern and kindness. "Adam, any time you'd like to share." He steps back, scrunches his eyes, fingers his hair, taps a foot, stares at the face of the oversize clock on the wall. The second hand moves smoothly through one rotation, a second and a third. Not a sound is heard. Neither the eyes nor the mouth open.

"A potentially fruitful avenue of research is rewarming. Some of Holzlohner's subjects were thrown into boiling water but frequently death resulted. Adam, do you think boiling water might help you speak?"

Bilak stares at the clock again, three, four, five rotations. No one in the observation deck above moves. Then he waves his arms like a conductor bringing in the vocalists in the Ninth. "The risks, all considered, are too high. As eager as I am to study such illuminating data, we'll forego the boiling water. Eppinger, another great mind, concerned himself with seawater. Our subject has been unable to receive nutrients in conventional ways, in order to increase receptiveness to suggestions. We have been hydrating intravenously but I propose to introduce seawater instead. Adam, does that jog your memory at all? Care to contribute?"

Bilak stares at the clockface. Even though the lab is freezing, beads of sweat appear on his forehead and he brushes at them with his left hand. His smile is alarming. "Our volunteer has given his informed consent to a continuation of our studies," he proclaims. His oversized eyes shine and he cocks his head as if to hear a sound no other ear has heard, to see what no other eye has seen. His hand stretches out, long fingers splayed and a white–coated assistant hands him a beaker. "Plain sea water," Bilak says. "Salinity of thirty–five parts per thousand, chlorine, sodium, sulfur, magnesium, calcium, potassium. Himmler was particularly interested in the research. Two research strands are here combined. Only fitting that a subject who himself had previously explored new realms should be under study. We will introduce the seawater into the intravenous. While we await its effects on memory stimulation, we will prepare the electrodes for the study of the cerebellum."

All eyes are fixed on Adam. Like spectators of an execution, they are gripped, willing a breakthrough.

Adam howls. His first sound since the beginning of the performance is high–pitched and inhuman. His back spasms. The body lurches sideways, back, frontwards, violent *grand mal* seizures as legs thrash and head repeatedly bangs against the tub. Fingers clench, wring, arch. The grey suits exchange glances. The Namer speaks into the microphone next to him. His deep voice echoes through the chamber.

"Stop, Bilak. Abort the experiments. We're done. He won't speak."

Bilak reaches out, the hand gripping the electrodes, then looks up to object, lowers his arm, teeters. The words are a blow he cannot bear. The voice from above says, "Release him." Two assistants place Adam on a gurney, cover him with a sheet. Adam shudders once, twice, takes a rattling breath.

The body lifts off the gurney. It is supine, as if still lying on a flat surface. It rises majestically, white face and white sheet, floats to the viewing area, rigid and weightless. Adam's eyes remain closed as the body propels around the expanse of the lab. This flight is nothing like those seen earlier. On his back, eyes closed, Adam circles, circles, circles. After an eternity, the body perches back onto the gurney, and Adam exhales.

An Eighth of Happiness

by Rachel Ambrose

Saturday, 8th November 2014

"There's a man in my bed!" I whisper–shout to Isa as we make coffee together this morning. She scoops the grounds, I fill the coffee–maker up with water. "A real man!"

"As opposed to those fake men you bring home all the time?" she replies, raising an eyebrow. "And … we're whispering so we don't wake him up, am I right?"

"Yes!" I reply, still whisper–shouting. "I met him at the collaboration last night and he was really nice and really cute so he kind of … followed me home."

"Is he a dog?" asks Isa, a smile twitching the corners of her mouth as she reaches for the cereal. "Tell me he's at least housetrained."

I roll my eyes at her. "His name's Finn, and I'm sure he is." Finn's a hell of a lot of other things, too, but I figure she doesn't need that much information before breakfast.

Just like clockwork, the smell of coffee and toast brings a rumpled Finn out of bed. His long dirty–blond hair hangs in his face, but he's at least put on his blue button down shirt from last night and his jeans. "Hi there," he says, surveying the kitchen counter. "Coffee? Please?" He stares at the pot thirstily, his brown eyes almost liquid.

"Sure," says Isa, pouring him a mug and handing it to him. "I'm Isa, by the way, Claire's roommate."

"I know you from the restaurant," says Finn between slurps. "I deliver your fish on the weekends, remember?"

"Oh!" says Isa, her hand flying to her throat. "I'm sorry, I didn't recognize you –"

"Without the Bellington logo on my t–shirt, I know," Finn replies. "Bellington Fisheries, for the best catch this side of your barstool." He grins rakishly at me and I pour milk in my cereal bowl to distract myself from the feeling that all my clothes have suddenly slithered off my body.

I didn't mean to bring him back home, I really didn't. But we started walking and talking after a few plastic cups of cheap pinot grigio at the restaurant and eventually we walked and talked our way onto a moonlit bridge, which led to making out, which led to more walking, which led here. And I have to say that Finn (no last name yet) was a pretty damn good catch. Kind and considerate in the sack, which led to me being even more, ah, considerate than I usually am, which led to more generosity on his part and ... yeah, let's just say it was a regular Kumbaya circle of awesome sexy times in my bed last night.

We all sit on the living room floor with our Frosted Flakes bowls watching the Today Show. "I can't believe I never got your number," he says, taking a pen and tiny notebook out of his pocket with a flourish. As we leave, he kisses me with abandon, and I try not to wiggle all the way to work. I still don't know his last name, but he's going to call me tonight! Come on, fun Saturday night out! It'll be a wonderful reward for having to pull extra hours at the gallery on a weekend.

Well, after a day of furious Finn–texting under my desk (for stealth purposes), I not only know his last name (which is Barrows), I know his shoe size, his address and his favorite color. I sidestep Frederico's invitation for dinner with his family by saying I've already got other plans, and immediately meet up with Finn at a Greek restaurant nearby. He, of course, orders the lamb gyro and I order a pita pocket with pork, and before you know it, we're making eyes at each other again across the blue marble table. We finish our food quickly, get baklava to go, and head back to his place, which is gorgeously messy (just like my room!) and features a skinny white cat named Dorado, and we light candles, sit on the floor and feed each other baklava, our fingers sliding across each other's tongues. I'm practically naming our children right then and there.

And then the door opens and this fantastic looking lady with honey–colored hair, purple glasses and tattoos up her arms walks in the door, and he says, "Pandora, this is Claire! Claire, this is Pandora, my wife," just as thrilled as can be.

"Your ... wife?" I splutter. "You want to run that by me again one more time?"

"We're polyamorous," he explains as she dives in for a bear hug and he kisses her on the neck. "I thought it would be a great time for everyone to meet and learn a bit about each other."

I slowly look between them, and I think about it for a few seconds. The idea of saying, 'well, sure, that sounds like fun,' occurs to me, but then it also occurs to me that this is not going to work in a million years. "I'm sorry," I say, shaking my head. "I just have no intention of being anybody's third."

I slowly pull myself together and give Pandora a hug. She smells like lavender and cinnamon, and I so wish we could be friends, because some of her tattoos are actually rad. I kiss Finn on the cheek and apologize again, and he smiles a little sadly and says, "It's better to know who you are than to try to be someone you're not," and Dorado gives a little mew as I'm walking out the door. Somehow, though, I know it's going to be okay.

I call Isa on my way home. "Why do the strangest things happen to me?"

Till Death Do Us Party

by Gill Hoffs

Sunday, 9th November 2014

Tonight I'm Shirley, and Shirley is cute.

I've seen the photos. She's what my dad would call a doll.

Tom was a lucky guy; knowing her, marrying her, hearing her halting "Yes ..." first while on bended knee then again a few weeks later at the altar in Vegas. He tells me all this repeatedly in his kitchen, leaning against the edge of the crumb-freckled worktop while his eyes drink me in through thick smudgy specs. His fingers are fiddling with his wedding band, somehow turning it round his pudgy digit without dislodging the mug of cold tea in his hand. From the pictures on the fridge, I reckon he's gained four stone since her death, easy, poking doughnuts in his mouth to distract him from the absence of kisses, to fill him with the taste of something other than bitter loss. To disguise the tingling awareness of where her lips have been. He sighs and I can smell cinnamon and powdered sugar on his breath. The Krispy Kreme boxes are piled high in the hall.

"Her wardrobe is as she left it, behind the mirrored door in the main bedroom. Top of the stairs, door on the right. I think she'd have chosen something red for tonight. She liked to dance with me to that Chris de Burgh song."

"Of course." I place my glass of water beside the crowded sink. "Do you want to join me upstairs? I'm a quick dresser and perhaps I could help you relax a little before the party?"

He freezes in place as I move towards him, fingers still, nailbeds pale as he pinches his ring. I smile and change direction as if this was always my intended route, walking past him to the stairs where his feet alone have left clear patches on the faded sage carpet, a thick layer of lilac dust covering the rest.

I'm halfway up the stairs, glad of my heels, of something keeping my feet away from all this, when he calls up,

"I know it needs a clean. I know she'd hate it, me living like this. But I read somewhere that dust is mostly human skin and I can't bear to lose any more of her. Not yet. Not to a vacuum cleaner and bleach."

I pause, turn my head enough so he can see I'm not *too* disgusted, and nod my understanding, before continuing my journey up. I don't look in the bathroom, but keep my eyes turned away from the open door, and instead walk into a comfortable shrine to Shirley.

Her perfume is one I sometimes spritz my neck with when wandering through the women's section in the fancier department stores, a light lemony pick-me-up with a classy bottle and three-figure price tag. Her eye-shadows have deep wells in the centre of each shade and are lying open, fluffed with dust, and her blusher brush stands askew in a chipped mug emblazoned with a photo of Shirley posing with a bow and arrow, Tom standing with an apple on his head behind her, and the legend 'My Mrs Never Misses!' in red.

There's a sleeping bag on the bed, spread next to several long dark hairs adorning the dent in her pillow and the thrown back covers of a long-gone hasty morning. I don't know how she died but I gather neither of them was expecting it. For once I have no smile for my reflection as I open the mirrored wardrobe door.

§

"You make *such* an adorable couple – tell me you're planning kids!" Tom's aunt is sweet but nosy, and I let him field her questions with a charming "Now c'mon, don't be rushing us, Jeanette," his arm warm round my shoulders and particularly welcome on this cold November night. He must look like a typical protective husband, guiding his shy spouse round the room at his grandfather's 90th, but I know I'm really his shield, his safety blanket, the prop needed to buy him some time so he doesn't have to admit to the world that she's gone, his Shirley's gone, and life is now a deep dark cave with only the taste of cake in it.

After two hours, three drinks, and four dances with male relatives while Tom fiddles with his wedding ring and twitches a smile in the general direction of his grandpa, we've done our duty and can go without tuts or frowns or any ill feeling. I accept kisses on the cheek and a pat on the bum from one randy relation with the same shy smile Shirley has on display on the fridge at Tom's – 'our' – home, then we're out into the sleet, skidding on the pavement a little as we walk to the car. The orange glow of the streetlights makes ghostly pumpkins of our breath, and you could hang paintings from my nipples. It's bloody freezing but Tom takes the edge off the worst of it, holding me close, and now we're away from the fug of perfume and deodorant (and cannabis on at least two of his nephews), I can smell the whisky on his breath.

When we get to his car we embrace and he shudders. Not desire, not cold, just plain raw *need* of another human being. Of Shirley. He leans his weight on me, pressing my body against the car, the damp seeping through her dress and chilling my back and bum. I hear him inhale long and hard, sucking in the scent of her perfume.

I say, "It went alright, don't you think? Your family seem really lovely."

And he looks at me like I'm speaking in tongues.

I squirm an arm free of his bulk and reach up, remove his spectacles from his face, and see his eyes blink, now totally out of focus. I smile at him, tilting my head to the right as his wife did in photographs, and think of how to tactfully confiscate his car keys so I can drive us the hundred miles or so 'home'. The whisky is sour on his lips as he kisses me, gently, and I don't say another word as I act the good girl and let the alcohol and optical fuzziness bring back his Shirley. Just for a few minutes, just for tonight.

Pus

by Susan Tepper

Monday, 10th November 2014

The thing about holidays is that they're a drag, Pedersen is thinking. In fact he can't remember a single holiday he ever enjoyed. Plus when there are holidays, the little kiddies, his little darlings, are off from school. It doesn't give him much to do. No point cruising the schoolyard to watch a bunch of squirrels hiding their nuts. "He–haw!"

His shout startles the white rat Swoon who dashes into the rat hole in the baseboard. "Hey you stink–face rat get out here!"

Rats, he discovered, living with one, are single–minded the way cats operate. If he had to choose between coming back in the next life as a cat or a dog (or a rat) he would choose rat. Hands down. Pedersen could see himself as an urban rat slinking along the ceiling pipes in restaurant kitchens once they've gone dark. Scouting out interesting morsels left behind by sloppy clean–up staff. A rat's life is a good life, he's thinking, scratching his leg.

That last kid – the one he picked up at the park – that kid was small but older than he looked. He bit Pedersen in his struggle to escape. The bite mark swelled his calf. It's itchy now and still has pus drainage.

Pedersen squeezes out the pus into a rag. He sniffs it. Pus smells bad. Strong yellow pus. He wipes the bite wound.

"Sweet," he says. The kid was sweet in his fury to escape. That kind of strength isn't lost on him. He respects that boy so much. Todd. He never got the last name. Didn't want it. This way no one can call him out on a missing boy named Todd. It's all a big mystery and will remain a mystery, as far as he is concerned.

He wonders how long the pus will continue to flow? Thinking of it as a putrid yellow river polluted by the corporations who let sewage in. A documentary on TV showed a big pipe with rushing brown fluid going into the Tennessee River. Kids swim in that river. Pedersen thinks about driving down to Tennessee to join the river protest. It could be a holiday type of thing to do. He isn't planning on buying a turkey and no one has invited him for a Thanksgiving feast.

He'll mull it over. The kid, Todd, had these long sweeping eyelashes that stuck together when he cried to be set free.

Careless

by Jessica McHugh

Tuesday, 11th November 2014

"Are you sure you don't want a drink? Most people who come here on Tuesday night have some troubles to drown."

Edward McKenzie swirls his cranberry juice as he lifts his eyes to the swarthy bartender.

"No thanks. Alcohol doesn't fix anyone's problems."

"You got a better cure?"

Tapping his pink press–on nails against the silver filigree crucifix hanging from his neck, Edward smiles.

The bartender dries a tumbler and drapes the towel over his shoulder. "Ah, so you're one of those, huh?"

"A big one," Father McKenzie says. "But I'm not looking to get rid of my problems or discuss religion today. I have bigger plans."

His eyebrows lifting, the bartender leans on his hand and trills. "Like what?"

"Like asking you on a date, Mario."

The bartender straightens his spine. When Edward's cheeks redden, he covers his face. "I'm sorry, I didn't mean to be so forward. It's something new I'm trying. Plus ..." Edward bites his lip and lowers his hands so he can meet Mario's gaze. "... I knew if I found someone like you, someone who could accept me, I had to jump."

Mario chuckles. "Did you just say you want to jump me?"

"I – no, I just ..." Edward fans his face with a bar napkin. "I'm sorry, I think I've made a mistake."

A smile spreads across Mario's face, and he lays his hand on Edward's.

"I've seen you here before. You asked Tricia about me, didn't you? About the people I date."

Edward nods, blushing harder.

"I thought you looked familiar. But I could've sworn you were a redhead."

Edward combs the bangs of his blonde wig over his eyes. "I was that night."

"But that was weeks ago," Mario says. "You didn't get cold feet about asking me out, did you? I know I'm cute, but I'm not *that* cute."

"Don't sell yourself short," Edward replies. "But no, it wasn't that. There was an incident back home. A man I know – his wife caught him."

"With you?"

"I didn't instigate it, but yes, she saw something that happened between us." An amused smile blooms on his lips. "It's funny, I thought things would get worse after that. I thought Charlie would lie, that he'd drag me down with him. But he didn't. He didn't involve me in his confession – which is strange, considering ..."

Mario's eyebrows scrunch, but his eyes brighten as he urges Edward on with a nod. As agitated as Edward had been by the situation, Mario's interest calms him. He exhales, and his shoulders relax as he leans forward.

"The point is, I decided not to press my luck. Like it or not, I had to cool off on being … me, I guess."

"But you're not cooled off anymore," Mario says, grinning. "You're red hot."

Edward rubs the back of his neck. "Ice blonde, actually."

As Mario chuckles, Edward's purse vibrates. He groans as he fumbles with his phone, pulling it out of his purse and squinting at the screen. Still awkward with the new phone, it takes him a few swipes to answer the call. He gives Mario a cutesy wave before facing away on the barstool.

Tossing his hair, he chirps, "Hello?"

"Father Edward, this is Roberta at Shady Grace."

He clears his throat and drops his voice an octave. "Yes, Roberta, how can I help you?"

There's a pause and some light chatter on the other end. When Roberta speaks again, her voice wavers.

"I'm sorry, Father. Your mother has passed away."

Edward blinks. Thanks to the false eyelashes, he's never been so aware of each flutter against his cheeks.

"I was just there for a visit this morning," he whispers.

"I know, I'm sorry."

He taps his knee, his veins running cold as he tries to secure a response through the garbled grief clouding his mind. Shaking, he says, "I'm away in the city right now, but I'll be there as soon as I can. Thank you, Roberta."

Hanging up, Edward sets his phone on the bar and removes his wallet.

"Not leaving, are you?" Mario asks.

"I'm afraid I have to," he says, laying a five–dollar bill next to his phone.

Seeing the screen alight, he realizes the call from Shady Grace is still connected. He swipes the screen, but nothing happens.

"Let me," Mario says. He ends the call with a few nimble swipes but taps the screen a dozen more times before handing the phone back.

"In case you feel like being forward again, you have my number now."

Despite his heartache, Edward doesn't have to force his smile. Looking into the bartender's deep, chocolate eyes, he says, "Thank you."

Kicking off his heels, Edward slumps into his car and looks in the rearview mirror. The fake lashes have left wet, black tracks under his eyes. He peels them off, drops them in the cup holder, and begins the trek across the state to Shady Grace Retirement Home.

Edward gives his face a wipe–down with a towelette in the parking lot and fumbling, pulls a pair of slacks over his pantyhose. He transfers his wallet and keys from his purse to his pockets, and wriggles his blue shift dress up to his waist. It snags on his crucifix as he lifts it over his head, creating a blind struggle until it tears free. Groaning, he tosses it over his shoulder and retrieves a long sleeve polo shirt from the backseat. The sleeves scratch like burlap against his freshly waxed arms; it's strange how unnatural the modest clothing feels, even after decades of wearing vestments. Removing his wig and tousling his mashed hair, he slides on his loafers and strides into Shady Grace.

Roberta's smile is tight as she speeds through her greeting and condolences. Her head bowed, she leads him to Betty McKenzie's room. The overwhelming smell of vodka smacks him across the face the moment she opens the door. A large stain on the carpet appears the culprit.

"She fell. Dropped a bottle. You know how sneaky she was about those things," Roberta says. "If it's too much –"

"No, I'm used to it," Edward says.

"We haven't touched anything else. Her personal effects are here for you to sort through, with three boxes. One for donations, one for things you'd like to keep, and one for items you'd like buried with Betty, God rest her soul." She squeezes his hand. "I'm sorry for your loss."

In the consolation, Edward notices Roberta's back stiffen. Still holding his hand, she gawks at the painted fingernails before casting him a baffled look.

Burying his hands in his pockets, Edward says, "Thank you for everything, Roberta. I'd like to be alone now."

She nods and shuffles down the hall as Edward shuts the door. The vodka smells thicker now. He opens a window and inhales the night breeze. Then, sidestepping the carpet stain, he empties Betty McKenzie's dresser drawers onto the bed beside the boxes.

There's nothing he wants to keep. He separates the clothes into the donation box, and scoops up liquor–stained photos to discard. But before dropping them in the trash, Edward notices a glimmer in the stack. Twirling his finger around the golden chain, he unspools it from the falling photos.

His grandmother's crucifix rests on his palm as perfectly as it always did. It even feels warm. As Edwards closes his hand around it, familiar fingers close on his shoulder.

His face flushes with a smile as he spins and embraces Grandma Eleanor. It's seemed an eternity since he inhaled the scent of her Duska powder, and he could easily lose another eternity to that comfort.

When she takes his hands, her body tenses like Nurse Roberta's had. *Oh Edward, your nails. After what happened with Charlie Kitner, why are you being so careless?*

"Because I don't care anymore, Eleanor. I'm actually a little disappointed Mr. Kitner didn't expose the truth about me. Now I have to do it myself." He sighs, then chuckles. "And for the first time, I believe I can. I believe this is who God wants me to be – whole, happy, and unafraid of a truthful future."

He clutches her crucifix so tight it stabs his skin.

It's yours again. Just like it always should've been. I never wanted your mother to have it.

Edward breaks away. His face crinkled by sorrow, he says, "Which is why she probably needed it. Even now."

With a nod and a beaming smile, Grandma Eleanor embraces Edward once more, kisses his cheek, and urges him toward the bed. He lowers the crucifix into the burial box and swallows hard as he closes the lid.

Illuminated by a new glory, Edward crosses through the empty room. He opens the door, and the antiseptic hallway flushes out the last waves of his mother's alcohol.

Passing by the nurses' station, he raps his tapered nails on the counter. "Everything's organized in the room, Roberta. Thank you. I'll be in touch."

Staring at the garish red fingers, Roberta's brow wrinkles.

"Is something wrong?" he asks her.

She lifts her eyes to him, her mouth agape. Edward offers a smile and touches her cheek warmly as he says, "The answer you're looking for is 'no'."

As he exits Shady Grace, he could swear he already hears the rumor mill grinding.

Bedside Manners

by Shane Simmons

Wednesday, 12th November 2014

We sit at Uncle John's bed, waiting. Waiting on a doctor, waiting on a nurse, waiting on a sign. Aunt Patricia strokes his hand gently. I look around the ward. There's a man opposite, dangling half his body off the side of his bed. I wonder if I should call someone. The television in the corner is stuck on a news channel and despite the time we've sat here, I have not a clue what is happening in the outside world.

"I'm going to go get something from the shop, do you want anything? Cup of tea?"

She shakes her head, but I don't pay her response too much heed. I'll bring her back a cuppa and a sandwich.

I wander off through the maze of corridors, all painted matching beige and white.

In the hospital's ground floor café I look over the drinks list.

"Large latte please, but can you do an extra shot with that?" The barista nods. He's not too harsh on the eyes.

"Course we can, what's the point of a café that won't sell you extra caffeine?" He smiles and turns back to his rumbling machine. I don't usually pay attention to blonds but my lolling against the counter comes from being knackered as well as half–

arsed flirtatiousness. But I'm too busy rubbing my eyes to *fully* appreciate the scenery.

I take my coffee (and a slyly purchased blueberry and oat muffin) to a table near the window. Hanging from the ceiling is yet another television with a perpetual rolling ticker tape relaying misery and doom. Every corner you take in this place there's a screen, a reminder that you or your loved ones may not be in the best of shape, but hey, the whole world's going to pot so man up because nothing you're going through is *that* bad. It's a cunning ploy.

This coffee's a tad bitter and a little too strong. But I did ask for that extra shot.

I can't tell Aunt Patricia the news. No, not the news on the screen. Other news, which at this moment in time is just not that important. Uncle John's had a stroke. They've kept him sedated while they investigate. Why am I even thinking about the content of yesterday's phone call?

But this news, it can't help but pop into my mind at the most inopportune moments. I'm not entirely sure what to make of it. It hasn't had the chance to sink in. And I want to talk to someone about it. Sandra's off the list. We haven't talked since we got back from Amsterdam and she had gained some sort of recall of what had happened. *I fink its best we dont talk 4 a bit* said her text. Aunt Patricia is understandably preoccupied. It's not important, not in the grand scale, yet I can't help feeling torn between the here and now, and what, according to that call yesterday, could be in store for me.

I stare out of the window at the smokers gathered by the hospital entrance, one leaning on the stand carrying the drip she's attached to. The caffeine hasn't hit my bloodstream yet, but an unexpected tap on my shoulder brings me out of my daze.

"Sorry, is this yours? A customer found it on the counter." I look at the phone in the palm of his hand and realise it is mine. "I think there may be a missed call on it, the screen was flashing when she noticed it." The blond bloke hands it over, smiles and walks away.

I open the call log. It was Aunt Patricia, two minutes ago. At that moment the screen lights up and it whirs in my palm.

"He's coming around, he's mumbled some words!" Her teary sighs are a mixture of both elation and exhaustion.

"I'll be two minutes aunty, I'm just in the café downstairs."

Quick–stepping past the counter I brake and take a few skips backwards. I wave my phone at the blond guy. "Thanks."

"No problem," he smiles, "you've perked up, good news I hope?"

"Yeah." I wonder if I should fill him in, but in this place he probably endures the traumatic stories of many a dull stranger. I thumb in the direction of the exit. "Best get going."

"No problem. Maybe see you in here again sometime," he calls as I speed off.

Dashing down the corridor, I follow the arrows on the walls back to the lift to take me up to the fifth floor.

There at his bedside, a nurse leans over Uncle John, and Aunt Patricia stands back as a pen light is shone into his eyes. The moment she sees me she grabs and grasps my hand. "He asked for a cup of tea!"

I look down at him and between blinks his bleary eyes focus on the two of us.

"They're getting him some tea and toast." She lets go of my hand and stepping forward, smooths the hair on his head. "They'll be here soon, don't worry, love."

Bearing witness to the relief beaming from Aunt Patricia's face, I know this moment eclipses any news I may have.

Postcards

by Michelle Elvy

Thursday, 13th November 2014

The waitress – *Jen*, as her tag announces with a Florida sunshine smiley face – brings a refill of coffee and a large breakfast plate. She tried to bring a side of grits – *breakfast of champions*, she said – but Stevie has not grown accustomed to this southern mainstay, so he has gently refused the generous offer made by the insistent and happy Jen. He finds himself grinning stupidly at the two eggs on the plate, as if Jen's name tag has some kind of commanding power over him. *Eat and be merry. Smile at your eggs, boy.* And why shouldn't he? It's an agreeable breakfast platter. The bacon rests crinkly on the side, the toast is brown and buttery, the eggs are cooked perfectly, golden yellow with just enough ooze when the fork breaks their surface ever so gently with a soft *pop*.

When the plates are cleared, Stevie asks for a refill and pulls the map and postcards from his backpack. The map shows an overview from Florida to Panama. Places that, up to today, have been exotic names on a page. Now they are within reach, and he's thinking even more about what's over the horizon. The Caribbean … Central America … Panama … Too many unknowns to count. And yet, every time he thinks about it, every time he asks himself whether he should go, the answer rumbles in his chest: *yes*.

For now, he turns his attention to the five postcards on the table: an alligator, some tropical fish, a beach, Cape Canaveral and a big yellow sun: *Greetings from the Sunshine State.* Missives for home.

Home. The Chesapeake. Mile after low mile of farms, sandy shores and grassy marshland. Corn and sorghum. Mosquitoes and fireflies. Assateague and Chincoteague. Baltimore and Washington. Places that make sense to him. Meaning and memories.

And people. Lucky and Manny. Ellie and Sylvie.

All his life contained in one brackish bay.

And now he's travelled nearly 1000 miles to get someplace else. And, despite overflowing with smiling, suntanned people, too many of them orange like the fruits that grow on their famous trees, Florida feels just about right.

"Where you from, sugar?" Jen drops off more creamer for the coffee.

"Um, Maryland."

"You not in school?"

"No. Taking some time off. Sailed down here with my uncle."

"Ah: snowbirds. I get it. Maryland that cold in winter?"

"Yes, cold enough."

"Good trip, then? You come down the ICW?"

"Yes, good trip. But no, we went outside." Outside meaning facing the frothy Atlantic rather than cruising down the relative safety of the Intracoastal Waterway. As he says it, Stevie feels the excitement again, something pulling him away. He doesn't say it because it sounds a little corny, but he feels it deep down: how, sailing out of the Chesapeake last month, he felt like Huck Finn, lighting out for new territory.

"You scared out there? On the ocean?"

"No." He's not surprised at the certainty in his voice when he answers this question. Some things scare him, sure – but being out of sight of land is not one of them. No, sailing offshore has turned out to be not at all what he'd imagined. He finds himself at home under the stars at night, and, despite being more alone than ever, he has also experienced the whole process of disconnecting – no iPhone, no television, no Internet – as strangely liberating. Being at sea was easy. Soothing, even. Plus, he adds for Jen's reassurance, they'd left the Chesapeake just in time; he's heard from his parents that winter has struck early this year and snow's on the way.

"Well. You write them postcards, sugar. You write your parents – and be sure to tell them about how good our breakfasts are, now."

Jen winks and sashays back to the counter. Stevie turns to the task at hand. Not a necessity, but a ritual, part of travel etiquette for as long as he can remember: drinking coffee in a diner booth and sending out small notes to the world is part of any travel plan. Something his mother has engrained in him, like marking a map with your existence, one small *x* at a time. Or, he thinks now, like a piece of the story, a hint at his existence. A flash of a moment in a blink of an eye. Proof that he was here: terra firma. He likes thinking that a postcard could mean more than what he would actually write, that there is more to the story than what fits on the page. He likes that this small excerpt, or hint, will tell a piece of a whole story – and that this one piece is enough.

First on the pile is the perfect postcard for his little brother, who has a telescope in his room and dreams of stars like Stevie dreams of the ocean. One day his brother will get to Cape Canaveral. One day Rob's life will orbit around a comet research center in California and he'll have many such postcards and photographs on his wall. And this one, a vintage photo from NASA's early years, will live in a small frame on his desk.

> Hey –
> Floating on the ocean is like how I imagine space. No line between night sky and sea, and stars like you can't imagine. Except it's easier to breathe.
> Maybe a better option, sky–boy.
> – Sea–boy

Stevie had seen *Gravity* with Rob just before he left. Stevie has always been afraid of space – but he's been a good brother and watched all the space movies with Rob, who gets a rapt look on his face whenever *Apollo 13*, *The Right Stuff*, even *Aliens* is the topic. Space appeals to Rob in a way that Stevie gets because he's also drawn away from land. But Stevie doesn't even like flying, much less any notion of leaving his own oxygenated atmosphere. He turns the postcard over and looks at the photo again. Flips it back again and adds:

> PS – Must have seen a hundred shooting stars out there. Even if I know they aren't stars.
> You'd have loved that.

Next card is for his parents: a beautiful long beach. The kind you write "wish you were here" on the back of. But Stevie doesn't write about the beach.

> Mom and Dad –
> Read *1984* and *Animal Farm* on the trip down. Spooky, your 'classics'. Kinda dry. Also found Norm's *Playboys*. Not so dry (joke, Mom). I guess Orwell makes a strong case for me writing you long–hand. I'm going to order

key lime pie before we leave. Big Brother, you
got my order?
Miss you.
– Stevie

PS Still don't like grits.

A huge alligator appears next in his pile. Grinning? Maybe. Just right for Manny.

Hey –
Haven't seen a single gator but I did see a guy
on a crowded boardwalk with a Where's
Waldo suit and a woman with a prosthetic leg
and an orange bikini playing volleyball and
kicking ass. No shit. Your kind of hot.
(Not the Waldo guy.)
– S

He misses Manny. And Lucky. He's spent all year trying to run away and now he's finally left them both behind. But the words "wish you were here" resonate more than he'd ever thought they could. If he were superstitious he'd write something about Lucky, but instead he keeps to the real world, to the here–and–now. To the living. He picks up his pen again, adds:

PS – Don't forget the road trip, fucker.
See you soon.

The Tropical Fish of Florida are for Ellie, who has just recently started her term as an intern at the Chesapeake Bay Foundation and is apparently counting fish, or something like that. She sounds good on the phone. Like she misses him, yeah, but also like she doesn't. Typical Ellie – he likes that about her.

And he likes that even though he misses her – of course he does – he was grateful when she said, even when he wasn't sure: *Go.*

Suddenly the challenge of fitting what he wants to say in such a small space is no fun. He always has a million things to say to Ellie. But he can't pack a million things here, so he writes:

> E –
> See you next month. Can't wait.
> – S

Finally, he has only one postcard left in the stack. It's the huge yellow sun. It's for Sylvie, Ellie's little sister. A girl whose presence is as strong as any other in his life, even if he's only spent time with her this year. Still, they have buried a pet canary together, eaten mac 'n' cheese off china, made Jello of questionable mixed flavors and colors – not the kind of things you do with just anyone. He looks at the sun and writes:

> Sun's coming up like a big bald head, poking
> up over the grocery store – and yeah, it's
> bigger here. You'll see one day. Love, Stevie

It's only years later that he'll think about that card again, and the Laurie Anderson song, the one always stuck in his head. Something inherited from his dad. Love. Fear. And strange dreams. Just what life is made of.

Jen's back to pour more coffee but Stevie places a hand over his cup and asks for the check.

"That for your girlfriend?" Jen asks.

Stevie shakes his head. "No, her sister. The fish are for her." He flashes the bright reef fish at Jen.

"Ain't they a lucky pair. But you lucky too, sugar. Don't you forget just how lucky you are."

Stevie flinches. Lucky. *Yep,* he thinks. *Lucky me.*

Callie and Company
by Len Kuntz

Friday, 14th November 2014

In Parsons, Kansas, a tiny place whose downtown is two blocks long, I find myself at a bar. Actually it's more of a saloon. Has a real gunslinger feel to it with swinging half doors at the entrance (how do they lock the place up at night?), a long mahogany bar, antlers framed on the walls, and patrons who look like they just left the state penitentiary. One bald guy has a neck tattoo of a dragon. His glum buddy has a worm–colored scar that runs from middle forehead, through an eyebrow and across the cheek. Knife fight, I'm guessing.

When I walked in, all ten or so drinkers turned but when they saw it was me they looked disillusioned, as if they'd been expecting a stripper who was very late for the party.

I took a seat at the bar, feeling a little twitchy. People had probably died in this place, maybe even recently. I was chum for any one of these barrel–headed guys if they got hot around the collar.

I ordered tequila. It reminded me of Mexico and my honeymoon, my wife and I on a private little dinghy manned by a squat native nicknamed Cannibal who would shout "Happy Hour" every sixty minutes, retrieve a bottle, fill a shot glass with tequila and 7 Up, slam it against the boat's roof, and pass the drink to me or my wife. We got so drunk I hallucinated, seeing sharks in the water that weren't there. My new bride became as frisky as I'd ever seen her and when Cannibal docked the boat at a small tropical island, she lured me away and we made love under a tree that kept dropping bombs around us as we went at it, two kids fucking like rabbits while dodging falling coconuts.

My memory is broken up by the arrival of a young lady who takes the stool next to mine, even though there are a dozen others empty.

"You're pretty deep in thought," she says, her voice sounding a little hillbilly.

"I guess so."

"My name's Callie," she tells me. "I was named for the calla lily. You know that flower?"

"Can't say I do."

The bartender, a huge refrigerator of a man whose name is Earl, says, "I thought your Daddy named you after a Cadillac."

"It's Callie, not Caddy. Come on, Earl. Don't give me any grief. It's been a long day already."

"I bet it's been long," Earl says, wriggling his purple tongue.

I hold up my glass to Earl. "Another, please."

Earl scowls, as if I've insulted him, but he gets me a refill anyway.

"Watcha drinking?" Callie asks.

"Tequila."

"Buy me one?"

I don't like how this is going, yet to refuse her would clearly be an insult. "Sure."

"That's so sweet," she says, patting my knee.

When her drink comes, Callie knocks it back and taps the rim and Earl pours her another, which she downs, just like the third one.

"Whoa," I say, though what I want to say is, *I'm not a fucking ATM.*

Callie starts talking a million miles an hour, saying she's had a patch of bad luck lately, she's a Scorpio, she likes dogs and especially puppies, her dad's an asshole, her mom's okay, Callie's self–employed, and would I like a date?

"Date? No, I don't think so."

She leans forward, massaging my thigh while looking down at some massive cleavage then back to me with a grin. "These are real."

"Great. Good for you."

"Want a squeeze?"

"Hey, I don't think –"

She grabs my hand faster than a striking rattlesnake, and when I try to pull it back, she screams.

Now several of the large felons in the room are up and out of their seats.

"He tried to cop a feel," Callie says. "He molested me."

"I did not."

Earl grabs a baseball bat from under the bar as Dragon Neck and his scar–faced buddy lumber over my way.

I put my hands up. "Look, I didn't do anything."

"I saw you," Earl says. "You grabbed her titty and were holding on for dear life."

"I did no such thing."

"Strangers come in here all the time thinking they can treat our women like dogs."

"I was just making some friendly conversation," Callie says "when he lashed out and groped me. It hurt, too."

"Fucking pervert," Dragon Neck says.

Earl stabs my back with the blunt end of the bat. "We don't cotton to sexual deviants in these parts."

I wish I'd been smart enough to bring the gun along with me. I wish I'd never stopped in this ratty shit hole, wish I'd never offered to buy Callie a drink.

"What're we going to do with him?" Scar Face says.

"I say we break a few bones."

"Please," I say.

Dragon Neck's face is only inches from mine. His breath smells awful. He's had sauerkraut for lunch, perhaps fried liver as well.

"Maybe you'd like to buy your way out of this," Earl says, nudging me with the bat.

I get it now, how this was a set–up. Probably happens any time someone from out of state is unfortunate enough to stop in.

Earl rams me with the bat and a sliver pierces through my shirt and flesh.

"Okay," I say. "How much?"

"How much you got?"

"Look," I say, fishing out my wallet, "I'll buy the drinks, plus how about fifty extra?"

"That wouldn't even pay for ten minutes with a good lawyer."

"Come on guys. Let's be reasonable."

Dragon Neck grabs my shirt by the collar and twists until we are almost a pair of Eskimos rubbing noses. My vision goes cross–eyed. Someone else takes the wallet from my hand.

"All right," I say, as if they need permission, "you can have it. Just leave me something for gas money. That's all the cash I have in the world."

Dragon Face grabs me under my armpits, lifts me off the stool, carries me to the door and tosses me quite literally to the curb. Someone steps over me and into the bar, but not before spitting on my forehead first. My wallet is chucked next to my bleeding cheek.

"Stay the fuck out of here," Scar Face says.

I get up slowly, first kneeling then standing up. Walking to the car I remember I have a gun in the glove compartment.

Inside the car I retrieve the pistol, holding it in my lap. With this gun, I could cause some serious shit, get my money back, even rob the place. I've never done anything so bold before and the idea excites me, the image of myself getting retribution and for once in my life being a badass.

But then a police car pulls over two spots ahead of me. An officer gets out with another cop and together they enter the bar. They're likely all in cahoots – cops, Callie, Dragon Neck. Heck, Earl is probably Callie's dad for all I know.

I drive off not feeling hoodwinked so much as feeling like a loser, cowardly like my wife often accused me of being. I watch the sun starting to set in the distance and remember how sudden the sun in Mexico would descend at a certain point in the evening, as if it got bored and decided to dive into the sea. I think about Mexico and my honeymoon, how it felt like life was just starting. I remember watching my wife blow–drying her hair naked in the hotel bathroom, her skin golden brown except for the places her swimsuit had covered. I remember thinking I'm the luckiest guy in the world, it can't get any better than this, and now as I drive off I realize just how right I was.

Eleventh Inning

by Michael Webb

Saturday, 15th November 2014

It has been a long Saturday, shopping and music lessons and soccer and a doctor's appointment putting us at loose ends and on opposite sides of our suburb. Angela's suggestion of a local restaurant for dinner brought enthusiastic responses. We find our way there separately, and after the customary fussing about seating and ordering and bathroom visits, we manage to get dinner into all four of us. The early round of the playoffs is playing on a television in the corner, and I follow it with distant interest. People assume I watch baseball when I'm not playing, but it's often the last thing I want to see when I'm off duty.

We follow our practiced drill, another bathroom trip for each child, then I settle the bill while Angela ushers the kids into the van, dealing with buckling and strapping and driving home to get ready for the bedtime rituals. I am thinking about the waitress' pert little breasts and the blessed 8–minute ride home, alone in the sedan with the windows open, playing Led Zeppelin into the night, when I push open the wooden doors and step outside.

There is a cute, pudgy brunette, the hostess, standing outside, her back pressed against the wall, her face taut and nervous, looking at a couple on a bench who are arguing furiously with one another. The woman on the bench has her head down, gasping for breath through wracking sobs. Her dirty blonde hair shakes as the man, a stocky guy with a round belly, muscular arms, and a crewcut wearing an Arizona Cardinals jersey pulls hard on the woman's arm. She is leaning away from him, and I can see the red streaks on the woman's arms where his fingers have been pulling. I can feel the fear and tension in the air.

"Come on, Alicia," the man says, too loud and drunkenly. "Come on. Enough of this bullshit. Come home. You're mine."

"No, Freddie," she says between sobs, her voice rising to match his. "I'm not yours. I'm not going anywhere with you. Not now. Not ever."

"You've got to come home," he says. "Come on. Cut the shit. People are staring."

"No I don't," the woman says. "I don't have to go anywhere with you. My sister is coming to get me."

"That bitch," the man says. "Fuck her. You're mine."

"You shut up," she says, looking up at him. Her face is almost purple, swollen and puffy with rage. I feel a heat building in my chest, a red swelling of misshapen rage.

He slaps her face with a suddenness that stuns all of us for a moment. She turns her face away from him and cries harder.

"That's the third time he has hit her," the hostess whispers behind me. "I already called the police."

I step towards the guy. I have a couple of inches on him, and I keep myself in shape. My heart pounds. I hate confrontation.

"Why don't you leave her alone," I say, standing up straight and settling my voice into a low register. "She doesn't want to go with you."

He turns at the sound of my voice, frowning.

"Why don't you mind your own fucking business, pal?" he says. He lunges towards me, his hands out to shove me backwards.

My body moves on its own, the shadow boxing of a million pretend punches at the Athletes Performance Center taking over.

I lean back, letting him stumble, then step forward, loading and firing a crisp left hand into his face, right into the cartilage of his nose. It feels exactly like the workouts do, except at the end I feel flesh giving way instead of the snap of canvas. The gorilla groans and falls backwards between two bushes, his face a mess of blood and mucus.

I hear the sound of sirens in the distance. The woman on the bench mouths the words "thank you," at me.

"Get out of here," the hostess says quickly. "He deserved that, but I don't want you to get in trouble."

I think about headlines on ESPN, how the story would get around the world before the truth gets its boots on, as the old saying goes. I think about getting a reputation as trouble, a nameless rumor drifting across the leagues, turning guaranteed contracts into polite refusals of interest, turning a firm career into becoming a baseball vagabond, pitching for rent money in Korea or Japan. I think about the look on Angela's face when I have to tell her that the gravy train has stopped, that the children's museum board will stop returning her phone calls. I think about the snarl on his lip when he looked at that poor girl, sniveling and crying on the bench, and I thank myself for the presence of mind to hit him with my glove hand and not my pitching hand, and I turn and walk to my car.

The Weight of Sadness

by James Claffey

Sunday, 16th November 2014

Weeks of constant drizzle have the Bird in the doldrums. The darkened days of the butt-end of the year might as well be a giant wet blanket as far as he's concerned. Only the other evening he was polishing the brasses on the front door when the streetlight bulb went out, leaving him completely in the dark, the tin of Brasso in one hand and the dirty cloth in the other.

Lonely is where he lives. This bitter place between bereavement and bachelorhood he has inhabited, a refugee from happier times. If he minds his unemployment money he might be able to take the train to Dublin on the weekend of the Feast of the Immaculate Conception and do a little shopping. He loves the city at Christmas, the lights everywhere and the shop windows so well turned-out and jolly. Might be nice if he could go with the French girl, but she's fallen off the face of the earth and won't reappear in his life again.

Even his own street will string links of white bulbs crisscross between the lampposts and make the place feel quite like another place entirely. Isn't it the most wonderful time of the year, as the song goes? Wonderful if you've family to connect with, or children to play Santa Claus for, or a love to buy a special gift for in the jewelry shops that blare holiday music into the street at a fierce rate. Too bad the Bird has such a weight of sadness crippling him and causing him little joy in his life since he spotted Melodie with her boyfriend.

When his parents were alive they'd have a big crowd in for drinks on Christmas Eve, before Mass, and afterwards presents would be opened in the sitting room before bed. No tree this year, he thinks, preferring to leave the room alone and try to forget all about the season that's in it. As it stands, with the town decked out for the holidays and little chance of his finding anyone to spend this time of year with, the Bird decides to remain desperately lonely and amuse himself with a bit of fishing and a few long walks in the countryside to catch sight of the winter creatures as they battle the elements and try to stay out of harm's way and the hunters' dogs.

In the aftermath of his fried breakfast the Bird makes a trip to the butcher's shop to replenish the bacon and sausage supplies. Behind the counter, red–faced Bartholomew Glynn is cleaving lamb chops from the carcass. The sharpness of the blade leaves a ringing in the tiled interior of the shop and the Bird inhales the scent of meat mingled with blood and sawdust.

"Go on, Bird," Glynn says, wiping his hands on the blue–striped apron. "What'll you have?"

"A pound–and–a–half each of rashers and sausages, thanks."

"Streaky bacon all right?" Glynn drops a slap of rashers on the scales and adds one more strip to even the balance.

"Game ball," the Bird says. He slips both packages in his overcoat pocket and slides a tenner across the glass countertop.

"Any plans for the Christmas?" Glynn asks. He drops the change in the Bird's waiting hand.

"Not a bit. With the parents dead and gone I'll likely stay close to home and heat up a bit of stew."

"God rest them. Didn't they go fast, now that I recall?"

The Bird winces and mutters a reply before turning on his heel and leaving before he can be drawn into any more reminiscences of his poor Mammy and Daddy. Maybe a trip out to the cemetery to put some flowers on the grave? Sure, there'll be no one there on a Christmas afternoon. They'll all be inside watching 'The Sound of Music' or some other bloody nonsense. Desperate lonely, he thinks. Desperate lonely, and awful to have not a soul to spend the time with over the Christmas. He pictures Melodie, all dolled up for the day, heels and lipstick and fresh-scented perfume. He should have held on to her when he had the chance and not allowed her to run like a frightened animal away from him.

Isn't he the fool for not pursuing her, and now her with the eejit from the band? In the door of the house he goes, stopping to put the meat in the fridge. Upstairs something thuds and he shivers a little. "Ah, Mammy, I hope that's not you tormenting me again." He slips along the narrow hall and up the stairs and into the bedroom. Nothing seems out of place, only the window a quarter open to let some air in to the room. With his desperate body odor and unwillingness to bathe more than twice a month lately, the Bird can barely stand his own pong. "Are you here, Mammy?" he asks.

Silence. Silence. Silence.

A quiet lie-down, he thinks. His overcoat as blanket, the Bird shuts his eyes and slips off into dreams. The scent of cooked turkey and fresh plum pudding fills the air and voices raised, interspersed with the small pop of crackers being pulled. Happier days. Downstairs he treads, loosing his belt expectantly for the big meal that awaits him. In the dining room the Mammy and Daddy are eating and drinking with abandon and wave him over, beckoning him to sit in his place. He sits and takes a large mouthful of wine. The soft French accent of Melodie asking him, "Bird, do you like the stuffing on the side of your plate?" Smile. Her gentleness. The warmth spreading about his heart a layer of insulation against the loneliness. How lucky he is to be in love, to have the parents he does, and to be content in all his being.

He pulls the overcoat tight, the cold air seeping in the window. Melodie's lips press against his cheek and she whispers, *"Joyeux Nöel,* Bird. *Joyeux Nöel!"* In happy dreams the Bird leaves the worries of the world behind and is taken away to a place where the unfairness of his life evaporates into vapor.

Live with That

by Gwendolyn Joyce Mintz

Monday, 17th November 2014

He just has to move the boxes out onto the porch for Goodwill to pick up later in the week. Then Aaron will go get Phil for the meeting.

Back in the living room, he stands before his posted 'to do' list. He makes a line through an item and then peels the paper from the wall.

He sighs with content.

All done, save for one and he could live with that.

Or die with it, as the case may be.

Stand Up

by Stephen V. Ramey

Tuesday, 18th November 2014

The clouds are heavy today. We haven't had a real snow yet, but the weathercasters are hopeful. Not enough drama in their lives, I guess.

We're cruising down Jefferson in our beat–up pickup truck. I've seen this street a thousand times, but it looks different today, probably because Anne is at the wheel. She offered to drive me to my oncology appointment on her way to work. She's been kind since my return, more than kind. Loving. The more I think about it, the more it's clear that she always was loving; it was my perspective that changed us. Resentment at the world, maybe. There's no grudge like a disappointed idealist's grudge.

"Do you need me to pick you up, after?" she says with a sideways glance. Her eyes are green. I never actually forgot that, but haven't really paid attention in a while.

"No, it's okay," I say. "Just an office visit. I'll walk back." The doctor is designing a new protocol for us, moving forward. He was stern with me for breaking our last appointment – how long has it been? Three months? Four? – and I thought he might even drop me, but he didn't. *People react in different ways* – this with a sigh as he's studying the latest scan – *I take it you're in now, Stephen, right? I mean all in. This is not going to be easy on you.*

Yes. I think of Mystery dying in my arms, her eyes on me, watching, expecting, the hole in my chest filling with grief.

"All the way."

Anne frowns. "What?"

"Oh, nothing. Just thinking out loud." A white billboard catches my eye. *Stand Up for New Castle* in bold red letters above a silhouette of people joining hands. "That's new, isn't it?"

Anne chuckles. "If you count six months as new." She drops one hand from the steering wheel and squeezes mine. "I swear you wouldn't see the sun if I didn't point it out to you."

I feel a sting of irritation, let it pass. "I've had a lot on my mind, I guess."

"True," Anne says, returning her hand to the wheel. "That's the group I've been volunteering with. We're working to save the Cooper building." She glances. "Your letter helped, you know."

"Letter?"

"The letter to the editor? Remem –"

"Oh, yeah. I just dashed that off." And I did, mostly. That was the day Rose touched my cheek, the day this all began. I probably should wish that day never happened, but I don't.

Anne sighs. "You have such a gift, Stephen, so much passion. If you'd just learn to channel it –"

"I'd be famous." I stare out the side window. "Has it ever occurred to you I don't want to be famous? I just want to be left alone, do my work, leave something meaningful behind."

"Yes, yes, I know. You're the great altruist, you don't seek validation from others – that's *my* flaw. We've had this discussion, I'm not dense."

Heat floods my head. "What are you saying, Anne? That I'm lying to myself, that I don't mean what I say? Well, I –"

"That's not what I'm saying." Anne looks straight ahead, blinking too fast.

"Then what?" I shake my head.

"What I'm suggesting," she says steadily, "is that you can't leave something behind if you were never here."

Everything crashes at once, the sky, my anger, the Stand Up sign; it's all falling around me, shrapnel from an explosion I never dreamed possible. *She's right. Exactly right.*

The truck starts across the downtown bridge. I glimpse the river churning below, deep and green and never ending.

I touch Anne's arm. "I'm sorry. I'm ... I may be dying. I'm scared."

Anne looks at me. For an instant I worry she's going to drive us off the bridge, then I decide it doesn't matter. As long as it's with her. I don't even notice the tears until they're sliding down my cheek.

In my mind, Mystery looks up from my chest, those golden eyes bright with some hidden fire. *It's about time.*

Returns
by Gay Degani

Wednesday, 19th November 2014

Mars slicks back his hair, damp from his shower, checks the thoroughness of his shave in the mirror, straightens his frayed denim shirt. Not bad, he thinks. The best he can do in a place like this. He misses Rita. At least, he misses her house, her hot tub, her bed. He grimaces, shakes his head. Better get going.

He strides out of First Light Mission into the bracing air and turns south. Cars rumble along the parkway, an old Beastie Boys song pounding from someone's radio. Mars lifts his chin. Beneath a cloudless sky, the peaks of distant mountains gleam white. The song he just heard repeats in his head. "You gotta fight for the right to parrrr–tee." He grins. With Thanksgiving just a week away, there should be plenty of work.

"Hey, man. Slow down."

Mars pivots, and waits as a short, solid man trots to catch up.

"Javi," says Mars. "How's that bambino?"

The other man rolls his eyes. "En español es 'bebé'. No sleep. Nada. My wife is, uh, es como un jaguar. Walking, how you say, how you say – when you walk up and down, up and down?"

"You mean, pacing? She's worried?"

"Yes, yes. She worry. She tired. No sleep. No money. No happy."

"Well," says Mar, slapping Javi on the back, "then we'd better get at it."

Three blocks down, a group of laborers mill around in front of the Home Depot, some sitting on a low cinderblock wall, drinking coffee, others smoking, kidding around, a few approaching pick–up trucks as they turn into the parking lot. A couple of guys linger across the street in front of the U–Haul, although a Wednesday in the middle of the month isn't prime moving time. The best jobs come from contractors and do–it–yourselfers, especially if a worker can hang drywall, lay brick, install a laminate floor. Mars can do all these jobs and hopes someone will take him on as a regular, at least through the holidays.

An Escalade slows to the curb and Mars and Javi look up expectantly. The passenger window rolls down and the woman behind the wheel leans across the seat, takes off her sunglasses, and smiles at Mars. "I need someone to remove some wallpaper?"

Mars puts a hand on the window frame, smiles back. He wonders if she's a realtor like Rita or maybe a house flipper.

Javi pipes up, "I can do that. Real good, real fast, real cheap."

She's still eyeing Mars. "Are you real cheap too?" but he backs away, glances at Javi. "This young man's the best you can get and very reasonable for the quality of his work."

Her lips part in surprise, her head tilts, and then she turns to Javi. "How much?"

"Only eight dollars an hour."

"Ten and he's a steal." Mars nods at her, and she nods back.

"Okay, Mr. Ten–Dollars–an–Hour. Hop in." And Javi does just that.

Mars watches the SUV speed away as another car, strapped with an empty trailer, bumps from the U–Haul lot over the curb into the street and up the Home Depot driveway, sending men scrambling.

"What the hell?" hollers Mars. He recognizes the driver, Ian Shane, at the same time Ian Shane recognizes him and Mars jumps out of the way thinking Rita's son plans to run him down. This is the guy he put in the hospital a couple of months ago, whose mother accused Mars of killing that woman down by the creek.

But the car and trailer screech to a stop and Ian starts laughing. "You should see your face. Like I'd try to take you."

"What happened just now?" Mars opens Ian's car door. The laborers bunch up around them.

Ian shrugs. "Saw you when I was getting the trailer, and I wasn't paying attention when I headed this way. Thought you might want some work?"

"What kind of work? Not with your mother."

"She's gone. You wanna help me move?"

"What do you mean, she's gone?"

"Get in and I'll tell you all about it."

Even if this is a trick, Mars knows Ian Shane is no threat. Gus calls him the shiny penny, the mama's boy. Mars says, "You'd better let me drive."

Once they're on their way, Ian says, "She cut me off, you know. Fired me, stopped paying my rent. Took off with some dude to Bali."

"I thought she was going to get rich on the Old Road development."

"Dead in the water. Hey, listen, I'm sorry she gave your name to the police. Sorry I had anything to do with it."

"Hey, the cops thought I did it because someone saw me talking with her. I didn't even know her name, but they pulled me in more than once. Dragged me out of the shelter a couple of weeks ago. They're probably watching me now."

"Why'd they let you go?"

"No proof," Mars gives Ian a hard look, "because I didn't do it."

"Her name was Charmaine Martin," says Ian.

They drive in silence for a while, the empty trailer rattling behind them, until Mars says, "Sorry you got cut when I hit you. I just wanted to hit you."

"It was okay. That was crazy all of us at the hospital in the middle of the night. Your dad seems to be doing alright."

"I guess. I don't see him much."

As Mars turns into the Old Road, he asks, "So where you moving to?"

"In with a friend. He's got a condo downtown."

"What are you gonna do, you know, for money?"

"Real estate. It's what I know. It's what she taught me. I just didn't realize she was such a bitch. Hey, who's that Sybil's talking to in the courtyard?"

Mars, busy thinking he should have come in from the other direction, to park on the same side of the street as the bungalows, glances up to see a group of people turning toward them, shading their eyes. Sybil, who owns the property where Ian Shane is moving from, stands next to a young woman. Another man is with them, and two children, a girl and a boy, chase each other around the adults. Gus German, Mars' father, watches from the front porch of his bungalow.

"That's Jamie," says Mars, pulling to the curb and turning off the engine, "and her kids."

"I thought she'd been, you know, kidnapped – or worse."

"No, not her. She just took off, I guess. She's safe." The break in his voice surprises him.

"That guy's the murdered woman's husband. Name's Sam. He's some kind of doctor."

"I never met him," says Mars. "You ever think he might have done it?"

"Yeah," says Ian. "It's usually the husband."

Nørthærn Lights

by Sally–Anne Macomber

Thursday, 20th November 2014

To: Milton Flaxmill, Red Cow Publishing
Bcc: Leonard Strauss Jr., Red Cow Publishing
From: Trudy Polaris
Date: November 20, 2014 2:06 p.m.
Re: Hilsænær frå Øslø!

Årt hås triümphæd øvær cømmærcæ!

I åm hæræ in Øslø in thæ læåd–üp tø thæ Nøßæl Prizæ–giving cæræmøny, which is ønly 20 dåys åwåy. Øsløviåns åræ væry håppy åßøüt this. (Thæy ønly givæ øüt ønæ øf thæ Nøßæls in Øslø – thæ ræst thæy givæ øüt in Støckhølm (did yøü knøw this?) – sø I åm høping thæ Nøßæl thæy givæ in Øslø is thæ ønæ with my nåmæ øn it.)

Læåving thæ Tyrøl wås væry drålmåtic. I snück øüt in thæ dæåd øf night! I tøøk sævæn gøåts with mæ, høming gøåts tråinæd tø find thæ Swiss ßørdær. I læft my hüsßånd å nøtæ ßæsidæ my cømpütær kæyßøård – *Gønæ fishing!* – ånd with thæ sævæn gøåts linkæd tøgæthær øn å løng røpæ, strück øüt før fræædøm! Wæ sång søngs åløng thæ wåy tø kææp øür spirits üp – søngs frøm my müsicål *Silås¡ Silås¡ Silås¡* – thæ nøtæs ßøüncing øff thæ cliff fåcæs, thæ high nøtæs ålmøst cåüsing åvålånchæs, ånd ßy thæ timæ wæ'd rün øüt øf søngs wæ'd jüst mådæ it tø thæ ßørdær.

Øf cøürsæ, it wåsn't thæ ßørdær with Switzærlånd – dæspitæ my tålænt før øriæntææring I cøüldn't find Åürørå ßøræålis ånd thæ gøåts læd mæ tø Liæchtænstæin instæåd – ßüt crøssing intø næütrål tærritøry, I wås nævær sø glåd tø sææ thæ ßåck øf thæ Tyrølæån tåx håvæn thåt øvær thæ præviøüs æight mønths håd ßæcømæ å tåx prisøn!

I søld thæ gøåts tø å tålænt scøüt før sømæ müch–næædæd æürøs øn thæ Liæchtænstæin ßlåck mårkæt ånd cåshing in thåt fræ flight cøüpøn frøm ßülgåriå Åir I'væ ßææn kææping før å råiny dåy, flæw tø Øslø.

Thæ ßülgåriå Åir flight wås tærrißlæ, ßümpy ånd cønfüsing (thæ ßülgåriån I læårnæd whæn I wås thæ Fættå Åmßåssådræss wås thæ wrøng ßülgåriån it türns øüt!) ånd thæ ønly føød åvåilåßlæ øn thæ inflight mænü wås sømæ sæcønd–hånd gøülåsh ånd rætsinå–infüsæd håsh ßrøwns. It wås likæ åll my præviøüs livæs cøming ßåck tø håünt mæ!

ßüt nøw I åm hæræ før thæ Nøßæl fæstivitiæs.

It wøüld ßæ ønæ øf thæ 10 møst impørtånt highlights øf my lifæ if it wåsn't før thøsæ snæåky Nøßæl Prizæ–giving ßåstårds! I cån find nø mæntiøn øf my nåmæ ør *Nüclæår Fissiøn in Thæ Himålåyås* ør thæ virgin–værsiøn *Nüclæår Fissiøn in Thæ Pyrénéæs* ør ævæn Ræd Cøw Püßlishing ånywhæræ. It's likæ Øslø is dæåd tø üs! Thøsæ Nørwægiåns åræ icy cøøkiæs indææd!

I åm wøndæring if måyßæ nøt håving å Nørwåy trånslåtiøn ræådy før thæ Præss ånd thæ püßlic ånd thæ Nøßæl jüdgæs wås süch å gøød idæå. Is sømæthing ßæing dønæ åßøüt thåt? Ånd whåt åßøüt thæ Frænch ånd thæ Itåliån ånd Gærmån ånd Swiss Gærmån ånd Åüstriån–Gærmån ånd Tyrølæån–Åüstriån ånd Spånish ånd Tågåløg ånd Süømi trånslåtiøns tøø? This is thæ stüff thåt's kææping mæ åwåkæ åt night in my süitæ åt thæ Røyål King Kristiån XVII Høtæl, which I åm chårging tø my Ræd Cøw Püßlishing fütüræ æxpænsæ åccøünt, Miltøn. This is thæ stüff thåt måkæs mæ tøss ånd türn in my swånsdøwn ßæd ånd sænd øüt tø røøm særvicæ før midnight hærring!

(I håvæ ßææn mæåning tø ßring üp this issüæ øf trånslåtiøns øf thæ ßøøk før sømæ timæ nøw, ånd ålsø ån åüdiø ræcørding ßæcåüsæ I think thæ hård øf hæåring will pårticülårly løvæ my ßøøk.)

My intærnæt cønnæctiøn hæræ åt thæ Røyål King Kristiån XVII Høtæl is rünning øüt sø I åm høping yøü cån wiræ mæ sømæ mønæy før thæ dræss I will ßæ wæåring tø thæ øfficiål cæræmøny. Thæræ's å løt øf øcæløt øn thæ strææts øf Øslø ånd it's clæårly thæ løøk dü jøür, sø if yøü knøw øf ånyønæ with cønnæctiøns in thæ øcæløt indüstry hæræ in thæ frøzæn nørth, thåt wøüld gø øvær ßig with mæ.

Øf cøürsæ, å ræspønsæ frøm yøü wøüld gø øvær ßig with mæ tøø, Miltøn!

Jüst kidding.

Wæll, nøt ræålly kidding.

Ånywåy, gøttå gø!

Yøür fåvøüritæ åüthør ånd minæ,

Trüdy Pølåris

The Retreat

by Mandy Nicol

Friday, 21st November 2014

Mum's being so nice, so solicitous, so unlike herself, that I don't want to force the facts on her. So I thank her for breakfast and say yes, I might stay in bed a little longer.

She thinks Charlie dumped me. She's wrong, it was me who dumped Charlie.

She shuffles out of my room. Persephone pauses in the doorway, sniffs the air, glares at me, then trots off down the hall. I can't see Peregrine, he's probably outside with Anthony. Anthony's been auditing the farm, whatever that means. I asked him if he had to count all the fence posts and he rolled his eyes at me. It stopped him asking me to help.

I shimmy up to a sitting position and rest the plate on my lap. Crispy bacon, boiled egg, toast soldiers. I fold a piece of bacon into my mouth and wonder not so much why I broke up with Charlie, but why I couldn't have waited a bit longer to do it. We were going to Tassie next month on holiday.

But Charlie has been scaring me a lot lately.

It started with babies.

Any kid in a pram or on a television nappy ad got Charlie grinning and winking at me. He was peppering conversation with irrelevant questions like how many children did I want and did I have any names picked out. Last weekend as we walked to his car after seeing a movie he paused a little too long at Bartlett Jewellers' window display. Yesterday he emailed me a dozen photos of houses for sale.

Yesterday I panicked.

I rang and told him it's over.

First he laughed, thinking I was joking. I said it was hardly something I'd joke about and he stopped laughing with a gasp. He kept asking why, even after I explained it five times, so I told him again and there was a long silence. Then he said I was over-reacting. His voice got high and I thought he was going to cry. He offered to slow things down until I caught up with him and I nearly gave in but I didn't. I felt like a bitch. There was another long silence and I started to say I wanted to stay friends but I knew that would be worse than the silence so I stopped. Finally he took a deep breath and thanked me for wasting six months of his life. Then he said he'd still go to Tassie and take his brother with him.

Last night I dreamed of frying pans and Tasmanian Devils.

I pick up the teaspoon and crack open my boiled egg. The yolk's hard and the white is, well, grey.

I shove the plate on the bedside table and wriggle back under the blanket.

Moving on Now

by Margaret Bingel

Saturday, 22nd November 2014

Nora never picks up on the first ring. To discourage telemarketers. She's in the kitchen, five feet away from the wall where she keeps the phone mounted, and lets it ring once. Then before it lets out another shriek, she grabs the receiver and whips it to her ear. And says nothing, breathing into the mouthpiece.

"Mom, it's Ned," says her son on the line, leaning against the counter in his kitchen. "You can say hi, you know."

"Hey Boy," Nora answers, her head tilting to the left, pressing the phone into her shoulder. "What can I do for you?"

Nadia pokes her owner's knees with her nose. Ned looks at his dog and reaches a hand down to pet her.

"Look, Mom, I was thinking." Ned scratches his nails deep into Nadia's furry neck. Nadia pants, wide–mouthed and happy. "As much as I would like to have Thanksgiving with you this year, I'm thinking we should do our own dinners." He holds his breath.

On the other end of the line, a solitary nail on her right hand traces a long–forgotten pencil line on the wall, Ned's last height measurement at seventeen. A small smile breaches the corners of Nora's mouth. "That's fine, Boy," she answers from a faraway place. "I understand."

One minute, the longest minute in their lives, passes between them.

Nora shatters the silence first. "I guess it'll just be me, Rob, and a candlelit turkey dinner." A weird laugh drops out of her voice, nothing forced, just embarrassed.

Nadia flops down at her owner's feet, and Ned bends down to rub her belly. Now Ned's mouth breaks out in a wide grin, thinking about the two most important women in his life: the one who gave him his first life, and the one who gave him a second.

"That's fine, Mom. You and Rob'll have a very nice time together. Nadia and I'll probably go to a friend's house."

Now Nora holds her breath. But she can't hide her wonder, her fingers entwining around the coils of the phone cord. "A friend? Who, may I ask?"

"No one you've met yet, Mom," Ned answers, thinking of Jeffery.

Nora turns her wrist to look at her watch, and frowns. "Ned, I have to get going. I'll have to talk to you some other time."

"Of course, Mom. Goodbye, I love you, I'll talk to you later."

"Love you too, Boy." And then Nora says, "Well, I'm certain we'll both have our own fun times for Thanksgiving."

Some Kind of Important

by Darryl Price

Sunday, 23rd November 2014

Hello, Doc. That's how you can tell it's me or else Bugs Bunny. One of us is always writing to you for answers for the big carrot questions. I guess that makes you some kind of important person in the universe, at least in the universe of me, for which I am grateful. Please don't ever doubt that thankfulness in me. Let me do all the doubting. I'm good at it. I would have made a good doubting Thomas for the Last Supper.

Now down to our current business.

How do I know if I'm still alive? I mean I must have been alive once, granted, because I remember so much of it, but, truly, Doc, how do I tell if you're a much–needed figment of my imagination, or just me spinning in my grave? You could be a ghost from head to toe conjured from out of my loosening mind to have someone to talk with while I'm breaking apart, spreading throughout the cosmos like some kind of foggy stardust. Maybe you're a sparkle on a grain of cosmic debris or something floating there, just out of the corner of my eye, so to speak.

What started me on all this was I can't seem to find any proof of anything anymore. Just because I think I'm here does that mean I'm really actually here? And if I'm not here where am I going? Can I take someone special along with me?

This whole thing really bothers me lately, mostly because I want to know if love is real, or not? I know that's a pretty big, silly question, but it suits the mood I'm in. If love is at least a very real possibility, that tends to make everything else well worth it, doesn't it? Does it not?

I won't go in the opposite direction. I can't. I'm not that person any more. I'm changed. I want to believe in things that are good for you.

I'm scared, Doc. I don't want to lose someone I love again.

Maybe we'd better get right to the letter's private little story and discuss all this deepening shit at a much later time in life: once there was a bright little ghost who was also a philosopher. He constantly argued with the other ghosts that being a ghost was a kind of life. They of course called him a liar and a crazy troublemaker. I only want to be your friend, said the little ghost, but the others didn't like him asking all those hard to answer questions about their natural feelings all the time, so they plotted against him. One night as he was floating through the gloomy forest three larger ghosts jumped on him and held him down. Ghost arms can hold down ghost shoulders, I guess. They splashed an awful smelling purple potion all over his sweet face which instantly disfigured him, but it didn't kill him, well he couldn't be killed, but it didn't make him permanently disappear like a pinched out flame on a candle either as they had been told it would by the witch who sold it to them for some freebie ghost sweat, which is hard to extract under any circumstance. Anyway the three immediately felt quite terrible for what they had done to their innocent friend and began to weep, moan and wail. The little ghost wiped off his wet face on a bunch of moon–lit leaves and just like magic it returned to normal right before everyone's astonished eyes. That witch cheated us, said the first ghost. Yeah, said the second, he's as good as new. The third ghost only continued to moan as if someone had dropped something heavy on his foot by mistake. The four of them became abandoned housemates after that, and still periodically fight over whether being a ghost is being something rather than being nothing.

Thanks for the listening radar ears, Doc. I await your many answers within answers, as they always bring me great relief and set me back on the immediate pathway to heaven.

Neighbor Relations

by Teresa Burns Gunther

Monday, 24th November 2014

Larry

My wife says I'm mad. I've been married to Joyce for twenty–three years; she has a big heart but a blind spot where it concerns the girl next door. I tell her she should be nice to Rachel.

"Why? She's a bitch."

"Nah, just awkward. Did you read the bits I printed out?" Joyce makes a face. "They explain a lot about her. And I just asked them round for turps."

Rachel is odd, but kind; she tries. Like the time she saved Joyce's rabbit, though it was already dead. I never let on that I knew, didn't tell Joyce either, she'd have used it as evidence to build a stronger case. But it means she doesn't know the girl's heart. "I asked them over to thank her boyfriend for his help yesterday, shifted all that timber and soil to the back."

"Boyfriend eh? Must be a fruit loop himself," Joyce says.

§

When the bell rings I squeeze her shoulders and press my forehead to hers. "Now give them a chance, wontcha?"

Rachel hands Joyce a pie in a bakery box. "Berry Cobbler, but it's not homemade."

"Looks a beaut," I say and give Rachel a one–armed hug. Kevin brought a bottle of Shiraz, from the Coonawarra. Nice touch that. Joyce gives him an approving smile. Rachel sees the loom in the corner and her big brown eyes go wide.

"These two are do–it–yourselfers!" she tells Kevin. He nods and grins, he's besotted and I want to hug the bloke for loving this awkward girl. She's a looker, though. Long legged and curved up just right, pretty face.

First glass of wine
Rachel

Joyce doesn't look pleased that I'm wearing a red dress too, though mine is short and has a belted waist. Her eyes run me up and down then study her own self. She's round and stumpy to my slim and long, but she finally laughs and makes a joke. She thanks me for the pie.

Larry's beaming, so proud of Joyce's woven blankets, pillows, and scarves. He says, "My Joyce can make anything beautiful."

They're a surprise, colorful with textures that make me want to run my hand over them. I ask if I can touch and Joyce puffs up, *of course* she says and presses her clutched hands between her massive breasts as I tell her how pretty they are. "I'd like to watch how you do it." She gives me a quick demo on her loom and I can see something new, something smart and sparky in her.

Larry leads us out to sit under their twinkle lights. He puts a match to wood in the belly of a Mexican clay stove that snaps and cracks in its belly. It's three days before Thanksgiving but it's warm tonight. I have the view they have of my back porch and kitchen window. I've heard them so many times with friends in their garden, laughing, playing music; now I'm the guest. The only time I was here I was sneaking their dead rabbit I'd washed back into its cage. I thought Stella killed it but she'd just dug it up after it was buried. I wonder what it means that I'm here.

"You have a beautiful garden," I say and I'm hit with a fizz of emotions that threaten to bubble into the open over the round metal table dressed in a hand-woven cloth, a jar of flowers and ferns from their garden sits at its center. "Maybe you could give me some tips." Larry's crook-toothed smile makes me want to ask if Australians are like the English when it comes to orthodontia, but I stop myself – people skills in action. Larry looks over into my yard and practically sings about my concrete slab's potential.

Second glass of wine
Joyce

She brought a pie, for cocktails? – odd that. Store bought, too. Her brows shot up when she gave it to me, nervous? Then her face lit up when I said I love berry cobbler, giving me a snapshot of what she must've looked like as a wee girl. She says she left the whipped cream at home, says she'll go get it.

"Honey," I say, my hand on her arm – she's almost a foot taller. I don't call anyone *Honey*, that's an American thing that annoys me but suddenly I get it. *Honey*, this tenderness that rises up in front of the words you thought you were going to say. "Honey, it's okay. Cream I have – just look at me." Larry grins like he's won me over to his side. He's been telling me she's one of those borderline autistic types. I always just figured her for rude but he downloaded these articles from the internet for me. Expects me to study before drinking with people? But I'm glad he did. I see now what he's been yammering on about. Her dog, Stella, now there's a problem. The creature's vicious. Went after me once.

Her new bloke, Kevin, says Stella's a sweet dog. "But it took her a while …"

"And a few bones," Larry volunteers with a laugh.

Rachel says Stella is just protecting her. That Kevin brought her dog a bone and now he's in. She beams at Kevin and it's sweet, this young love. Larry watches them holding hands with a big grin. Goofy, that's my man. That's what I thought the moment I met him. My mother said, "Bad teeth, bad future," but she never really knew him or the feel of his loving arms. Larry has proved her wrong all the way around. But Rachel's dog, I'll keep my distance thank you.

Goodnight
Kevin

I'm keen on this friendship, they're interesting; good people. I think it would be good for Rachel to get to know them. She has no family, except her cousin – unless you count her mother who doesn't know her anymore or that father. The asshole missed her birthday. I wanted to hunt him down and feed him a slice of my furious logic. But Rachel says she doesn't care. She's always so pragmatic. She just said, "That's the father I got." I love her more just for that.

Larry and Joyce stand on their porch, calling goodnight to Rachel and me.

I wrap my arm around Rachel. "So?" I ask.

She says, "It was fun. I think Joyce just needs to get to know Stella. I'll take her over this weekend and surprise her."

Morgana Malone and the Sign of the Boisterous Horse

by Matt Potter

Tuesday, 25th November 2014

"I feel as though I should read it, everybody's talking about it," her voice trills above the hushed crowd. She smiles and the brim of her black straw hat dips over one eye. She must have practiced the move hundreds of times in front of the mirror, it's so perfect, her blonde blunt–cut falling across one side of her face, and draping down across her shoulder on the other, just as her eyes look up. She laughs. Well, neighs almost, shaking her nose and mouth and whinnying. Then she points her toe and hoofs at the carpet.

Perhaps she isn't hoofing at the carpet but her hair is what I *thought* I was getting way back in January when I had mine dyed orange and bobbed. (Which is still half–grown out.) Under her straw hat her mane is sleek and lustrous.

I don't know who she is but then, I don't really know who any of these people milling and chatting and smiling and reminiscing are either.

Turning my gaze to the framed photo of Mr Rubinstein resting on the table beside the condolence book, I raise the teacup to my lips and shift my weight from my left foot to my right, with what I think is a faraway look in my eye. Like I do this every day, this weight–shifting, faraway–looking, standing–beside–the–piano–all–on–my–very–own–looking–slightly–uncomfortable in a room with 200 other people sort of thing.

I drain the cup and place it on the saucer on the polished, upright piano, which unlike the piano Marco Garibaldi uses when he struggles to teach me singing every Saturday afternoon, is completely free of stacks of sheet music.

I can't imagine why anyone would want tinkling piano music playing as the mourners offer their condolences to the family, but then I've never been to a Jewish funeral service before so everything is novel.

"Whoa, sexy glasses," Seth says over my shoulder.

(Actually, everything is novel because with my new glasses, I'm seeing *everything* for the first time in I don't know how long.)

Seth steps around me and I breathe in his treacly cologne as his arms envelop me in a hug. It's nice to know he thinks he can still do this, eight weeks and five days after we broke up. Although "broke up" implies something that, I don't know, maybe it wasn't.

Seth looks at the grey and brown regrowth spreading across my head and says, "You are one seriously foxy woman, Morgana." And now he looks in my eyes. "And your glasses are so (and here he stops as he considers his words) … *becoming*."

If I didn't know better I'd think he was joking, but I do know better, and a smile creeps across my face.

"Opi would be very happy you're here," he adds, with just the vaguest, slightest, tugging catch at the end. His eyes are ringed red and the tip of his nose is pink and I look at the high cheekbones on his thin face and short dark hair atop deep brown eyes and I am struck again by how much he looks like Grigor. Even Grigor after his plastic surgery.

And I can't help it, it just flies out of my mouth. "Mr Rubinstein was a wonderful man and he adored you."

Seth smiles, that 1000–watt grin he flashes the moment he first wakes up. "Yeah, well, he was Opi and he was special."

"He was, he always made visiting him in hospital fun."

We both nod, hands clasped in front of us, like some sort of mirror–action game.

"Are you seeing anyone?" he asks.

I want to say, *And your grandfather loved how polite you always are asking after people* but instead I lie. "Yes, no, well … you know, sort of, it's … (and here I shrug) … early days."

"Yeah, me too."

I don't really want to hear that so I listen for any other sound floating around the room, which happens to be the horse–woman saying, "I'm only becoming a doctor so it will make me a better mother." Followed by a trilling bray.

Seth says something else to me – something like well, it's great to see you or have a nice life or please sign the guestbook or I hope you're enjoying the singing lessons I gave you as a breaking–up gift (or maybe he says goodbye gift) – and I nod (again) and he walks through the crowd which shows no sign of leaving, to the other side of the room and sidles up beside horse–woman and slips his arm around her waist.

Hmm, so there's a downside to being able to see better.

"If I don't have a baby soon I think my ovaries are going to burst," horse–woman says to a man in a yarmulke.

A dark suit steps into my line of vision so I bend at the waist and through the crowd, watch horse–woman slip her arm around Seth. He nuzzles his chin into her shoulder and I wish I could dislike her but … they look quite good together. He's a little shorter than her and she's older than him – maybe thirty, maybe she was a nurse before she started studying medicine, or a hair / hat model in a previous life, or a jockey before she grew too tall – but physically they look in proportion.

Still, I wonder what Seth sees in her. And even more so, listening to her conversation and watching her cock her head and drape her sleek and lustrous mane, and pose.

And I wonder what he ever saw in me. Just an older woman pity fu –

"How are you, Susan?"

I turn to see Barry, Grigor's brother, just as he takes a blini from a tray offered by a waitress wearing crisp black and a crisper smile.

"Morgana, I mean Morgana," Barry adds, as the waitress disappears with her tray into the crowd.

Barry, whose high cheekbones on a thin face and short dark hair atop deep brown eyes also remind me of Grigor. Grigor before his plastic surgery. Grigor before he had his nose chiselled and his wrinkles blasted away.

Barry, who I worked for a few months back, in the therapy practice he shares with Grigor and who had appointments with Mr Rubinstein almost every day, which is how I came to know Mr Rubinstein in the first place and how I came to be here at Mr Rubinstein's funeral.

"*Susan* is okay," I say. "It's my real name."

Barry – his mouth full of blini (the half uneaten portion he clasps in his fingers as he waves his hand in the air) – looks at me, eyes shining with new interest. And swallows.

"You're just not a Morgana to me, you're always a Susan. I never worked out why you changed it."

Oh, it was another life ago …

"How's Grigor?" I ask. (God, I can't help myself, I don't *care* how Grigor is yet I still do the polite thing and ask about him.)

"Fuck him, fuck whatever his name is even if he is my twin," Barry says. "Fuck him if he's just got out of prison. How are *you*? *Really*, I mean. I want to know: how are you *really*?"

And now the blini and napkin are on the piano beside my empty teacup and he's flinging his hands in the air.

"I mean, I'm a little late for the wedding rehearsal and suddenly I'm not best man any longer and you're not matron of honour and the wedding is off and I'm told you've resigned your admin job at the practice and I have no idea what's happened and I really enjoyed having you in the office …"

I smile. His intense unblinking gaze might put some people off but I've always liked that about him, even when he was my brother-in-law, even when Grigor was still called Greg. And Barry's enthusiastic hand-waving is infectious, another mirror-game. I'm stirring the air too and I don't know why.

"… and now here you are," he adds, with a sigh and a smile, "ready to tell me."

I don't know what to tell him.

"But it's old news, isn't it?" Barry says. "*Old* news." He picks up what's left of the blini and the napkin from the piano and looks around the room. Perhaps Jewish funerals are popular, because the room is still full, and shows no signs of emptying soon. Even with heartbreak, I think, something can be learned.

"I guess Mr Rubinstein must have been one of your favourite patients," I say.

"Favourite patient?" Barry says. "God no, he was my favourite *bookie*." He laughs, like he's been caught with his hand in the biscuit jar and is trying to charm his way out with disarming honesty. "And not a great bookie either but he was a nice man and nice men his age and with his life experience are few and far between."

I nod. And Barry waves his hands in the air a little more.

"But he was never my patient, he was too switched-on for psychotherapy."

I nod again, just as I see the horse-woman pass behind Barry, swiping the straw hat from her head as she smiles. And there I see it, in broad daylight, or as broad as daylight gets inside well-attended funeral refreshments at a well-appointed funeral home: her very own racing stripe, dark brown regrowth through the blonde mane.

A smile spreads across my face. Somehow that regrowth makes me feel better.

Gabrielle

by Gary Percesepe

Wednesday, 26th November 2014

We cross into New Mexico on US 84. After Durango, Gabrielle talks nonstop. About her ex, who is hooked up in some bad business – some high–wall white–collar Greenwich crime that I can't quite fathom. About her bitch goddess magazine editor with the signature blunt cut. She talks about Andrew, who had rented the Range Rover in Denver and driven the three of them to New Mexico for Anna's Thanksgiving Break from NYU, only to leave them there because of some business deal he had to wrap up in New York. Which is how she and Anna happened to be in Telluride on the night I met Anna at The Last Dollar Saloon, after I had finished my dinner with Henry and Kate. Andrew is being re–evaluated, Gabrielle says. She talks about her job in the city and how she was coming to dread it, and her days as a rocker and her nights out with Deborah Harry and her Blondie mates.

Two things happen as she talks on past 2 am. Three things, if you count me trying to calculate where in the hell we are going. First, I miss Anna. And second, I begin to understand where Anna comes from. Gabrielle is funny, tough, and beautiful. She's whip–smart, cutting, ironic, and very New York. She doesn't ask about Anna, which I appreciate. She does ask about Frankie. For the fourth or fifth time this Thanksgiving week I try to explain, and get exhausted. I throw up my hands. She doesn't interrupt. She gives me that.

She takes her eyes off the road to look at me. Then makes the dual motions for zip the lip.

We drive. I study the pavement. The road looks more and more attractive. I like how it lies there, mile after mile, year after year, how it serves the needs of others without complaint, the traveling citizenry, how it sees everything, but from its limited perspective. It's road. It knows what it is and doesn't try to be anything more than that. It's variable. It sticks to earth, or is suspended above water. It doesn't care about us, but still makes itself available.

At two thirty we enter the mineral springs resort at Ojo Caliente, not far from Taos. Gabrielle reaches into her purse and produces a key to a cliffside suite. "I never checked out," she says. I nod and head for the bathroom, rubbing my eyes.

She raps on the door and hands me a swimsuit. "It's Andrew's. He left in a hurry. You're the same size," she says.

It's a black Speedo and a perfect fit. I find a robe hung on the door and put that on too. She throws me some flip flops.

Gabrielle hooks her arm through mine. We walk outside, into the clear New Mexico night. The door seals shut behind us. Our flip flops slap the pathway. She wears a black bikini under her robe, and carries her purse on her high shoulders.

We enter a large iron pool. There is not a soul in sight. The warm water bubbles up beneath us, rising upward from an underground vault. A massive rock looms over our heads. We shed our robes and dip beneath the steaming surface of the water.

Gabrielle reaches back to dig in her purse. She tells me to open my mouth, and then places what looks like a brown earthen button on my tongue and tells me to swallow. I do.

"What is it?" I ask.

"Peyote." She swallows a button, and fastens her purse.

"Fuck, Gabrielle, what's this shit gonna do?"

"Relax. Slide back into it, Gary. You have to trust me, OK?"

We sit there and soak, studying our skin. She takes one of my hands in hers. We are three handed. Our hands have tiny clear bubbles on them. I look over at her and nod.

"Native American legend tells that the giant rock guards the place where the ancient people of the mesa once received food and water during times of famine. It's said that the iron in this pool prevents fatigue. It's considered beneficial to the blood, and to your immune system."

We lie back, braced against the side of the pool, and look at the stone citadel thrust upward into the starry night. It looks like the Acropolis, a miniature city in stone. We take it in, our necks stretched up like tourists at the twin towers in lower Manhattan. Off in the distance a coyote barks. Our four legs, crooked in the water below, rest on the pebbled floor.

"I could use some immunity," I say.

Gabrielle laughs. "If you're referring to Anna, relax," she says. "I encouraged her."

I raise an eyebrow.

"I trust her judgment."

"You do?" I ponder this.

"Of course, she's my daughter."

"So how'd she do?"

Gabrielle punches my upper arm. "She did fine. She made a good choice. You're harmless, Gary."

"Thanks," I say. "I think?"

"My ex may not see it that way, of course."

We bump hips like salsa dancers under the slippery water, and she smiles. Anna was right, she has cover girl teeth. I like the way the skin of her mouth moves. Her lips part slowly, pulling up her cheekbones slightly.

"In Italy, the age of consent is sixteen," she says.

"Ah, Italia."

"Besides, I was fourteen when I made it the first time," she says.

"Four years younger than me," I say. And seven years older than Anna, I start to say, then check myself, figuring that Gabrielle knows how old her daughter is.

"I was in Italy, actually. In Venice, with a museum guide at the Gallerie dell'Accademia, while my parents were gamboling. His name was Francesco, oddly enough. He took me to a back room where they were restoring a Tintoretto."

"I was in America," I say. "At prom. At a Westchester country club. I came in my cummerbund."

Our laughter echoes off the rock. I feel my heart rate speeding up. The water, or the peyote, is making me perspire. My skin feels slick and metallic. Underwater, Gabrielle places one foot on top of mine. She has long narrow feet, like Anna's, minus the black toenail polish.

"You've got feet like Anna's," I say. I think about that a minute. The peyote is slowing me down. "Oops. That didn't come out right, and is probably inappropriate. Hers are like yours, I mean."

"Yours are hairy," she says.

"I forgot to shave."

"There's only hair on top of your feet, I hope."

"Far as I know." I pull my wrinkled foot up to eye level. It takes some effort. I let it plop back into the water. She reaches over and grabs it, pulls it into her watery lap.

Gabrielle sits up straighter in the pool. She let's go of my hand. She waits until our eyes make full contact.

"Anna likes you, Gary. You do understand that, right?"

"I do," I say.

"And you like her too," she asks.

"Very much," I say.

Gabrielle twirls her hair a second. Then she stands to her feet, and pulls me up with her.

"See," she says. "That's what we've got to work on."

Gabrielle steers me over to an old pump. She places a hand at the back of my neck, pushing my head down, and then pulls the pump handle. Water pools at my feet. She guides my head under the flowing water. I drink deeply.

"This is the Lithia spring," she says.

When I've had enough she takes a long drink herself. We look back at the lighted pools, shimmering. Everything is lovely in the pale light of stars and moon.

Gabrielle steers me back to the room. We walk carefully. "The lithium," she says, "relieves depression and aids digestion."

We reach the room. I collapse on the bed. I see Gabrielle pour herself a pretty drink in a heavy glass. She opens wide the windows. A light breeze blows cool against my fevered skin. The breeze blows the curtains. I close my eyes and see sunken tubs with copper fixtures, linen rugs from Arabia, the red mountains of Sangre de Christo, the lemon trees of Capri waving against the azure sky.

I wake at first light. Sitting next to me in the ruined bed is Gabrielle. She sits with her back against the wrought iron headboard in a black lace bra and unzipped jeans, smoking. She stares into the middle distance and listens, I am guessing, to the gentle beating of a drum, coming from somewhere outside.

This may be a dream. Or not an actual dream, but surely something with dreamlike features? A small bird flits in and out of the open window. At the base of the window lies a suitcase of snow. A twisted strip of bed sheet is knotted around my ankle. Gabrielle sits smoking more peyote. I hear her lungs work. It is snowing outside, and then it isn't.

Samford Tries to Die

by Nathaniel Tower

Thursday, 27th November 2014

On a Thursday in November, Samford ingests what might be a lethal dose of Drain–O.

He downs half the bottle, which, if the bottle is any indicator, is way more than enough to kill him.

He does not call the emergency number for immediate attention.

Samford's consumption of the thick drain declogger is not performed by accident. Nor is it an act of homicide. It isn't necessarily an act of suicide either. It's more of a "let's see what happens" sort of thing.

Based on all the crazy shit he's experienced in the past ten months, he expects anything could happen.

Not that he necessarily *wants* to be saved. Dying wouldn't be the worst thing that could happen to him. After all, it would put an end to the rapidly exploding population of Samford clones. Samford just can't keep his dick in his pants. It's almost as if every woman on Earth is trained to fuck Samford as soon as his genitals have reloaded enough sperm to impregnate them. Samford recalls a biology teacher in high school informing the class it only takes one sperm for this miracle to occur. Samford sees nothing miraculous about it.

Within five minutes of swallowing the last gulp of Drain–O, there is a knock on Samford's door. He expects the clone police, or some crazy ass clone doctor, or maybe something incredibly odd, not that anything would be odd to him anymore.

But instead of seeing something batshit nuts, he sees Sarah – or at least *a* Sarah – standing in the doorway of the fly–by–night hotel room.

"I finally found you," she says. Samford instantly knows it is her, the real Sarah, which must mean it isn't the real Sarah, especially since *his* real Sarah is a clone, or at least claims to be one – and since he could never find a serial number in all his hours spelunking in her asshole, she must be a clone. It's too confusing for him to even think about, especially with the Drain–O starting to rip away his insides. It doesn't really matter though. He knows he will fuck this woman until another Samford bursts forth from her vagina. Maybe it will be a mutant Samford.

"You aren't the right Sarah," Samford spits through the gargling slobber that is forming in his mouth.

"Of course I am," she says as she takes his convulsing hand. "I can prove it to you."

"How?" Pain radiates in his stomach and he wonders if this pain is what the women feel before they give birth to the full–grown Samfords.

She puts her finger on his lips, sealing off the bubbles of foam. "Just be quiet and let me show you."

Samford stands still and doesn't say a word while the Sarah slowly kneels to the floor and slides down his pants. Even in a dying state, he knows that sex will overcome the seething anger and disgust he holds at the sight of this imposter Sarah. For a brief second, he also hopes it will feel the pain.

The Sarah blows on his penis, then bites at the air. Samford thinks this is something from a really shitty porno movie, something called *Clone Fucking* or *Clones Giving Blow Jobs.* The type of porno movie that doesn't even use a clever title. If

Samford is going to die while getting head, he wants it to be something from an A–list porn movie.

But the Sarah is not interested in sucking his dick. After two more puffs of air – which have elicited a raging hard–on – she says, "Now bend over and let me show you I'm the real Sarah."

What happens next is something Samford would rather not anyone ever know. He bends over, prepared to accept his fate. What the Sarah does is magical, but before Samford can fully enjoy it, he drops to the floor, thick green bubbles bursting from his wide–open mouth and onto the filthy hotel carpet.

Welcome Home, Jacaranda

by Kimberlee Smith

Friday, 28th November 2014

I'm naming my half–sister Jacaranda, after my favorite flowering tree. Jacaranda has been with me for a month to the day and, like me and my daughter Etheline, she didn't have a chance to meet her mum nor for her mum to meet her. She was stillborn and her mum, who was close to death herself whilst giving birth to Jackie's brother – they were twins but only the boy was born alive – didn't have a moment to even see Jackie before my dad, Brother Tom Bend, hoisted her lifeless body into the air, praising God for delivering to them an angel. Brother Tom stepped right into his evangelical mode of preaching to deflect what was really going on, right there, right then.

Jacaranda came to me; not as a gift from Heaven, but as a gift from Earth. My husband Dean is sulky about the new addition to our family. Ever since his buddies, those German Tourists, left – to spiritual levels unknown – his energy is stormy and unpredictable. Today he's distracting me from the wee one by whinging how lovely it would be if we could just zip up to Heaven together. We two, not with Jacaranda.

"For Christ's sake, Melodie," he pleads, "we've been hanging around here in limbo long enough. There's got to be something more than this … remember what Doreen said when she passed through?"

"Doreen was a horrid spirit. I got a very bad feeling from her," I counter. "Why are you so desperate to leave? I feel more fulfilled than I have since we died. We can look over our flesh–and–bone bub and also have Jacaranda here with us." I feel Jacaranda lean into me, warm me, soothe me. The storm that usually builds up when I lose my temper is a steady breeze with mist … no thunder, no downpour, no blizzard, no tornado. Jacaranda steadies me. But Jacaranda will never know what it is to be a baby. All she knows is the womb. Having been pregnant with Etheline, Jacaranda and I have a symbiotic relationship.

I think that perhaps if I were to agree to travel to Heaven or somewhere like it – maybe our marriage will be perfect, our problems will disappear, our worries and miscommunications will turn into a blissful, harmonious fusion of love. Like how life was during our first years together. But I feel such a strong pull to Etheline in the living world and to Jacaranda in this afterworld that I cannot risk losing that for a chance of improving my marriage: I am dead. My husband is dead. And finally our marriage is dead. When all you have is a spiritual connection to someone and that perishes, there is nothing left.

"Come on, baby, let's go. This here bub isn't ours. She isn't even a real baby, for fuck's sake! She don't need to be changed or fed or nothing. She's dead. Don't you get it?"

As Dean does when he gets in a snit, his aura is changing from a dull stone color, which is mainly what it is these days, to a flickering like a telly with bad reception. Before the flickering felt like static with intermittent drum beats to me; his unnerved spirit was usually sharp and simple. Today it has weakened to a sluggish flicker, like energy draining from a corroded battery, and the drum beats are more like faraway echoes, traveling across mountain ranges through soupy fog. Dean's not going to give in.

"I don't mean to be harsh, but you never took care of a *live* infant. I was the one who did. Your mum, she spent a fair amount of time helping out, but I was the parent. Not you. You never even met her. You don't even know her. You're creating a situation in your emotional mind that just can't exist. You never met her, which, I am sorry to have to tell you, is proof positive you can't possibly love her. It's a fantasy, babe. For the sake of you and me, give it up."

"My *emotional* mind? As opposed to the mind that was housed in a bone cage, in a swirl of gray matter, before your snake bit me? Chewed on me until it killed me? You're the one who's lost his mind."

He ignores me by shutting down the thoughts I've put out there for him to absorb. He's in deep denial. We never had these complicated issues when we were alive. Or maybe we did but I was the one ignoring the warning signs. Sex made up for all the shortcomings in our relationship. Regardless, I'm not leaving either of my bubs.

I know when you die, time stops. I know Jacaranda will never grow up. I know she's not a real baby, but she's all I've got. She will never play peek-a-boo with me, like Etheline does with Mum. She won't smile when she sees me. She will never open her eyes. She knew nothing of the world, and as I feel her with me, the difference is so clear between life and death. The only one here who got a taste of what it's like to love and be loved on earth, to be held and to hold, is Dean. This is as close as Jacaranda and I are going to get to that.

Having Jacaranda with me is like being pregnant again. I'll never know what it's like to raise a child, but one thing I do know about Jacaranda being here is that she can feel the only world she ever knew, and I can remain in this glorious state of what it feels like to have a baby inside me, forgetting where I am now and feeling the anticipation of being a mum. Dean is not taking this away from me. Not again.

"I got you loud and clear. You're thinking it was all my fault. I kept those snakes as securely and responsibly as I possibly could have." He moans and turns blackly iridescent, like when oil and rainwater mix.

"Damn straight. It was your carelessness keeping them in the house when I was fully pregnant in the first place."

Jacaranda is hiding in me now; her spirit is burrowing like she's afraid. I let her in. It's like I'm full of life again, but that's only because it's what I wish. Two spirits together are strong. Sacred. Dean and I never felt this close, in life or in death.

"You sure didn't complain about moving out of your mum's old caravan and into a home of our own, with air conditioning and waterbeds and everything. You know I worked my ass off to provide those things for you *and* your mum."

Jacaranda shudders, just like the trees do when a wild wind kicks up.

"She ain't my baby. She ain't your baby. All we three got in common is we're dead," Dean says.

I've heard enough. He's free to go. I don't think there's anything, or anywhere, better than this place for a spirit turned bad like Dean's. Difference between the two of us is that he wants to know what else is out there, but I'm afraid to know. Jacaranda is right here with me. While I'm thinking hard about us, and our situation, I stop to realize that Dean has gone.

Nobody, Somebody

by Vanessa Weibler Paris

Saturday, 29th November 2014

"You're nobody 'til somebody loves you," I hum quietly as I pull open the refrigerator door.

The air inside the refrigerator buzzes, *hmmmm–hmmmm–click–click* on repeat. Its bright white sides are studded with drops of condensation, concave holes, perfect little mounds like candy buttons on paper tape. I trace them with the darts of my eyes, drawing zigzags and diamonds and finally a star.

The shelves are filled with nothing but bottles of water.

"Close it," says Iris. "Close it. Close it!" It becomes a single word.

I am Iris's muse. Her love. Her art. Her exhibit.

There's no more food for me now, just water. I must become thinner: Iris' art has *clean lines.* But I keep forgetting, keep going back for the food.

"Close it!" she repeats.

The condensation drops are warming now, stretching and tearing. Some start to roll down the sides, snail–trailing into neat vertical stripes like overlapping prison bars. A bulb flickers in the back.

A housefly coasts in smoothly, landing on a white bottlecap, expiration–dated far beyond my own. Its eyes shimmer red. The fly buzzes in competition with the cooling system, trying to win a battle the fridge isn't even fighting.

My leg is bleeding again. The bandage Rorschachs in slowly seeping shapes. I stare at a big blot of red: is it a head of lettuce? a lotus pod?

"I just need to know how deep it is," Iris had said last night, razor blade in her fist. "Until I hit bone."

"The exhibit?" I asked.

"The exhibit," she said.

I take out a bottle, try to open it. Iris grabs it from me, cracks it with a quick twist. I lift the bottle, gratefully, and sip. She slams the fridge shut.

"I'm going out for a bit," Iris calls over her shoulder, heading for the door, and then she's gone. She's gone a lot lately. It seems. Or maybe it's just that I'm sleeping more.

When I was in school, they used to say that everyone should drink eight glasses of water per day. I'm not sure that's true any longer. It's like the Four Basic Food Groups or catching a cold from being damp and chilled, the science that was shoved down our throats and then later quietly discarded.

I finish my water, open another, and gulp. I'm feeling stronger now. Fuller. If I grow, though, Iris will leave me, and I'll be alone again. I'll be Slim Jim again, poor pitied Slim Jim, who has family and friends and co–workers who love him but nothing more.

I throw my empty to the floor, where Iris won't like it. Open another.

I once read an article on what it's like to drown. At first you panic, try to hold your breath. That goes on for a while. When you can't hold out any longer, water gushes in. Your lungs feel like they're tearing and burning, but that doesn't last long. Finally, you feel calm and tranquil, then go slowly unconscious. Your heart stops, and finally, your brain dies.

What time is it? The wall clock is gone.

I can feel myself gaining weight as I continue to drink. It hurts to swallow, and makes a hard noise in my throat, *nnunnk nnunnk nnunnk.* I pick up the phone and dial.

"I'd like to request a song," I tell the woman who answers the phone at the radio station. "It's by Dean Martin." I open a bottle of water, leaving the refrigerator door ajar. But they don't accept requests now, haven't for years.

I feel like vomiting, but I breathe and I breathe and it passes.

I take another, open it with shaking hands.

The red–eyed fly buzzes in tune with the song in my mind. "*You're nobody 'til somebody looooooves youuuuuuuu.*"

Close it, I can hear Iris saying, and so I do. Maybe I'll let the fly out in a bit, see if it can come back to life. Or maybe I'll leave it there, dying slowly, without even realizing.

Sunday Brunch

by Joanne Jagoda

Sunday, 30th November 2014

"Mom, what time are they coming?"

"They'll be here around eleven. I need you to pick up some eggs. I thought I had more, but I only have a half dozen. I hope the guys will like mushroom omelets."

"They will Mom, and no one can resist your home–style potatoes. The onions browning in the butter smell so good. "

"Oh, Cass … forgot to tell you and Rob. After brunch, we're going to the De Young Museum. I got us tickets for the Impressionist exhibit. It's supposed to be fabulous."

"Count Rob and me out."

"We'll talk about that later. Get going. I need those eggs."

"I'll get her lazy butt up."

I want to pinch myself. I've been on a roller coaster since January. Just like Eli said, Sandy called me on Halloween. Who would ever believe that a Mossad agent could be a matchmaker. He had a feeling we would be right for each other. I know he felt badly about how I was used by Damon Southeby, because he saw it all happening but couldn't do anything about it.

When Sandy came to the door he had a cute smile that crinkled his eyes. He wasn't drop–dead gorgeous but nice looking, built solid and taller than me. He was checking me out and I was glad I got my hair cut and looked good in my new burgundy sweater.

We went to my favorite pizza place, Tomaso's in North Beach. We talked so much over our pizza and bottle of Chianti that the waiters were piling the chairs on tops of the tables until we got the hint. Then we picked up ice cream and ate it in the kitchen standing up at the counter. We felt comfortable like we've known each other forever and laughed until two in the morning. I insisted he not drive home, and he slept in the guest room. The next morning he left quietly. Breakfast would have been too much too soon. He got that.

We've been seeing each other often. Bike riding, movies; I cook dinner or we take long walks. And we've spent one yummy weekend at a quaint Bed and Breakfast in Half Moon Bay. He's a sweet lover. It's only been one month, but it feels like a lifetime with him.

I was tickled when Sandy said he wanted to be with us for Thanksgiving. He came over early on Thursday and helped with chopping. He carved the turkey too. His son was with his wife's parents, which was fine. The girls had just come home from school. At first it was strained. They were civil but quiet and not themselves. I know they don't want me to get hurt again. I'm touched by that. After my horrible experience with that liar, Damon, they are acting like guard dogs.

"Why are you sitting on me, Cass? Leave me alone."

"Rob, get your butt out of bed and come with me to Safeway. Mom needs eggs."

"Oooohh … I had way too much to drink last night. My head is pounding."

"No one told you to down three margaritas. You over–did it, Rob."

"I can figure that out for myself, Cass. I'm the one feeling like shit."

"Sandy and his son are coming for brunch."

"I don't want to make small talk. I feel like crap."

"Rob, I'll get you some Peet's Columbian, the best hangover cure. I'm excited for Mom. Sandy seems real. He's going bald; his pants were falling the other night. In some ways he reminds me of Dad. When he was carving the turkey for Thanksgiving I had a flash of how Dad used to do it."

"I know what you mean, Cass. He feels comfortable and he's funny. I loved when he was telling stories about some of the weird women he's met through online dating."

"Rob, do you think he and Mom have a future?"

"I don't know, but I feel better about him compared to that other jerk–off. He was too smooth, too good–looking, I didn't trust him from the start."

"Yeah, well you were right. Come on, get dressed and let's go."

"All right all right."

"*Cass and Rob, I need those eggs.*"

"*YEAH MOM, we'll be right down.*"

"Smells *delish*, Mom." Cass grabs a chunk of pineapple from the bowl.

"Kids, pick me up a sour cream and make it two dozen eggs. Robin, sunglasses in the house?"

"It's bright in here. Mom, anything else? Tell us now …"

"No, that's it."

§

I wonder where the girls are with the eggs. I bet they stopped for coffee. Rob must have another hangover. I want to go away again with Sandy. Our weekend at the B&B was perfect. It all just feels right with him. I hope the girls will like Josh. I better finish setting the table. Where are my blue placemats? Oh, here's my favorite picture of the four of us in Maui on the beach.

Paul, I've met a good man. He's a lot like you. Give me your blessing.

Finally they're back. "Thanks kids. Leave the eggs on the counter."

"Mom, we were talking. Do you like Sandy? I mean really like him?"

I was afraid they might ask me. I need to crack these eggs in the bowl. Where's the salt and pepper? They come out better when I use a whisk. Got to grate the cheddar. Mushrooms are cleaned and washed. I'll assemble everything for the omelets.

Cassie watches me whisk the eggs. "Mom, you didn't answer. We want to know."

"Well, if you must know, it hasn't been very long, but I do like him … a lot. I think it's even more than that. I feel like it is the beginning of something good we can grow in to."

The girls come over to me and we hug and hold on to each other. We've been through an ordeal that is all too fresh. "No sweats guys, puh–lease???"

"Yeah, yeah."

Robin can be such a brat. I'm going to finish the potatoes. It's ten minutes to eleven. They'll be here soon.

§

"You guys look nice and jeans are way better than sweats. There's the bell. Rob, get the door."

"I see Josh through the window. He's cute. Looks like Sandy but taller."

"Hi Sandy. Mom, Cass, Sandy and Josh ARE HEE … RE!"

"Hey, Anne." He gives me a hug and peck on the cheek. The three kids are embarrassed. Then he bows at the waist like a gallant knight, and they laugh.

"Donaldson Ladies, meet my son, Josh. Josh, meet the Donaldson Ladies."

I'm relieved Sandy broke the ice. "Come on everyone. Let's hit the table. Just tell me what you want in your made–to–order omelets. Cassie, serve the home fries. Robin, bring the fruit salad to the table."

We eat and laugh and I quietly observe the three kids talking about school, football and music. Sandy grabs my hand under the table and squeezes.

"More home fries, Josh?" He hands me his plate.

"They definitely don't serve these on campus." He continues the heated football discussion he was having with Robin. "You know that the 49'ers are going to make it to the playoffs and the Super Bowl."

Robin shakes her head, "No way, Josh. The Seahawks are going all the way and would you like to make a little bet?"

Sandy pipes in, "Don't do it, Josh. She knows what she's talking about."

§

After brunch everyone helps clear the table, then the twins and Josh head upstairs. I hear noise and arguing but it sounds like they are having fun. I let my breath out. "I think they are getting along well, Sandy."

"I knew they would." He puts his arms around me at the sink. I turn and kiss him full on the lips, dripping soap bubbles on his sweater. We don't hear them walk into the kitchen.

Josh clears his throat. We break apart, and Sandy whistles like we've been caught making out by our parents.

Robin takes the car keys from the counter. "Mom, we don't want to go to the de Young. Got other plans. Hope you won't mind. Now, you two behave ..."

We smile and Sandy answers before I can, reading my mind. "That's fine. See you later." The door slams.

It feels like a cyclone left the house with a whoosh. Sandy helps me dry the rest of the dishes. It's a rare quiet moment, and though we don't speak, we recognize something special is taking place between us. I feel a rare contentment that I haven't experienced in a long time.

I dry my hands on a kitchen towel and Sandy leads me to the sofa. He massages my feet in my socks. I don't need to ask if he wants to stay and hang out at home. We curl up on the sofa with the Sunday paper. The Impressionists can wait for another day.

December

The Miracle of Small Things

by Guilie Castillo Oriard

Monday, 1st December 2014

Monday nights are always crowded at De Heeren. Not a single empty table inside, not even on the patio. Familiar faces turn my way, hands raise, fingers wiggle hello. Nudges make more faces turn, even from tables full of strangers. *Look, Curaçao's crazy dog lady.* Too late for regrets. Not many places to pick from on a Monday, anyway.

The hostess gives me a bright smile. "Goeden avond," she says. "Inside or outside, Ms. Solak?"

Inside there's more light. Inside, the hum of conversation will cover awkward silences. Which begs the question: why should I care? "Outside," I say. Dagger of awkwardness, find thy sheath.

"Just five minutes while we set it up."

I wander over to the bar and make small talk, ignore the veiled once–overs the glitzy women give my jeans and my flip–flops, until the hostess taps my arm. "Your table is ready."

Dekko, the manager, is waiting outside, full of apologies. The table barely catches the edge of the patio lighting. In the darkness, its candle centerpiece hollers *romantic.* "I have better spots inside," he says.

And then I see him, striding into the restaurant with those long legs. His hair is longer, his shirt is untucked, the sleeves rolled up, but it looks freshly ironed. His feet, though, are the key: the great Luis Villalobos is wearing *flip–flops* to a restaurant.

"It's okay, Dek. This is fine."

He says something about sending over a bottle of wine and I nod, say thanks (I think). Luis is scanning faces in the half–light. When he sees me, he grins, and it's that same arrogant hot–shot attitude. The flip–flops lie; he hasn't changed.

"I wasn't sure you'd come," he says as he sits down across from me.

I give him what I hope looks like a non–committal smile. "How are you?"

"Good. You?"

He looks happy. More relaxed even than in Bonaire that one luscious weekend. Maybe it's the tan, the weight he's lost. All that lugging around of tanks in the sun. "Enjoying your new career?"

He nods, looks down at the table. "So far, yeah."

"Being a dive instructor was a lifelong ambition?"

He laughs. "I'm not an instructor. And no, not remotely. But I do love it."

"So far." A gibe. I can't help myself.

He lets out his breath with a *whoosh.* "So far."

Where the hell is Dekko and the wine? A waiter at least, maybe some water? "How's Al?"

"Great." He smiles that tender, childish smile of his, the one that gave me faith in humanity. "Our neighbor has a Rottweiler puppy – well, not a real one, a mix, but he looks Rottweiler–ish – and he and Al totally hit it off."

"I'm glad he has company while you're working."

"Actually, he comes to work with me."

I want to frown, to show I disapprove – Al isn't exactly the world's most socialized dog, and Luis isn't going to win any trainer awards any time soon – but the sheer absurdity of the image trumps everything and makes me chuckle. "You bring your *dog* to work?"

He laughs. "Pretty awesome for the guy who didn't even like dogs, right?"

Pretty glib for the guy who was going to leave his dog behind is what I think. But I don't say it. Anger is nothing but hurt; revealing it makes us vulnerable. And I'm done being vulnerable. "Where are you living?"

"Montaña. Tiny place. Big yard, though, all walled in. At night the stars are amazing. And rent's affordable on my new salary."

Montaña? How far the great have fallen. "Is it safe, though?"

He chuckles. "I'm from Mexico City, remember? This island is the safest place on Earth."

"Don't get cocky, Luis. It's the –"

Dekko arrives with two bottles. "I have an Argentinian merlot and a Spanish tempranillo, both excellent. If you're having meat, I'd suggest –"

"We're not eating," I say, in English. "The merlot –"

"The tempranillo sounds good." Luis puts a hand on mine. An apology for interrupting, or is he marking territory for Dek – or me?

"Bit heavy, no?" I slide my hand away, disguise the movement by rummaging in my bag for my phone.

"This one's very light," Dek says, and for once I resent his solicitude. He does offer the half measure to me for tasting, which is somewhat appeasing.

"I wasn't being dismissive," Luis says as Dek moves away to check on another table. "I know it's not the best area, which is one of the reasons I bring Al with me to work. They want to break in, let them. There's nothing to steal. But Al wouldn't see it that way, and I don't want him to get hurt."

"You have savings. It doesn't have to be the lap of luxury, but –"

"It's not bad. You should come see for yourself sometime."

I mean to take just a sip of wine, but I can't stop. I drain the glass. Luis watches, but in the candlelight his expression is unreadable. He pours my refill in silence. I wait until he's done, until he looks at me again. "I don't do repeats," I tell him.

"I made a mistake."

"Just one?"

He grins, but there's no arrogance in it now. "One after another. But here's the thing, Pélagie. Every one of those mistakes – and they go back all the way to law school, maybe even before – they brought me here. To you, to Al." He reaches across the table, his open hand asking me for – for what? Forgiveness? Acceptance?

I ignore it. "No cheesiness. Please. It's the ultimate insult."

He nods, turns his hand palm down on the table, but leaves it there, invading my space. "I don't want a do–over. I wouldn't take it, except maybe on leaving Al. And I'd do it for him, not for me. These mistakes have been my saving grace. I need you to see it that way, too."

I sit back, as far away from that hand as I can without leaving the table. "How long are you going to do this? Play at this hippie fuck–the–corporate–world shit?"

"I don't know. I –"

"Will you go back to being a lawyer?"

"I don't –"

"Will you stay in Curaçao? In that rented Montaña shack? Will you buy a house?"

"I don't know." He holds my gaze, and I see discomfort.

Finally.

"What will happen to Al when you get tired of diving, the way you got tired of lawyering?"

"Wherever I go, he goes. China, Timbuktu –"

"What if you get tired of him, too?"

His eyes darken with anger. "What I got tired of was playing a game where every win is a flash in the pan, nothing's enough, ever. I got tired of living by a measuring stick of achievements that mean nothing except to a tiny group of people. I got tired of working my ass off so some rich dudes could cheat their government."

"Oh, I see. And teaching those same rich dudes to dive is so much loftier?"

He finally pulls his hand back to his side of the table. "I didn't leave, Pélagie. I didn't leave Al, and I didn't leave you."

"This was never about me."

"Then why can't you forgive me?"

I hold my wine glass aloft in a toast. "I can, and I have. What I can't do is trust you."

"Because I don't know where I'll be next year, next month?"

"Because you can't be trusted! Because I'm not a dog. Because, hard as I try, I can't live just in the moment. The future exists, it's coming, and I don't want to get chewed up and spit out."

"You were the one who said no one has a lease on the future. Promises are the worst kind of fallacy, remember? Isn't that what you said?"

I need something to swallow, but my glass is dry. Again. Luis beats me to the bottle. His fingers graze mine as he picks it up.

"Come with me to Bonaire next weekend," he says as he pours.

"No."

His eyes stay on the flow of red. "I'll be diving most of the time, even at night, so you won't have to see me much. Maybe just at breakfast. If you're up early enough."

"No."

"The diving people are great. You'll love them."

"I probably know them already."

He slides the glass, a perfect third full, towards me. "Maybe not. Maybe I can still surprise you. And maybe, if you want, we can stay one more day. Just the two of us. I'm off on Mondays."

He's searching my face with that naive moxie of his.

I take the coward's way out. "I'll think about it," I say.

A lazy afternoon in Bonaire, hammocks, Luis asking me to teach him more ridiculous Dutch expressions. *Now the monkey comes out of the sleeve. They're talking about little cows and little calves.*

Things never go back to the way they were. And perhaps it's for the best. We've no business, none of us, trying to return to the places we were once happy in. All we'll find is blighted hope.

Perhaps all we can do is build anew.

La Ronde / Frank and Madge

by Townsend Walker

Tuesday, 2nd December 2014

A month has passed since Frank figured out Madge had a price on his head and not one of those days has passed without him thinking about how to do her in first. It had to be tight: he knew, no–doubt–about–it, she'd told her friend Gina–the–bitch about how he'd slap her from time to time. Not that Madge didn't deserve it, but it wouldn't look good if they also suspected him of her death. He pretty much had it figured out, but then Thanksgiving rolled around and there was the traditional feast at his family's place upstate near Rhinebeck. He'd do that, but he was damned if he'd go through another Christmas and New Year with her, especially since it was her family's turn this year and her sister Ann was having folks out to their place in Queens. *Queens, for god's sake.* And Ann's husband, what's–his–name, short weasely guy, always wanting inside tips, not understanding (for how many years now) that he was the last person he'd tell. Frank could see it. What's–his–name would make money off the tip, then buy the house rounds. *Got this brother–in–law, horse's mouth, inside scoop.* Sayonara career.

Frank had picked up an old Dell laptop on the street corner the week after seeing Alexei and started to do a bit of research on poison. He tossed the laptop in a dumpster two weeks later.

Settled on thallium salts for his conniving Madge. No taste, no color, no smell, no change in food texture, and a tenth of an ounce does the job. His problem: how to get hold of it. Not commercially available. But. As part of his due diligence on the Time Warner/Comcast merger deal he had visited fiber optics manufacturers. (Frank was nothing if not thorough.) The guy who took him through the Corning plant in Wilmington, NC was also named Frank. They hit it off: names and shades (both wore them all the time). Wall Street Frank was Frank the Tall; fiber optic Frank became Frank the Short; FT and FS to each other. After the tour, they had drinks at the City Limits Saloon down by the river and FS told FT about how they used thallium salts to make fiber optic cable. *And we keep that stuff in a special place, toxic as shit; remember that alcove off to the side on the main floor?*

After Thanksgiving FT called FS and said he needed to check a couple more details, flew down, while making the tour: excused himself, dipped into the alcove, grabbed a vial of thallium salt, pocketed it. FT took FS to dinner at Aubriana's downtown where for the third time FS told him how the thallium worked *like a dopant in the lenses, prims and windows of repeaters to speed the signals on their way.* FT nodded politely and moved the conversation to basketball. That carried them into the night: FT was a Buckeye; FS, a Tar Heel. And nearly on to the next morning when FT had to catch his flight.

He came home early today. He knew Madge was meeting Gina for lunch and drinks, and if past history could be depended on, she'd roll in about seven or so. For dinner, he decided to prepare his specialty, Julia Child's stew a la façon de Frank Cabot. Years ago, he discovered he could substitute lamb in her bœuf bourguignon recipe. He assembled the bacon, olive oil, cubed lamb, carrot, onion, red wine, beef stock, cloves, thyme, bay leaf, white wine, butter. He was sautéing the lamb in the hot oil and bacon fat when the kids came home from school, got a car for them to go over to be with Alexei, Sally and their kids for a Hanukkah ceremony (arranged last week). *Even if they're not Jewish, they ought to know about it if they're going to live in this city.*

"Listen up you two, you're going to be doing something different tonight. I want you to be very respectful of what they do and how they do it. Their tradition goes back thousands of years."

"Do we have to eat everything?"

"Take a small bite first. If you don't like it, leave it on the side of the plate. Oh, bring back a potato latke for me, okay."

"Bye Daddy."

Frank adds in the other ingredients, slides the casserole into the oven, pours himself a glass of '07 Cote du Nuit, puts on the CD of Donizetti's *Lucrezia Borgia* (soon to be his favorite), and waits.

Madge clambers through the door, shopping bags akimbo, smelling the stew.

"What a lovely surprise." She drops her bags in the entry and saunters over to him in the chair, leans down and kisses him warmly.

"I thought I'd make us a grown-ups dinner since the kids are out. It will be ready in half an hour."

"I'm famished. I only had a salad for lunch."

"Martini?"

"Why not? Sure."

"How's Gina?"

"Fine. Why? You never ask about her."

"Just wondering."

Madge has a puzzled expression on her face; him asking about her?

"Here's your drink. Cheers to us!"

"Huh?"

"To us." He lifts his glass with a flourish.

She slowly brings her glass up to clink his, her expression now one of curiosity.

"Bonus time in a month. Should be a big year."

"What you going to do with it?"

"Buy a boat, maybe, an ocean racer. I sailed as a kid, haven't much since I got out of college. Thought I'd teach Molly and Lance. They had fun last time we were out on Dad's."

"Isn't that kind of dangerous? People fall off. Storms come up out of nowhere, especially these days."

"Things do happen when people aren't careful … I think it's ready. Sit down."

He brings the vichyssoise (from Gristedes) out from the kitchen.

"Nice, just the right amount of salt." Madge spoons her soup. "I heard this story last summer about a guy sailing with his wife, claimed when he changed course she didn't hear the command, wife was hit by the boom, knocked overboard, he tried but couldn't rescue her."

"The moral is?"

"I don't know if I'd feel safe."

"Aren't you going to finish your vichyssoise?"

"It's feeling heavy in me, not agreeing with something."

"Well, if anything was going to happen, it wouldn't be like that, with the kids around."

Frank excuses himself to serve up the stew.

"What would it be?"

"Something more domestic, probably something slow and painful."

"Did making the stew make you so grim?"

"Hey, you're the one brought up the wife–killing story."

Madge takes a bite of the lamb stew. Frank sits back, as if waiting for her to enjoy. She spits out a mouthful. Chunks land in the middle of the table.

"What the hell did you put in this stew?"

Frank goes down the list of ingredients.

"And what bottle of white wine did you use?"

"It was that half bottle of Chablis left over from last week."

"That was ouzo, you dolt, left over from that Greek meal. Couldn't you smell the difference when it was cooking?"

What a royal screw–up this is. Shit. I cannot believe how fucked up this is. Dammit. He manages the semblance of a straight, please–forgive–me face.

"Hey, it's okay. I'm not gonna die over ouzo–ed lamb."

"How about I go around the corner and pick up some samosas? You like that?"

"And I'll open some real white wine."

Frank grabs his coat, takes the elevator down, thinking *still have enough for another try*, says "How ya keepin', Sammy," to the doorman, turns right, walks about fifty feet, sees a woman: young, tall, long blond hair, high heeled black boots, big coat. Her hands are tucked into her pockets. As she approaches, he moves to his left, she moves to his left, he moves right, she moves right, she comes face to face, eighteen inches apart, icy blue eyes.

"You Frank Cabot?"

"That's me, how'd you ..."

She pulls a compact black gun from her pocket. She fires three shots into his heart.

Farewell to Loved Ones

by Derek Osborne

Wednesday, 3rd December 2014

"No Eddie, I will be fine," Rebecca says, "I just need this time to be alone."

Eddie closes the cabin door. Rebecca can hear him walking back down the passageway. It is freezing cold aboard *Gadabout* but she does not feel it; she is wearing the foul weather gear Max had specially made for her, the brown knit cap they bought that day on Martha's Vineyard, the silk t–shirt her mother insisted upon.

The cabin is just how they left it, the bunk made up with the patchwork quilt, the pillows piled high along the bulkhead. All the fittings have been polished bright, the mahogany and painted white millwork detailed to perfection. The desk and the drawers – the drawers – she fumbles with the thing inside her pocket. Rebecca is here to complete the contract. They have a buyer. *Gadabout* will have a new captain. Tradition dictates the owner's drawer must hold the one thing he could not do without, the one thing they cannot let go. It weighs there in the cargo fold of her jacket. As Max's wife, it is Rebecca who now owns *Gadabout*, Rebecca who will sign the papers. The nights they spent together drift through the cabin. The gray winter day shows through the skylight. Rebecca stands as if on an empty stage, the performance done, the echo of a standing ovation drifting across the proscenium.

"I hear you, my love. I hear you."

The wind pushes the hull. It snowed a bit this morning, only a dusting, but enough to cause her mother to make a fuss about her coming out to the boat.

"So now your baby will be motherless as well."

"And you call me the drama queen."

"I'm afraid you inherited your father's common sense."

"Do not go there, Mama. You married him for it. And I know you loved that in Max. Do not tell me otherwise."

This made her mother grow quiet.

Rebecca is taking in every detail, every moment – their love–making, their fights, the quiet times; their talk that last evening – their pact. Baby Max, though premature, is the picture of health. He has his father's hair, his mother's lungs. Andi enjoys calling him little brother.

Rebecca can feel the wind outside. The mizzen creaks in the mast step, another gust. *Gadabout* swings to face it. She scans the ship's library, all the books she intended to read, all those evenings curled up together snug and warm and sailing the great, wide ocean. This cabin was to be home, a sense of generations, more than anywhere else on the boat the place of so many lives completed, the empty chair at the desk, the mirror hanging over the sink. She looks at the drawers again. The fifth drawer, what was to be Max's drawer only, now hers as well. Max never said what to put in it. He never discussed it with Eddie. Eddie could not, or would not, help. She feels again the thing in her pocket. She hopes it is the right choice.

"Is it, my darling? Did I know you that well?"

Eleven months, a lifetime in eleven months. Touching the drawer is not easy. Pulling it open even harder. Like peering down into an empty grave. The wind will not back down. Outside the light has turned leaden and gray.

"The sun for all its sorrow …"

The bearers are coming, the graves men stand to one side. Rebecca takes the SAT phone from inside her jacket, its weathered red case and black stub of antenna strange in her hand. The weight of it, heavy and solid. She folds the antenna into its little niche, pressing the instrument down between the sides of the drawer. Her hand is shaking. She cannot bring herself to close it, not yet.

"Are you here with me, Max? Am I the good shepherd?"

Gadabout shifts again. Rebecca leans back against the bunk.

"I had no idea what would come of a single kiss. Driving home that night from the restaurant. Sitting in your lap. I only knew I had found you – again – after all this time."

She takes one last look around the cabin.

"And now you are gone, and now we will have to find each other again."

Reaching back, she pulls the patchwork quilt off the bunk. She promised the girls she would bring it. Folding it over and over, clutching the worn and bulky softness to her face, his scent fills her eyes, his warmth flows inside her. She knows it is time to leave. If she does not leave now Eddie will have to carry her. The open drawer awaits the final rose, the fist–full of dirt, the turn and walk from the pastor's stranger's smile. The SAT phone's screen is blank, lifeless. Max once told her the sound of it coming alive was the sweetest thing he has ever known. She reaches into the drawer, pushing the big red button. The backlight warms, searching for satellites. STANDBY appears in the upper right corner. Gently, she pushes the little drawer closed. Go now, the boat whispers. At the cabin door she waits before turning the latch – not hoping it will ring; knowing it will not ring, but giving it time nonetheless – giving Gadabout the chance at one more miracle. Who better than Rebecca to know such things only happen in the movies, and after all, she was only a cable TV star, and even then, only a little while. All will move on, now. All will move on.

Chanukah

by Gloria Garfunkel

Thursday, 4th December 2014

Bipolar Ralph here. It's a month since my father's death / suicide. My father always loved Chanukah the best of Jewish holidays because it was totally joyous despite the Destruction of the Temple in Jerusalem. He loved the miracle of one candle in oil lasting eight nights and the renewal of the Temple. He always bought everyone presents, me, my five siblings and their kids. Manic toys on all eight days.

My father's gift theory for kids was quantity over quality. It didn't matter if it broke the next day, just get them a lot of things.

I decide to take over his job and do the same thing. I have plenty of time to spy on what everyone wants, all ten nieces and nephews. Chanukah is eight days starting Thursday the 16th. I think about Chloe. She's the best thing in my life. I'm just numb for now, for a moment, though I know I'm on my way to euphoric, but for now content and calm. A blessing. I'm probably due for some mania around New Year's. It always precedes a depression. I can see what Chloe's father's suicide has done to her. I could never hurt her like that again.

There's a Jewish custom on Rosh Hashanah to go to a river and throw away your sins in crumbs of bread. I drive out to the river and throw in all my suicide paraphernalia so it's never a temptation: my gun, my years of hoarded pills, my noose, the knives, razor blades, and the thick plastic bag for over my head. I swear my bipolar will never kill me or my kids.

We'll do our best like everyone else. Who cares some say bipolars shouldn't have kids? We'll educate them early about the illness. We'll medicate them. I'm buying the ring I picked out and I'm going to ask Chloe to marry me tomorrow.

Ivory

by John Wentworth Chapin

Friday, 5th December 2014

A tote of cleaning supplies rests on the kitchen counter above a messy bundle of coat hangers and an over–filled trash can. White rectangles pop from the walls, nuclear shadows of dethroned artwork outlined by dirt and grease. Everything he's taking with him is in his car.

"You need a therapist," Stephanie drones through the invisible speaker of Charles' phone.

"No, I need a philosopher," he answers. Moving is usually a terrible chore, but not this move.

Charles' terrible watercolor portrait of Esther sits propped against the wall by the door. He took it from his closet and put it in the *garbage* pile, then moved it to the *keep–it* pile, then tossed it to the *donations* pile, then pulled it back out. Now it's in limbo. He puts it back in the *garbage* pile.

Stephanie's voice is thin, powerless. "What if you move and it doesn't solve anything, but now you're unemployed and alone?"

"I'm not moving," he reminds her. "I'm leaving. I will be traveling, and when I stop, I expect to end up in a different place."

On the kitchen counter, atop a mound of desk debris, lies his little memory book. Charles picks up the book and flips through it while Stephanie monologues. So many things dear to him are jotted inside. He writes down important events and then looks back to celebrate. So he is always looking back.

Stephanie continues. "I don't think it's particularly healthy to slam the door closed on your life."

"I look backwards too much, don't I?" he says.

Silence. Then: "Are you even listening to me?" Stephanie asks.

Charles isn't listening to her. He's staring at the page for today, December 5. He sees the note for today, carefully drawn with a box around it and three stars, which in his important-events rating system is a Top Event.

"Charles?"

"Holy shit," he murmurs.

"If this is a ploy for attention, it's working," she says.

"Today's the one-year anniversary of the accident."

"Are you okay?" Stephanie asks.

"I'm fine," he says. But he's alarmed that he didn't realize until now what today is: a momentous day.

The evening waterfront is dark and cold and desolate except for a few joggers, women with strollers, women jogging with strollers. It's quiet down here, only distant traffic breaking over the murmur of water lapping the pilings. Charles ambles along the harbor's edge, saying goodbye. Fell's Point is his favorite – or was his favorite – place to walk with Stephanie, an unbroken stretch of the water's edge meandering around the ritzy condos and highrises that replaced the dilapidated maritime mess of his childhood. *Maybe I'll come back. Eventually.*

A stroller rolls across in front of him, so fast it almost hits him. Then it careens into the harbor.

Charles spins, but there's no one around. He looks over the edge to see the spot where the stroller floats on its side in the black, trash–speckled water. He's certain enough that there's a baby in the stroller that he jumps in next to it; the water rushes up cold and black and he can see nothing, but he feels something pushing against his leg and he grabs: a length of metal. He then catches something squishy, an arm or leg. He tries to pull it up to his chest. Kicking with all his might, he manages to hoist it out of the water.

He's holding the metal side of the stroller and a small foot swaddled in what feels like a wet pot–holder. Charles tries to lift the baby out of the stroller, but it is strapped in. He puts both hands underneath to lift baby and stroller out of the water together. It's nearly impossible to keep the baby's face and his own mouth out of the water. The baby issues a blood–curdling scream; Charles kicks to keep himself upright while he fumbles for a clip or buckle to get the baby out. Then he hears a woman's voice and a splash and more hands reaching for the baby. Charles shouts for the person to grab the stroller and keep it up. He puts his hands under the baby's armpits and then pulls it up, now free of the stroller. He sets the baby on his chest and kicks backwards toward the bulkhead wall. The baby alternates shrieks and deep gasps for air.

It's cold, and the weight of the water in his shoes, in the baby's clothes, is beginning to wear Charles down. The young woman asks if her baby boy is all right. Charles says he is but they need to get out of the water quickly, and he works his way along the bulkhead until he feels the cross–bars of a ladder. The mother splashes along behind Charles cooing to her son between sputters of fear and grief.

When they've clambered out of the water, the woman takes the baby from him, wrapping her body around it. She's sobbing, and the baby is screaming. Charles reaches for his iPhone to call 911, but of course when he hits a button, it's dead, waterlogged.

He flags down help and a small crowd gathers.

"He saved my baby!" the woman shouts. A man in the crowd removes his sweatshirt for the baby, and now it's swaddled in a cream–colored hoodie. When Charles hears sirens approaching, he quietly slips away from the crowd, wet shoes sloshing beneath him on the cobblestones.

“I’m looking for Chuck,” Charles says. He’s soaking wet, but he has one more goodbye, so he’s back at Eastern Antiques for the last time.

Deonna stands in the back doorway with her arms crossed and a sour look on her face. “If you find him, tell the cops. They’re looking for him, too.”

She could be bluffing, either trying to scare Charles or keep him away from Chuck. Then again: *Chuck*.

“Holy fuck! You’re dripping all over my floor! Get out.”

“I rescued a baby from the harbor.”

“Jesus. Sure you did. Time to hang a youie and go back to rehab.”

“I never stole anything from you,” Charles says. “Do you have a phone number for him? My phone is … messed up.”

“Just get out. Don’t come back or I’m calling the cops,” Deonna replies, jabbing at the air with her finger.

“You’re awfully quick to call the cops for a drug smuggler,” Charles said.

Deonna says, “I’m telling you, take a hike or you’ll be sorry.”

He picks up the phone next to the register. “9–1–1. They’re required to come, even if I hang up. Maybe you don’t have any drugs in the shop. Maybe you do. But you’ll be on their radar –”

“Put down that phone,” Deonna says. “I got a pistol in my office.”

“And if I know you, it’s probably not properly registered,” Charles answers. He knows better than to take his eyes off her. “You fucked my asshole father, and he stole from you. Threaten me all you want, but nothing changes that. Just give me his phone number."

She scowls at him, thinking, then leans back into her office. Charles steels himself, but she turns back around holding her iPhone. It's swathed in an oversized, pink and purple, jewel–encrusted bumper that stretches around the edge of the phone for protection. Deonna peers closely at it, makes a few swipes, and then lays it on the counter by the register, her recent call list with CHUCK and several other numbers facing him.

Charles has a glorious moment of clarity.

He asks Deonna for a piece of paper, and while she turns back to the office, he pops her phone out of its bumper and replaces it with his own destroyed phone. His is black and hers is white, and he can only hope she doesn't notice. He slips her phone into his pocket. When she returns with paper, he writes random numbers quickly.

"Thanks," he mumbles.

"Tell him to fuck himself. And don't you come back, neither," Deonna shouts after him.

Once outside, he quickly retrieves Deonna's phone to make sure it's still unlocked; it is.

Hallelujah! With her unlocked phone, Charles has carte blanche to wreak havoc. He calls the police from Deonna's own phone to make an anonymous tip about some hash smuggling.

He giggles as he texts his father on Deonna's behalf, begging for a couple of cocktails and one last hot screw. If all goes well, Chuck will show up at the shop. He emails himself Chuck's contact information for future reference. He can unload all the old Chuck debt once he knows where to find him.

Charles forwards himself a few incriminating emails between Deonna and her shipper in Vietnam. When he gets around to it, he'll forward them on to U.S. Customs. With such lovely technology, it doesn't take him long to do a lot of damage.

He calls his mother and tells her he's leaving; she insists on saying goodbye in person, despite his objections. He sighs and agrees to meet her back at his apartment. Instead of ending the call, he tosses Deonna's phone into the harbor.

Ah, revenge. Esther would approve.

The walls, the floor, the doors: everything shabby, dingy white. His mother stands with her arms crossed in his kitchen, radiating disapproval and Shalimar.

"Why do you have to leave tonight? Why would you start such a big trip at *night*?"

She doesn't want to hear his answer, so there's no point explaining. "I rescued a baby from the harbor," Charles said.

She furrows her brows. "When?"

"Just this evening. I was walking and a stroller zoomed by with a baby in it and rolled into the harbor in Fell's. I saved its life." A year ago, carnage. Now this.

"I'm very concerned about you, Charles," she says. She clearly doesn't believe him; Charles doesn't quite believe himself.

"That's probably wise," he answers. He indicates the door that he wants her to depart through. Charles' mother walks stiffly out into the hall.

Charles takes a final look around. He leaves the key on the kitchen counter and spots the memory book, lying there undecided. Charles lobs it atop the *garbage* pile on the floor, where it knocks into the watercolor canvas. Charles stoops to collect his painting and walks off into an opaque future, the portrait of Esther tucked securely under his arm.

Fleeting
by Lynn Beighley

Saturday, 6th December 2014

"You're her, aren't you? That one from that reality show, *You Tell Me*?"

I turn from the rack of blouses to see a skinny, overly made up sales girl smiling at me.

"You are! Oh. My. God. This is so cool! Look, can we take a selfie? No one will believe this."

I shrug. Maybe I'll get a discount on the clothes I need to buy for my new cubicle job. I could use it.

She stands next to me, puts her arm over my shoulder and cheek next to mine, and we smile as though we are best friends having the best time ever. Best. Ever. The.

Photo shoot done, she glances around. Seeing no one but me watching, she taps on the screen sending the proof of our giddiness out to all the sites where such things go today. Done, she turns back to me.

"God, thank you soooooo much!" She glances at the clothes draped over my arm. "Oh, let me get you a fitting room. Those are going to look soooo great on you. I just adore your red hair." She's beaming at me. I nod and she takes my clothes and sets me up with a dressing room.

I let her help me find some more clothes. She seems thrilled to help me look good, and I'm happy to let her. I'm optimistic that a discount will happen.

I'm trying on a blue shirt that she swears will bring out my eyes (taken literally, that's an alarming image), when she laughs.

"My boyfriend wants to know ..." she pauses. "He's asking about Bill Plover's nickname. He wants to know." She's giggling so much she has trouble talking. "Okay, so on the honeymoon, was he Bill Dozer because he slept a lot? Or Bill Dozer because he was, um, unstoppable?"

Shit. She thinks I'm April, the Jessica Rabbit–looking woman he married last month. She doesn't realize I'm the evil redheaded woman who turned him down. Crap.

I take a deep breath. I really want that discount. Okay. I can do this.

"Ha ha," I pretend laugh. "Both. Tell your boyfriend it was both."

I try on a few more outfits, and with the help of my new best friend, end up with a nice work wardrobe. I let her think I'm the newlywed. And it pays off, I do get a nice discount. She wraps my clothes in tissue, as she chatters on about the show and how it changed her life and how she wishes she could be on a show like it and how she's applied for a bunch of them and they never call her back and how she's put some of her business cards in my shopping bag in case I hear of any shows that might be looking for someone like her, someone with some acting experience (she was the lead in tons of plays in high school and just loves acting) and she hopes we can go out to lunch some time (when Bill has let me get enough rest, heh heh) and talk it all over.

I smile graciously and nod, and say yes, of course, and you'd be perfect. I take my bag of work clothes and drape it over my shoulder and leave the store. I walk out to my beat–up yellow car, and shove the bag in the bag seat.

My phone rings. I see it's a Los Angeles area code. I listen to it ring three times. My finger almost presses the mute button, but instead I tap the Answer button.

"Season two of *You Tell Me*, Jenn. We want you."

Ant

by Andrew Stancek

Sunday, 7th December 2014

The body is leeched of colour. The creases around the eyes and nose have smoothed; the mouth is freed of the howls.

The monitor blips brain activity but the chest does not rise and fall.

Antiseptic silence. A pale blue vase on the night table holds wilted remnants of a white sweet pea, edges curled.

An eyelid twitches. The darkness outside breaks with a ray of light. A chirp. A rustle of wings.

From a corner of the room a six–legged wingless ant, indistinguishable from billions of its brothers, marches three steps and stops. It lifts into the air, circles, circles, circles. The human body shudders and the monitor flatlines.

The ant soars through the crack in the open window, towards the sun, and disappears.

It is only the beginning.

Christmas Fettucine

by Rachel Ambrose

Monday, 8th December 2014

"It's coming on Christmas, they're cuttin' down trees ..." The melancholy lyrics of Joni Mitchell's 'River' wend their languorous, sad way out of my sister Molly's speakers. We've decided to have a classic tree–trimming party complete with English crackers (which explode), American crackers (which hopefully do not), and altogether too much mulled wine for a Monday evening. But Molly's longtime girlfriend has just walked out on her. Sometimes an older sister needs a younger sister to watch *Miracle on 34th Street* with her and feed her inordinate amounts of alcohol to help her get over life's setbacks. I've taken the liberty of inviting Isa, because we cannot be expected to subsist only on Triscuits and cheap booze.

"Do you have any tinsel?" I ask Molly as we unearth the last of the ornaments from the dust–covered Christmas Box. "Or stale popcorn?"

"I think there might be some up in the attic, in the New Year's box," she replies. "I moved it somewhere last year after we pulled it out for a party ... Michelle wore it like a feather boa ..." Her eyes well and she presses a crumpled tissue to her face.

I hug her. "Please forget about that loser, okay? You'll be fine. You can't possibly be less successful than me, and I've become pretty darn successful this past year. The world just wouldn't stay on its axis. You're a lawyer, for goodness sake."

It's true: my gallery job is still going well (although I have given up forever on trying to figure out what Frederico does with those four–hour time gaps; I figure it's one of the great mysteries of the universe, and that I'm somehow better off not knowing). Diogenes is still creaking away and leaving fur trails all over the apartment, and I've managed to find myself still single and, rather miraculously, not hating every second of it. I've become a voracious reader in my spare time and have even started to hand in little blurbs about the books I read to the local paper.

The fake tree is almost toppling with our childhood ornaments, which Molly insisted on taking for herself when we were going through our parents' attic. She thought she would keep them for when she and Michelle got married and had kids of their own. Clearly that's not happening now. I wonder briefly if I might be able to steal a few. I'd forgotten how cute our youthful efforts at arts and crafts were. So many Popsicle sticks. So much glue peeking around the edges of ancient glittered macaroni.

"Pre–Christmas fettucine is almost ready," says Isa from her perch at the stove. "Where do you guys keep your bowls?"

I dig out the good bone–china bowls from Molly's sideboard and swipe a few forks from the dish drain as Isa pours us more red wine from the bottle on the counter. "You know," she says as she peppers the pasta, "it hasn't been a half–bad year."

I raise a glass at her as Molly comes back into the kitchen, draped with enough tinsel to make a drag queen cry. "It ain't over yet, sweetheart," I say, taking a gulp and squeezing Molly's shoulder as she passes me on her way to the tree. "There's still just enough time for a dance party."

Realationships and rules

by Gill Hoffs

Tuesday, 9th December 2014

I'm meant to be seeing Trudi at the salon today for some festive fanny-hair, probably a Christmas tree or a snowflake, but instead of a wax I'm sat in Zoe's chair in the office, spinning round while she nips for a wee or worse and I cover the (thankfully silent) phone. We'd been discussing the best manicure for a work-wank, which finishes would survive a strum, whether glued-on crystals can come off, and the horrors of acrylics and nail piercings, so perhaps it's just all the mental images of yours truly getting her hot under her hemline.

Though her vibrator's still in her stash drawer, nestled beside the emergency Maltesers and Tampax, so perhaps not.

Wondering whether a snowflake's sexiest, I type '2318008' on her calculator and as I turn it upside down to check I spelled 'boobies' right, the phone rings. I learnt my answering voice from *Madmen*.

"Good morning, might I ask what services you require?"

And it's him. Rory.

"Hello, yes, good morning. Is it still morning? Feels like afternoon but I've been up ages."

There's a bit of a quiver in his voice, and he's rambling – nervous? Could he be nervous? – but it's definitely him.

"Indeed, sir. And how are you today?"

I've spent enough time chilling out here with Zoe, eavesdropping while she takes bookings and doles out assignments and flirts, to know her standard lines and repeat the script word for word. Just as well. My cheeks are burning and I doubt I'd string a sentence together otherwise.

"Fine, fine. Bit busy but fine. I was wondering if you still had a certain girl working for you – I, um, spent some time with her in March."

I swallow what feels like a pint of saliva that's suddenly swilling about my mouth and hope to goodness Zoe's got a magazine in the loo with her. Something with an article on Will and Kate and babies and whether every parent should have their own version of Lupo blah blah blah. Something to get her daydreaming about princes, princesses, and dogs the colour of my (over)cooking.

"Can you be more specific? I can certainly check that for you."

I can hear him gulp, but no sip or slurp beforehand. *Is* he nervous too?

"She's beautiful." He coughs out a little laugh. "Sorry, that hardly narrows it down, does it? Um, she had long dark hair, freckles on the bridge of her nose, green eyes, and a slight Manchester accent. She went by Jennifer."

No mention of my boobs or my fabulous arse? Fuckssake.

"Jennifer ... yes, I know who you mean. Would you like me to arrange another meeting with her? Do you have a particular date in mind?"

Whenever it is, I'm free. Even if I have to plead food poisoning to Zoe and whoever I'm already booked with to make it.

"Tonight, if she's available." Yes! "Or any evening this week. I can be flexible." Him and me both. I click at Zoe's keyboard with my sex–safe French manicure, typing his name and mine for the sake of a sound effect and making Zoe's screensaver of the bald guy from *Masterchef* holding an enormous cucumber vanish, revealing a spreadsheet of things going in and out in more ways than one.

"She's free tonight. Where and when should she meet you?"

"If she can be ready for collection at six from wherever is most convenient for her to be picked up then that would be great."

Six! I don't know if I can wait.

"Certainly. Is this for a special occasion or setting? Will you be emailing any information for her to read or any particular requirements?"

I wonder what he works as. Vet? Scientist? Surgeon? Something caring, anyway. I wonder if this a business date?

"No, no, nothing like that. I was hoping to take her for dinner in Sheffield then, if she cares to, to a spa for the night."

Oh!

"Should I check her schedule for tomorrow?"

"Yes, of course. Sorry, yes. Actually, could you check it for the next couple of days while you're at it?"

Hmm … I know I've a Christmas business do to go to on Thursday but the client's only requested a slim brunette in her 20's so I can always swap with Sophie or Kim if I need to.

"Her schedule is free or flexible through to Saturday. Shall I suggest to her an overnight case?"

"No, no, I can buy her whatever she needs. Unless you think she might prefer her own things?"

Dammit, I can hear a toilet flushing.

"I'll mention the situation to her, sir. She'll be waiting for you at the agency at six."

"Great, great. Thank you."

I'm clapping my hands and spinning on Zoe's chair, full circle, full speed, when she returns from the loo muttering about Harry and the Queen.

"What's *that* smile for?" she asks, staying well out of range.

"I've … got … a … *date*!"

§

Trudi sorted me out as best she could. I definitely did *not* want to look like I'd slipped a freshly plucked chicken breast in my knickers but equally I'd no intention of turning up for this date with spider–legs creeping down my thighs. It's amazing what a woman with tweezers and strong glasses can do.

After two hours of rejecting outfits, emptying my wardrobe, and shooing my cat off the piles of clothing on my bed, I'd decided on a pale jade sweater with a deep v–neck to show off the pearl pendant Rory gave me at his ex's wedding nine months ago. Nine whole months. Enough to grow a baby, perhaps someday a mini–me. It shows off my cleavage a little too, but not overtly, and the skirt is a rich purply velvet swirl around my knees. The boots are black suede, comfortable but sexy, my makeup subtle and a little bit student–y, with a smudge of lilac glitter sparkling round my eyes. No perfumes or scented lotions. I feel jittery but confident, or so I tell myself.

And unlike any other work–night, I'm dressed as me.

Zoe keeps looking at me from behind her desk, I can see her reflection in the glass as I peer out the window at the busy street below. I don't know what he drives but it seems a waste to miss a moment of him, so I watch it all.

"New look for you tonight. Suits you."

I don't turn round but I do meet her eyes in the glass and wink. It's like she is actually seeing me, *me* not Jennifer.

"Thanks, Zoe."

She opens her mouth to say something else but the phone on the desk rings the abbreviated *brrring* that warns her someone's approaching our door and I nearly giggle or sing.

The door opens and he's here and gorgeous.

He nods a quick hello to Zoe then his deep–denim eyes fix on me. There are about five million hair follicles on the average human body, and every single one of mine seems to be vibrating like a happy bee.

"Hi …" He steps closer and smells of sandalwood incense.

"Hi … great to see you again." *I'm-a-fool-I'm-a-fool-say-something-BETTER* runs through my head. I need to make sure this is what I hope it is. "Are we meeting colleagues or family tonight …?"

He shakes his head, and I love how his smile crinkles his face and moves his freckles into fresh constellations on his cheeks.

"Would Italian suit you tonight, Jennifer?"

I blush and grin, my cheeks like tomatoes.

"I'm Carla, Carla Donovan." I hear Zoe gasp at my breaking house rules but I really don't care. "Anything's fine with me."

Oranges

by Susan Tepper

Wednesday, 10th December 2014

"When your mind is made up, it's made up," Pedersen tells the white rat. Swoon, on the arm of the chair, nibbles Frito crumbs out of Pedersen's palm. "If you were a man I'd expect you to understand. But you're not. You're a third–world rodent. That white fur won't save your ass."

Pedersen rests his head back. The Barcalounger, from the year of the flood, has the same type of headrest as a dentist chair. "What a piece of shit," he says, dusting his hands together. The white rat, Swoon, flees.

"Good–bye," he tells it.

Frankly, he'll be glad to be rid of it. The rat has become a nuisance. It used to appear occasionally, when it smelled cooking, or when there was take–out food in a bag on the table. Lately it comes out of its rat hole whenever he's home. Even when he'd rather be alone with his thoughts. His mind drifting now to warm skies with sunshine bearing down and palm trees along the roadsides. Not this slushy sludge of winter. Winter being the worst time of the year. Winter they keep the kiddies locked in the school, no coming out for recess. God forbid they should catch a sniffle. His little darlings.

Florida will be a nice change of pace. Down there it will be warm most of the time and the kiddies will be everywhere. They'll be bright in their little kiddie clothes and flying around like a bunch of colorful kites. Running, screeching, squealing, laughing, shouting. He can park his car outside the schoolyard (per usual) almost the entire year down there.

Pedersen's knees creak when he gets out of the Barcalounger. Good oranges down there, too.

All the Little Labels

by Jessica McHugh

Thursday, 11th December 2014

Nelson Wade loads a box into the moving van. Falling snow hits his nose, and he rubs the cold spot as he faces Edward McKenzie.

"It's going to be weird without you around, Father."

Edward clamps a pink mitten to Nelson's shoulder. "You don't have to call me that anymore. I'm just plain old Edward now." He flips his blonde wig and bats his eyelashes. "With a touch of flair, of course."

The altar boy laughs, and Edward's heart warms in the frigid December afternoon. After resigning from his position at St. Peter's, and the backlash following his explanation, he's grateful for any kindness offered. Nelson is one of the few who stuck by him when he entered the church garbed in a Sunday dress to rival the most fashionable ladies in the congregation. For the first time, he spoke his confession outside of the confessional and felt no shame, even after those he'd once counseled cast their aspersions. Since his mother's death, Edward McKenzie has refused to hide, refused to be unhappy with his truth.

He assumes he could've loaded the boxes alone, but now that he stands among them, he's glad for the company. Especially when he realizes how many he's marked with 'Eleanor' and 'Betty' instead of 'Edward'. All the boxes, all the little labels.

Each one contains a portion of a life he built from the lives of others, too afraid to live his own.

Not anymore. Fairvale will have its close–minded people, too – he's certain of it – but it'll also have its Nelson Wades. And Mario.

His heart flutters when his boyfriend's face fills his mind. His boyfriend, his boyfriend. He can't stop thinking it. *I have a boyfriend.*

Edward's phone rings, and he digs it out of his coat. Ripping off his mitten, he swipes the screen, presses the phone to his ear, and says, "A whole hour without talking to me. That's a record so far."

Mario chuckles. "I just wanted to let you know I'm leaving the office to come help you now. I'll be there in thirty."

"We're nearly finished. I'll be ready to leave for the new place before you get here."

He sighs. "I'm sorry, babe. I should've been there to help you. I just got hung up at work."

Edward had figured Mario wouldn't be able to make it in time to help him move, but as he's become used to such disappointments, he'd prepared himself for the letdown.

"Really, don't worry about it. It's okay."

A car horn catches Edward's attention. Mario's car pulls to a stop at the curb, and he says, smiling, "It is now."

Edward's grin shines from his entire body as his boyfriend jogs over to embrace him. He twirls his fingers through Edward's golden waves as they kiss. Mario's lips taste of espresso and spearmint, and his breath fills Edward with heat until he no longer feels the snow.

When they break apart, Edward glimpses Nelson's averted eyes.

He blushes. "Sorry, Nelson. You can go on home if you want. Thank you for all the help."

"Glad to do it, Father – whoops, sorry. I know that's not who you are anymore."

Edward squeezes his crucifix with a smile. "Man or woman, I'll always be a child and shepherd of God. I'll always worship and love Him. He made me who I am. He gave me strength and illuminated my path to a better life."

Mario hooks his arm in Edward's. "And brought us together."

Edward can hardly believe his joy. Fear still dwells in his heart, but it feels different from the fear that's haunted most of his life. Instead of terror inspired by his mother's insults and threats, instead of needing the ghost of his Grandma Eleanor to assuage him, instead of believing he has no place in God's heart, he sees hope in not knowing the future. He might not find it in a new church, maybe not even with Mario in the new town, but he believes a happy future lies in his ability to take the first steps on his own.

Edward hugs his former altar boy, his chin quivering as he thanks him again. "God bless you, Nelson. Without you, I might not have had the courage to begin this journey."

Nelson pats his back, grinning. "You would have. It just might've taken another year."

As the altar boy disappears around the corner, Edward wonders if they'll cross paths again. If not, he knows Nelson will grow into a wonderful human being. He is another man's child, another social circle's friend – in theory, he shouldn't have given Edward McKenzie anything but service in the Lord's name, but he gave more than anyone. It's amazing how something as small as acceptance can change a person's life in such colossal ways.

Mario slides the last box into the back of Edward's car, and pulls him into his arms.

"Have I told you how beautiful you look today?" he asks.

Edward blushes and toes the frozen ground. "I look like a big fat bell in this coat."

Shaking his head, Mario links his arms around Edward's back and kisses his nose. "You look like a beautiful woman in the snow. A *princess.* My girlfriend is a princess."

He thought “boyfriend” was a great word, but “girlfriend” sounds even lovelier.

“Princess Edward,” he continues. “Hmm … that doesn’t really match your beauty, does it?” Tapping the box labeled ‘Eleanor McKenzie’ in the back seat, he says, “How about Princess Eleanor?”

He smiles. “No, not Eleanor.”

“You’re going to need a new name sometime, don’t you think?”

Gazing into his boyfriend’s eyes, he says, “Yes. And when I pick one, you’ll be the first to know.”

High and Bye

by Shane Simmons

Friday, 12th December 2014

"You did what?!" I ask. I'm standing in the doorway, an empty cardboard box in my arms.

Sandra sits there, one hand grasping the obligatory glass of wine, her other arm wrapped up in a sling.

"You heard me," she says. "I climbed out of the window."

I walk into the room and pause to look her in the eye, just to see if she's bullshitting me.

She's not.

Shaking my head, I continue to the corner where I sit on the floor and start lifting handfuls of books from the bottom shelf, into the box. "I've said it before and I'll say it again. You are absolutely fucking barmy."

"I don't know what I was thinking."

I shake my head again.

"That waste of space was more upset about his Xbox smashing to pieces when I threw it out of the window than when I was threatening to jump. But hey, whatever. I've seen this Sherice he was sexting and believe me, I'm his loss."

I want to let her know that from the moment I met Marlon I never saw him as anything but a trussed up little prick. But I'm certain I don't need to. "Then what happened?"

"Well, a few people stopped on the pavement and were watching and some knob even shouted for me to jump! Oh, and someone put a photo on Twitter! Hold on, I favourited it ..." She pops down the wine glass and with her one available hand, rummages through her handbag and pulls out her phone.

"Here!" She turns the screen to me and sure enough there's a blurry shot of her flat and as I lean in closer I see a pair of legs hanging from her window ledge.

"That's just before someone called the police! You won't believe this though, remember that shoplifter, in the shop across the road?"

"Oh yeah, tied back hair, council estate facelift, millions of kids. What's she got to do with this?"

"No! Remember the officer who turned up?"

I shake my head, "No ..."

"Yes you do! I know you do because you were staring at him! You do realise that you do that, don't you?" She leers at me with googly eyes.

"I don't do that! Okay, yes, I remember him. Really tall, amazing eyes, blondish hair?"

"Yeah, well he was one of the officers and when I saw him coming up the path, looking up at my fat, pale dangling legs, well I felt a right tit. So I thought, fuck this, I better get down."

"Hmm ..." I've barely cleared half the shelf and I need another empty box so I spin around on my backside to face her and give her my full attention.

"So while Marlon was kicking off about all the stuff of his I'd chucked out ... his clothes, Calvins ... And maybe his laptop ... and the Xbox ... Anyway, so I swung around to get back in, twisted and turned, and then I made a right arse of it."

I point to her bandaged arm.

She draws out a "Yeeaahh ..." and fixes her eyes on her shoes, embarrassed.

As I pick up one last book to try and cram into the box, I wave my other hand to prompt her to continue.

"Well, I fell into the room from the window sill. And you know how high the windows are in these flats!"

My howl bounces around the room.

"Yes, yes, laugh all you want!"

"Sorry," I say, but my snickers continue.

"I put my arm out to stop myself but it twisted around under me and ended up between my chest and the floor! I've bruised three ribs as well you know!"

"I'd have thought your boobs would've cushioned you."

"Ha–bloody–ha."

I give her the two–fingered salute.

"Anyway … an ambulance came, they took me to *MY* hospital! All the girls kept popping by to poke fun at me and then they wouldn't let me out in case I was 'a danger to myself'! Oh, and then they called my mother …"

"You Sandra, are one prize twonk."

She shrugs her shoulders and winces, touches her sore ribs. "Aren't I just?"

Now we're sitting in a room dotted with chock–full packing boxes. "Here, you finish this." Sandra holds the bottle in my direction. "I've had enough. And stop packing things because you're hardly going anywhere."

She's only a couple of glasses through the bottle and I wonder if she didn't bash her head too during her mock–suicide tumble.

"I've told you Sandra, I am. And I don't have long to pack."

"No, I'm not letting you leave here. You can potter about, putting all your things into these bloody boxes – WHY?! WHY DO YOU HAVE TO GO?!" Her shrill bounces off the walls and the vibrating shakes my eardrums.

I weave around boxes and sit down on the sofa next to her.

"I applied for that job. I didn't get the job. And then, at the last minute, the guy they chose pulled out. And not just that, it's not even the role I applied for, it's management. Nearly double what I'm earning at the moment. I could hardly pass up that opportunity!"

"Nah, it's not that," she shakes her head. "It's because it's Scotland, isn't it? It's that boy? The half–Scottish one? Mark! You think you're going to meet him again, don't you?"

I stand up and navigate around the boxes to the TV stand in the corner of the room, and start picking up DVDs from the floor around it and stacking them one on top of the other.

"That wine has gone straight to your head," I say. "You don't know what you're talking about."

"Oh, but I do. See, I know we're both fuck–ups. You know I can't help but keep attracting these cheating, bastarding wasters and I know you've not *really* let him go as yet, have you?"

I turn around to face her just as the tower of DVDs topples like dominos between the boxes. "Sand, if Mark walked past me right this minute, I probably wouldn't even recognise him, and I'm sure he's all sorted in the romance department by now. And just because he's half–Scottish doesn't mean he's going to turn up in Scotland. The world is a big place, you know."

"I know that, but do you?" Her eyes bore holes straight through mine. And I want her to stop.

"I know, Sandra." I bend down to gather up the scattered DVD boxes around my feet, "I know all too well."

"I think I should come to Scotland for Christmas. It's not that far. Or how about New Year's? We can each find our own cabers to toss! I'm not leaving without your new address!!!"

Picking up the notepad and red pen from the coffee table, she rips my 'to–do' list off the top and stretching across, brandishes the blank sheet and the red pen in my direction.

Dust

by Michelle Elvy

Saturday, 13th December 2014

"That's us," says Ellie at the sound of the boarding call. She takes Stevie's hands and pulls him close.

"Yeah." Stevie laces her fingers in his. "You take care of Manny, right?"

She smiles. "You know I will."

They lean their foreheads together. They are exactly the same height and they close their eyes, noses touching. They inhale and exhale and remain this way for a few long moments, each feeling the other's breath, warm and familiar. He will not feel her breath on his skin again. Ellie is his first love, and his last for a long time. When she turns to walk through the gate and fly back to Maryland and he exits the airport and heads to the boat that will take him farther south, their paths will diverge into separate universes. She will return to the Chesapeake, looking both inward and back through time, focusing through a microscope at organisms of the Tidewater region – and her personal and professional life will be nurtured by roots extending down through generations entrenched in those low sandy shores. He will spend the next few years journeying outward and all over the map, sailing seasonally with Uncle Norm in the tropics and getting a degree in linguistics up north. He'll study German and French and will be an exceptional student. He'll have an occasional short–term girlfriend. He'll fly to Europe. He'll go on to grad school and a good career. He'll spend summers with Norm aboard *Nightingale*, island hopping in the Caribbean and Central America. And he'll even traverse the Panama Canal one day and cross the Equator. Occasionally, he'll dream of Cape Horn.

When their eyes open, Stevie and Ellie know there's nothing else to say. This is when Ellie kisses him. This is where their story ends.

When a story ends with a long goodbye and a kiss in an airport, you can bet on it being over once and for all. There will be tears and nose–blowing and public emoting. There may be last–minute jitters: *don't go*. There will be onlookers looking on. But that's not where this story ends, because this is not the story you think it is. Sure, it's the story of a boy about to light out for new territory. It's the story of a boy and a girl who've both been lost, just a little, whose love has grown from grief and brought them here, to the domestic departures gate of the Miami International Airport. It's a story of friendship, too: Stevie, Ellie and Manny. An alliance deepened by remembrances of a friend gone forever and a common history reaching deep into the soil in which they buried him on a cold February day.

But this is not only a story about all that. This is also a story of a small girl who has spent the year not exactly in the middle of the story but somehow, strangely, at the heart of it – a girl growing up too, with dreams of her own.

Stevie is not choked up. He's saying goodbye to Ellie, but he's smiling. He's remembering every detail of her body, her hair, her eyes, her hands. And he's happy.

But when Sylvie pulls on his sleeve and gently tugs him down to her level, when he drops his backpack from his shoulder and kneels to look her in the eye, something breaks inside. She is not crying, but when she hugs him hard he feels his face wet with tears. His. Her lemony hair tickles his nose and the year washes over him. There's no sequence to it, but it's all there, from the car crash and Lucky's funeral to Ellie standing naked in his bedroom and Manny swan diving (also naked) off a dock on the South River. And there's this small girl, too – the girl who befriended him one rainy day when she asked him to help her bury her canary. The girl with no family other than a sister to get to school each morning. The girl who served him mac 'n' cheese on china plates and drank lemonade from Waterford crystal. The girl who gave him a bottle of sand from the beach and dirt from her own back yard to carry with him on his journey.

The girl who makes him cry.

"Hey, you know what?" he sniffs and pulls away, placing his hands on Sylvie's shoulders. "I met a boat with two kids on board – two small girls, one your size. Their boat is canary yellow."

"Really?"

"Yeah. And they eat cake off china plates."

"Well, it shouldn't be eaten any other way."

Stevie and Ellie laugh. Sylvie is an old soul, but she seems downright grandmotherly in her exactitude about cake etiquette.

"Yeah," Stevie stands as he continues. "We went and visited one day – Norm was borrowing some charts – and the mom served coffee in small white cups with silver trim, and plates with tiny grey flowers around the edges. She said it's her grandma's china, and she's had it with her all the time they've been sailing."

"Nice mom. I guess she knows how to keep things safe."

"Yeah," marvels Stevie. "Not a single one broken."

§

When the two sisters disappear down the corridor, when he can't see Ellie and Sylvie any longer, Stevie lets out a long sigh and turns on his heel.

Time to let them go. Time to go.

He's back on board *Nightingale* within an hour, tucked into his snug berth. He has not slept much in the past four days. Long days with Sylvie and Ellie, even longer nights with Ellie. He is worn out, body and heart. But he's also exhilarated. He can't fall asleep, so he pulls a book from his shelf: *Beautiful Swimmers*. A gift from Ellie, secured just above his bunk with a few other favorites: *Huck Finn* and *Walden*, Vonnegut and Bukowski, a stack of old Marvel comics and the collected works of Emily Dickinson. Beside the books there are also a few other items from home: a small stuffed Sulley from Monsters, Inc (a pet he's had his whole life, tossed in his duffle bag by his kid brother), a harmonica he's promised himself he'll learn to play, a Baltimore Orioles cap, a carton of Lucky Strikes – a parting gift from Manny ("'cause what else you gonna do on the high seas? May as well smoke, yeah?") – and a photo of his family in a small wooden frame: Mom, Dad, Rob, him.

He doesn't even get to the bottom of the page before he's drifting through a layer of golden dust and floating on a distant ocean. He's on the bow of a boat, swaying up and down with the motion of the gentle swell. The dust is everywhere. He sees each individual particle, and they are beautiful. The air is warm and golden. Through the glow, off his starboard bow, a shape forms. A ship. A ship on tumultuous seas. He looks harder as a grey haze replaces the golden light. The sky darkens now and a chill runs through his bones. Stevie is afraid of the heaving sea. He is afraid of the shape in the clouds. Then it comes into view, suddenly, and he recognizes Great Grandpa Gus. Gus has been prowling Stevie's dreams for over a year, luring him to sea from his whaling ship somewhere in the Southern Ocean. He appeared during the car crash back in January, the event that took Lucky's life and spared Stevie's and set the whole year in motion. And now, he's waving.

But there are two figures there. Standing beside Gus is someone else. Stevie squints to see better but just then his boat heels hard and he has to hold on for balance. He grabs a stay and turns to see Norm at the wheel of *Nightingale*, smiling and shouting happily over the howling wind, "Ready about?"

Stevie jumps to the cockpit to trim the sheets as the boat's bow comes through the wind. He concentrates on the task just a few seconds, releasing the starboard sheet and winding the winch to bring the jib to port.

Nightingale has tacked away and is steering a new course.

Stevie scrambles to the starboard side again just in time to see the other boat's stern. And there's Gus, still waving. Stevie can't make out the name on the transom but the other man comes into view quite clearly now, standing beside Gus. Stevie sees his jeans tattered at the knee, his flannel shirt with a yellow smiley-face tee peeking from underneath, a joint hanging from his lips. He's grinning and waving. A stupid, happy grin.

Lucky. Fuckin' Lucky. Dead Lucky.

Stevie hesitates, hears his heartbeat pierce the deafening wind. In one flash of a moment he feels guilty–angry–sad–pitiful–scared–relieved … and something akin to happy. He can't help himself now – he grins back at his friend. And waves.

And then, the other ship is gone and the heaving seas settle. The black clouds disappear and *Nightingale* sails south by southwest over a glassy sea. The air is sparkling with that golden dust again. Stevie sees each tiny particle. In this one moment, in this dream, everything is beautiful.

Time to go. Time to let go.

§

On the northbound plane, Sylvie watches small ice crystals forming on the window. She sees each individual one, and they are beautiful. She leans her head into her sister's shoulder and falls to sleep. She sleeps hard most of the flight and it's only when Ellie nudges her awake that she remembers she's on a plane. In her dream, the vibrations and whirs of jet engines were blocked out. There was no turbulence, no crackling captain's voice with weather and geography updates. There was no one but her. She thinks she glimpsed Stevie once – but only for a moment and the moment's gone. In her lullaby dream, she was a particle of dust over a cornfield in a storm cloud, spinning dark and angry like something out of Kansas, then she was a drop of water in the sky, raining down into an endless golden ocean. Then – the way it happens in dreams – she was somehow herself again, a small girl gently rocking on a southbound boat, canary yellow, with china plates tucked safely in the cupboard.

Cracked

by Len Kuntz

Sunday, 14th December 2014

It's not even dawn. I'm broke, somewhere in the middle of East Jesus, Wyoming, and all the radio will pick up is twangy honkytonk or stations playing rambunctious Mexican music. Not only that, but my gas gauge is leaning its elbow on E.

This little joy ride of mine – almost a year now – has been an adventure, but it's done nothing to transport me out of the funk of having been dumped by my wife. If anything, I feel worse than when I first set out. Seeking adventure is fine, so long as you have a safe harbor to return to afterward. Without an anchor somewhere, a man might as well keep driving, fly his car right off a cliff, or drink himself dead.

The dashboard lights up in the far right corner, flashing strawberry red: *Get gas now!*

I'm not sure what to do. I check my wallet and pockets. I've got a buck twenty. That'd get me a third of a gallon of gas. But I need to eat because I'm starving.

Get gas now!

The landscape is a shroud of darkness. I'm going to run out of gas and die in the desert, be eaten alive by lizards. Panic sets in, as if termites have invaded my chest and are trying to gnaw their way through my flesh.

I try to keep my eyes off the dashboard but it's like trying to ignore your favorite pornography rippling across a computer screen.

Get gas now!

A spark of rage ambushes me. I feel the urge to break something, hurt someone, leave a life in ruins.

Get gas now!

Up ahead, the craggy, bone–dry land shows the semblance of a town coming into view – barn–shaped buildings and flat–topped domes.

I pull off at the first exit. It's December and chilly yet my armpits are drenched and I reek.

I find the gun in the cubby and tuck it between my waistband and belly. I have no idea what I'm doing but as soon as I enter the AM/PM mini mart the smell of scorched wieners reminds me that I'm ravenous.

I grab a basket and fill it with Ho Hos and Hostess fruit pies (cherry and chocolate) and toss in a six–pack of Budweiser and some Doritos and aspirins and bags and bags of beer nuts, plus rolls of SweeTARTS and an enormous sack of gummy bears.

At the counter, the teller rings the items up as if in a trance. He's got a shaved head, a stud through his nose, and gauges the size of quarters in his earlobes.

"Thirty–seven fifty–nine," he says, without looking me in the eye.

I whip out the pistol and point it at his forehead where a yolk–yellow pimple stares back at me.

"Hand me the money in the till."

"Are you shitting me?"

"I'm going to be shooting you in a second."

"There's a camera," he says, calm as can be, pointing up over his right shoulder.

"Do I look like I give a shit?" I jiggle the snout of the gun at him, hoping he doesn't notice that my hand is shaking.

"Suit yourself," the kid says, bored as death, stuffing bills into a brown paper bag that might have once contained his lunch.

"Change, too," I say, feeling greedy and desperate, thinking if I'm going to go through with this, I might as well get it all.

"Where's the duct tape?" I ask.

"Duct tape? We don't have no duct tape."

"Fine, then step around and get on your knees."

"There's no way I'm giving you a blow job."

"You're getting a little wishful," I say. "I need to tie you up."

When I cock the gun, it makes a teeth–scritching noise, and the kid obliges.

Once he's on the floor, I realize I don't have anything to tie him up with. I am probably the worst criminal ever.

"On second thought, get up. Give me the keys and your cell phone."

The guy hands them over. His phone cover is a Hello Kitty logo. "It's my sister's," he says, reading my expression. "I dropped mine in the toilet."

I lock him in the back office and stuff a stool up against the door knob so there's no way he's getting out on his own. I grab my money and goodies and fly out the door, waving at the camera on the way.

The only other car in the lot is the kid's and so I take it instead of mine. His is a vintage Volkswagen Rabbit, painted purple, that smells like a combination of Lysol and sweaty feet. Surprisingly, the gas tank is full. Surprisingly, the car has some guts.

I head west doing ninety–five, keeping my eyes peeled for lurking state troopers. My idea is to go as far as I can until the gas runs dry, then catch a bus. I figure it's the last place the cops would be looking for me, and besides, all they know is what the kid can tell them. My image on that camera won't do a bit of good.

I take a big bite of a cherry fruit pie, pop open a can of beer and take a swig to wash the fruity taste down. I'm feeling confident now, burning with a felonious high. It's the best I've felt all year. Even though I've committed a crime, I've accomplished something, something brave and daring. I wonder if my wife would be proud or scared or what. I wonder why I still care about her and what she thinks of me. Her new guy is probably doing her doggy–style right now.

Then I get a picture of her and him in bed, him mounted behind my wife, grunting and thrusting. My eyes sting. As I cross the border into Idaho, I start to bawl. It's only the second time I've cried in a decade, but now that I've started I can't stop. I don't know who I am or what I'm doing. I think about the gun I've stashed in the kid's glove compartment, next to his book of cigarette rolling papers. I could blow my brains out and not have to worry about my next move or how to make something of my life. I could fly off the curve up ahead where the road winds around a mountain. I've got a hundred different choices, and none of them are good.

It's nightfall and I'm on a Greyhound bus seated next to a young man with two prosthetic arms. I want to ask how he got them, how he lost his others. When he catches me staring, I shift in my seat and stare out the black window.

"IED," he says. "Afghanistan."

I look back. He's actually grinning.

"Could have been a lot worse," he says. "The guy that actually stepped on it, PFC Raymond Williams from Kentucky, he lost everything."

"God, I'm sorry."

"It's true what they say; war is hell."

"But you made it out."

"Most of me did. I'm thankful for that."

I feel a sense of shame wash in. Here I've been feeling sorry for myself all year and this guy lost two of his arms yet wears a bright smile.

We make small talk for the next hour. When I tell him I robbed a convenience store earlier today, he laughs. Nothing seems to faze him.

So I tell him about my last year, how I've been searching for something all this time since my wife left me.

"That's a shitty deal, a woman cheating on a guy. Not much worse, but you've got a choice to make."

"Yeah?"

"You can let it haunt you forever or else burn all your memories of her and start fresh."

"Is that what you did, with your experiences in the war?"

"I guess so. Of course, I've got these two reminders," he says, lifting his fake arms.

I feel guilty again for all my self–pity, yet it's easy to say, *burn all your memories*, and another thing doing it.

"Look," the guy says, "it's your life and who am I to say, but maybe what you went searching for was something that was in you all along."

"Like what?"

He punches me lightly in the chest with his fake fist. "Heart."

I'm not sure what he means exactly, but all the same he's got me thinking about courage and renewal.

The bus driver comes on the speaker telling us we're twenty minutes from Seattle.

"Say, did you really rob a convenience store?"

"Yeah," I say.

"Man, you're a real crack up."

Cracked, I think, but with luck and a lot of hard work, fixable.

Twelfth Inning
by Michael Webb

Monday, 15th December 2014

I drive the babysitter home, drink a diet cola in the kitchen, then sneak upstairs, trying not to wake the kids, padding into the bedroom in socks. Angela is facing away from me, looking at her reflection in a full–length mirror. She is topless, wearing only soft green sleep pants that ride low on her hips. I watch her turning, looking at her body in profile, and then straight, and then turning the opposite way. I stand and watch her. She seems focused on her belly, the gentle swell that rises below her ribs and above her wide hips. Despite our bickering now and then, she still makes my heart stop. Angela puts her hands behind her back then, pulling her shoulders back, her breasts full and round in front of her. Two children, but still as beautiful as a postcard, as precious as a love song.

"Hey," I say softly.

"Hey," she says. "Marcy proposition you yet?"

"Of course," I say, "you know I'm always beating her off with a stick." Our babysitter Marcelline, the 15–year–old daughter of one of the trainers at Athletes Performance Center, has become a running joke between us, after an offhand comment I made about how mature she looked. Angela now teasingly insists that she is about to seduce me every time we are alone for more than 30 seconds.

"As long as you keep that stick handy," she says. She turns to face me, her breasts sagging but full, glorious and round, her nipples enormous and brown. Angela's hands are still behind her back for another second, then she exhales, roundness returning to her stomach again. She walks across and into our bathroom.

"Did you talk to Jacob? He said he'd try you on your cell."

Jacob Feinberg, of Feinberg Sports Management LLC, is my agent. He is busy fielding and evaluating the offers for my services for next year, and hoping for the largest number possible that he can then take 10 percent of.

"I did," I say. I hear her brushing her teeth, so I continue. "He told me Seattle called, and Houston, and Cleveland made an offer. He's going to wait a few more days, and then if nobody blows him away, he thinks we should go with Seattle."

"Is it a good offer?" she asks with her mouth full of toothpaste.

"Pretty good. Three years. It will be nice to not be going hat in hand for a while. And the money is good, because I may not get another long one like this."

I hear her spit. "Sure you will," she says cheerfully.

"I appreciate your confidence," I say. "But the list of 35–year–old pitchers making big money is … well ... it's not long, love."

"I'm sure you'll be on it," she says. I hear her washing her face. As I sit on the bed, with the bathroom door open a crack, I can still catch flashes of her bare skin as she moves around. I spy on her openly, still as thrilled as a 12–year–old who finds the hole in the fence where the neighbor's wife is sunbathing. Even with folds and wrinkles, perhaps because of them, she is still the most beautiful woman I have ever seen. I feel the throb under my pelvis. Maybe tonight, I think. We make love a fair amount, but I'm never averse to more.

She comes out, her face slightly red but looking clean and smooth, droplets adhering to stray hairs that circle her face like a halo. I feel need for her, acute and full, watching her hips sway as she walks across the bedroom. She slides her pants off her legs, leaving them beside the bed in case of some kid–fueled night time crisis.

"Are they good?" she says.

"Seattle?" I say. "No. They're young. Lots of promise. But they won't contend until the end of this contract, if even then. Lots of handholding, showing kids the ropes. Which sucks, but for the money they're offering, I'll do whatever they want."

"Oh," she says. She turns out the light on her side of the bed, then climbs under the covers. She finds her usual spot, her head resting on my chest, my hand down her back, her thigh thrown over mine. It is a subtle negotiation. Neither of us like to say no, even when that is the answer.

I spread my fingers out wide, feeling the muscles of her lower back and the delicate curve of her buttocks. Smelling her is an intoxicant. I think about the line I love from Joyce, about her name being a "summons to all my foolish blood," and the desire for her runs through me like a current. I can feel myself getting full, and growing, and beginning to press against the skin of her thigh.

"Oh," she says, swallowing a chuckle. "Hello there."

"Hi," I say. She shifts against me, opening her legs, her softness now on my skin, wet and intensely hot.

"I'd say someone wants something," she says. She moves her thigh slowly, rubbing the soft inside against the outside of me, a delightful torment.

"Someone wants something," I say, my voice growing thick. "That's for sure."

"Are you ready for another baby?" she asks me, her tone serious for a moment.

At this point, I felt hard pressed to refuse. I would say anything to get her to agree to what I want. I still don't think it is a good idea, but as my mother likes to remind me, not to decide is to decide.

"If you are," I say. She slides herself on top of me, getting into position, lifting one leg slightly to guide me into place. I ache for her now, feeling lust and greed filling my head like popcorn in a bag.

"Good," she says, letting me have her, her weight coming down as I slide inside her, strong and velvety smooth and wet, surrounding me delightfully in our practiced rhythm. I sigh with pleasure.

She groans. "Good," she says again, "I tested this morning. I'm pregnant."

Alive and Kicking

by James Claffey

Tuesday, 16th December 2014

The Shannon burst its banks a week ago and sheep, cattle and the odd goat float bloated and lost in the middle of Ireland's great start–up lake. Farmers wring their hands in McKettrick's snug, drowning their sorrows and totting up the EU compensation they'll collect in the New Year. The Bird knows plenty of them will invent numbers the way the government seems to do on an almost daily basis in order to put a rosy look on the unemployment figures. Only the prior Monday he started a new course in Athlone at the technical college, a Postgraduate Diploma in Business in Cultural Event Management. He likes the sound of it and daydreams about leading large groups of foreign travelers about the countryside searching for fairy forts and Leprechaun troves. He also conjures up the idea of a lovely single French woman to replace Melodie in his heart's desire.

This afternoon the nuns are all in a dither about the visit of the Archbishop to the convent. Bunting and flags are put into place and the narrow triangular fabric that last saw air when the Pope visited in the 1980s now adorns the railings of the church grounds. A great honor, the Mother Superior told the Bird when he inquired as to the occasion. If he can have the Archbishop's ear for a minute, the Bird will put a stop to the Mother

Superior's gallop and tell the man about the nun's swindling ways and property acquisitions. Shite and onions, the Bird thinks, as the bloody Church is as crooked as the road to Baltrasna. He left the nuns in "high Do" and wished the miseries of the world to be heaped on their crow–like shoulders.

Maybe he'll whitewash the doors of the convent with the words, 'Thieving Bitches', or worse?

In the dim light of the snug he orders another Guinness and watches the dark liquid settle in the glass, layers of time collapsing on top of one another. No one speaks to him and he sups alone and unhappy in the corner. The racing from Kempton Park is on the television and a horse takes a terrible fall as the Bird watches the final furlong unfold. Maybe that's how his own life will end, in a tragic fall, legs broken, heart pounding out the last desperate beats. Worse ways to die, he thinks, draining the Guinness and making for the door.

On the street a few hardy souls wait for the bus to Athlone, the wind blowing hard and the spits of rain a promise of more to come. Those nuns, he ponders. "Don't tread on me," he whispers. Yes, he'll show those crones who the boss is when push comes to shove. Hands thrust in his pockets as he walks, the Bird pushes into the wind and makes towards the river to see what might be floating by in the water.

A trip to Clara to listen to the music isn't out of the question, and the Bird lingers on the picture in his head of the lovely French girl he might have wooed had fate not slapped him for his insolence. Melodie. She was some looker and no mistake, he thinks. The time she almost smothered him between her breasts, and him as useless as a broom on a beach to clean up the sand.

As he steps out the door of the house to cycle over to Clara, the Bird stops to gaze up past the rooftops of the town. The velvet December sky gives the Bird some solace, though, so many pinpricks of light shining in the heavens. Love is not something he's had much luck with, one way or the other, and he wishes it were different, but at least he'd had a sliver of opportunity with Melodie, until he'd scared her away with his talk of the Mammy's ghost.

The river is fast flowing, bushes and branches of downed trees tumble by as the Bird flies by with the breeze on his back. Fast out, slow home, he thinks. Across the wide expanse of water lights flicker in the night. Maybe cottages of farmers cut off by the high floodwater. Or, maybe, faeries afoot on these last nights of the last month of the year? He'll have to keep a wide berth of any of the supernatural creatures abroad, and with his own mammy prone to dropping by unannounced, the Bird is no stranger to the weirdness of this life.

Hogan's is packed to the rafters and the Bird doesn't recognize any of the musicians tonight. Melodie might be back in France for the holidays, or off with her damned boyfriend, the fortunate cur.

As he takes a seat by the bar a hand on his shoulder startles him and he prays it's Melodie, but Father O'Hehir's sober face stares at him. "Bird, isn't it well you're looking?"

"How are you, Father?"

"Never better. Though I'll be mightily relieved when the Archbishop is come and gone. That Mother Superior has me driven distracted by her constant phone calls about this, that, and the other."

"Can I buy you a drink, Father, for the holidays?" The Bird lifts a hand to hail the barman.

"A small whiskey, thanks very much." The priest sidles into the spot next to the Bird and plants his behind on the stool. "I prefer the company of men, Bird," he says. "Not that there's anything wrong with the fairer sex, but sometimes I don't have the patience for all their insignificant blather."

The Bird shrugs, lifting the glass to his lips. "*Sláinte*, and a *Nollaig Shone Dhuit*," he says to the priest.

"And to yourself, Bird. May the coming year bring you better luck than this one did."

The reels and jigs commence and the two men turn their backs to the bar, feet tapping along with the music. Voices join in the chorus of the songs that play between the dancing tunes and for a moment the Bird imagines his life not to be too shabby after all. Across the room the musicians sit in a semi–circle, instruments blazing, cigarette boxes on the table ready for their break. A middle–aged woman pours sweat and wrists the *bodhrán*, her eyes tightly shut, the strains of a familiar tune filling the air. The Bird recalls the music Melodie played the first night he saw her in here, and he draws a deep breath and believes he can catch her scent still lingering in the pub.

Nothing in his life is the way he wants it, not work, not love, not family, and least of all not Melodie. The Bird shifts on his stool, only realizing the priest is no longer beside him, and he searches the room for the man. Never around when you need one, he thinks. He raises his hand to order again and when he turns back to face the music he feels the beginnings of a tear traveling down his cheek.

"Would you send over a drink to the woman playing the *bodhrán*, like a good fellow," the Bird tells the barman. When the set ends the barman delivers the Bird's gift and says something to her. The woman raises her eyebrows and lifts the glass to the Bird in thanks. "Sláinte," she mouths, silently, winking at him. In return the Bird raises his own drink to her and says, "Alive and kicking. Alive and kicking." He slips off the stool and makes his way across the packed bar to the players, a battered old boat navigating the choppy and dangerous waters of life and love. The Bird shouts, "My name is Mahony, the Bird Mahony, nice to meet you."

"By the hokey, that's a name worth remembering," she tells him. "Rose. Rose Conroy."

The Bird feels the leaky boards of his craft lighten a bit. He pulls at his ear, grins, and realizes he has some living to take care of before he too fades and sinks beneath the overflowing Shannon waters.

What It Feels Like To Have Your Friends Dying Around You

by Gwendolyn Joyce Mintz

Wednesday, 17th December 2014

Mora makes her way across the parking lot to the front door of Kelly's, all the while telling herself to go elsewhere. At the threshold, she stops and gives the idea serious consideration.

"But I promised Aaron," she says aloud, her words a whispered white breath in the cold air.

She pulls the door open.

Another time, her heart would have been tugged by the deep green wreaths and garland decorating the walls and doors. The mistletoe placed strategically above the hostess podium might have made her smile. The boisterous rendition of 'Joy to The World', one of her favorite songs, blaring through the speakers might have had her joining in. *And Heaven and Nature Sing*. Another time –

She heads straight for the bar where she orders a glass of champagne. The bartender takes her money and is about to leave but Mora stops him by holding out one hand. Tossing her head back, she downs the drink. She pushes the empty champagne flute across the bar counter.

"Another one," she tells the bartender. "And some water."

She pays for the second glass, and then takes her drinks to a nearby cocktail table to sit.

She watches the servers interacting with patrons and she wonders if Lindsey is working. She hopes she is and she hopes she isn't.

Lindsey wasn't working when the group last met.

It was then Aaron had announced, "This is gonna be my last meeting."

"You're finally doing it?" Phil had asked.

"Yep."

Aaron was heading out of town for the Thanksgiving holiday, to Dallas, where his parents lived.

"Decide how?" Phil had continued.

Aaron had had a paper napkin in his hands and he had folded it and then again. Again. Unfolding it, he had said, "Did you know you can search the internet for quick ways to die? I always meant to tell you guys about this one site ..."

His attention had drifted to the tables around them. Then he'd slowly turned back to them. He'd tossed the napkin toward the center of the table and said, "Guns are messy. Pills take too long. Some other ways invite your body to fight for survival, and from what I've read, the struggle is not pretty. So it's down to carbon monoxide –"

"Your car is being picked up by the new owner after the meeting," Mora had interjected.

Aaron had frowned. "It wouldn't've worked anyway, low emission. But my father has two cars. Old ones. And a garage." Aaron had picked the napkin up again and began twisting it tight. "And then there's hanging."

"Seriously? You weren't disturbed by that book in high school – the way they described John hanging there? Why would anyone wanna leave that kind of image in someone else's mind?"

Aaron's sigh had been loud enough to have people from other tables turn to them. "Mora –"

"I'm sorry," she'd quickly said.

"You don't have to be here."

She'd said she did. "I promised to be with you guys to the end."

"Then you're going to need to shut up," Phil had told her.

Later, when Aaron sent the text, he used a previous thread that had been a group message. When Phil sent a response to Aaron, telling him that he had been a good friend and that perhaps it was time for him to check out as well, Mora got a copy.

She got a copy of Aaron's reply to Phil and then Phil's next reply. There were a few more texts and then Aaron sent one that said, "Unfortunately, this was not a *fan* club. Goodbye."

Phil sent another. "Later."

And then the texting stopped.

It was only days ago that Mora was able to take a deep breath and search for their obituaries online. She left a comment in both of the visitor books although she believed what she'd written was trite in the face of what she knew.

"Hey?"

Mora blinks and she's out of her thoughts and back in the restaurant.

Lindsey is standing there.

"Hey, hi," Mora says.

"You alone?"

Mora nods. "No one else could make it."

"Can I get you something? This isn't my section and I'm off in a few minutes but I could run an order in for you."

"I'm fine," Mora says, "but thanks."

"Just here to celebrate?"

"Huh?"

Lindsey points at the champagne flute. "Someone in your club has accomplished their goal."

Mora tilts the flute slightly and twirls the remaining champagne around. "Yeah, something like that."

Tell her.

Mora sets the glass upright and looks at Lindsey. "Can I talk to you before you leave?"

"Sure. I'll be right back."

Mora nods.

When Lindsey returns, she drapes her coat over the back of a chair and sits down. She slips the elf cap off her head and shoves it into her purse which she sets on the table.

"I hope you get paid extra for that," Mora tells her.

Lindsey grins. "We do, but it's fun too." Her hands smooth the sides of her green costume. "Unfortunately it's impossible to find non–slip, pointy–toed shoes so the look is just a bit off." She lifts her foot and wiggles it. "But you wanted to talk to me."

"I was wondering if Aaron ever told you what our club was about."

"He said you met to talk about life and death matters."

Mora smiles and shakes her head. Aaron. "That's close. We were interested in suicide; we met to figure out how to die."

Lindsey's expression moves to stoic as her gaze sharpens on Mora. She nods as she begins to understand. "So, when someone didn't show up, it was because they were dead?"

"Yes."

Lindsey's eyes shoot to the champagne flute. When she speaks, it's slow like she's using words for the first time. "Is … he … dead?"

Should have used a buffer –

Mora is surprised by Lindsey's sudden tears. Maybe there had been more than Aaron said. "I'm sorry. I –"

"No, no," Lindsey tells her. "It's not like that." She swipes at her cheeks. "I liked you guys, you weren't just a tab." She takes a breath. A few more. "I'm from a small town and when I was in middle school, our town made the national news because our suicide rate was bigger than the nation's average. Kids were just killing themselves. My sister's friend. The boy next door. Our dad's boss's daughter." She takes the napkin Mora holds out to her and blows her nose. "Our parents got scared and they were always talking to us about it, to make sure we weren't considering it but they never asked what it felt like to have your friends dying all around you." She pulls strands of hair from her wet cheeks. "I just never dealt with it." Lindsey takes a breath. "Aaron is dead?"

Mora can't stop the tears that come to her eyes. "Yes. Phil too."

"Wow," Lindsey whispers. Wow, her mouth forms the word again. She leans back in the chair and stares at Mora. "Are you next?"

Mora shakes her head. She may not have the life she wants but she can live with the life she has. "I tried two times before to kill myself and while there are days I don't want to live, there are not days when I want to die."

"I'm sorry," Lindsey says, sliding off the chair and reaching for her jacket. "Thank you for telling me but I just can't do this right now."

From her seat, Mora places her hand on Lindsey's arm as Lindsey reaches for her purse sitting on the table. "This is hard, I know. But listen, since you're off, why don't we go somewhere else and talk?"

Flow

by Stephen V. Ramey

Thursday, 18th December 2014

The room is like a cathedral, dark panels, painted ceilings, brass everywhere. A polished bar runs the back half of one wall, bottles stacked along the mirror behind it. The tap is a glory of levers and logos.

You might wonder how Lanigan's Irish Pub ended up in a place like New Castle, with its Italian tradition and economic woes. While you're at it, you might wonder how a 50-something guy who never drank much, never smoked, was reasonably athletic, ended up with aggressive prostate cancer. You might wonder any number of things, but sometimes stuff just *is.*

"What do you say to another Guinness?" Jimmy says. He and Rose and Anne and I are sitting at a table, winter coats draped over our chairs.

"I say if you're not with us, you're a Guinness," I answer. It feels good to smile.

Jimmy rolls his eyes. "Leave the comedy to professionals."

"I think two is plenty," Anne says. "You have your appointment in the morning."

"They won't care if I'm hung over. It's the other end that concerns them." I signal to the server, avoiding Anne's glare. "Another round, please."

"What's this thing called again?" Jimmy says.

"Cyberknife," I say. "It's an experimental radiation protocol. I have to fill out the paperwork tomorrow."

"Cyberknife," Jimmy says. "That's cutting edge, right?" He stares at Rose as if expecting her to laugh.

Rose turns to me. "I'm sorry, Stephen. Sometimes I wish he came with an *OFF* button."

The server approaches in her plaid skirt that shows off those firm white thighs. *If only I was younger, and not dying.* She sets the drinks onto the table, one by one, and picks up the empties. Mine is in a wooden tankard.

Anne watches intently as if she's afraid I'll fall off my chair, or maybe forget my promise to fight this thing. It irks me that she would doubt me after what we went through with the cat, but it's a passing irk. A buzz has settled nicely into my brain. I drink once and set the tankard down.

"Let's go. I've had enough."

Outside, the air is sobering. The moon, a mere sliver, hangs above the parking lot. I pause to gather my bearings and a thought beams bright across my brain.

"When this all began," I say, "I went to the tent city along the river and spoke to a woman named Tomorrow. She told me to come back when I was –" I make air quotes "– *ready.*"

"Oh, how interesting," Rose says. "Why don't we take a stroll down there now?"

"It's darker than Obama's nutsack down there," Jimmy says.

"Afraid you'll fall in?" Rose says. She gets that playful look, wide doe eyes, brows arched.

Jimmy laughs. "I'm afraid you'll fall in and melt, you're so sweet."

"You're my Cinnabon." Rose pinches Jimmy's butt, then he's chasing her through the parking lot, across the street down the slanted path to the river.

Anne watches stoically, but I see a hint of smirk.

"Pathetic, isn't it?" I say.

"Let's pretend we don't know them," she says.

"Agreed." Holding hands, we stroll after our crazy friends. "Jimmy's a little drunk to be driving anyway."

We follow a path, graveled but not yet asphalted. Rose's laughter echoes beneath the bridge. When we reach the river bend, we find two coats hanging from a tree limb and two sets of shoes standing along the shore. Jimmy and Rose are splashing in the shallows.

"Aren't you guys freezing?" Anne says.

"No, it's fine," Jimmy says. "My wife's so hot the water's starting to boil."

"Come in," Rose says. "The waning is a perfect time for letting go."

"Of what?" I say.

"Of everything unnecessary." Rose slides her blouse over her head. Jimmy unbuttons his shirt.

"I'm not taking off my clothes," Anne says. "It's supposed to go down to thirty tonight."

I nod absently, but the truth is I do feel the river calling. *Come to me, Stephen, come…*

I sit on the bank and pull off a shoe. A Velcro rip staccatos. I remove the other more slowly, then my socks, roll up my pant legs until they're cuffed at my knees.

"You're not actually going in," Anne says.

"Why not?"

She watches Rose in her black brassiere, Jimmy bare-chested. Breath steams from their mouths.

"You're going to have to be careful once you start chemo," Anne says.

I stand. "I haven't started yet. Are you sure you won't come with me?"

She shakes her head stoically.

I leave my coat on in deference to her concern and step in. Icy water hits like a sledge. I gasp. Cold becomes numb, becomes a strange kind of warmth moving slowly up my legs, my hips, my spine, revealing me to myself. Healthy tissue glows. Disease is banded gray or black, a topography of linked valleys and mountain nodules. I shudder – there's so much – and then I think of Mystery breathing in and out with such resolve. *You can kill me, but I will not make it easy.*

The river flows around me, dark and steady. My hands dip reflexively into my pockets. I feel a keychain and pull it out. Dangling amid the keys is the flash stick Frank bought for me. My novel is stored on that drive, at least the portion written since Frank, which is most of it, really.

I turn, pulling the flash stick out from the keys to show Anne. "Remind me when we get home to save this –"

Something shoves me. My foot slips. Hands flailing, I fall. The flash stick twists. The key ring flies off. I hit the water with a cushioned splat. Tendrils of cold water flow across my hands and neck.

"Are you all right?" Rose and Jimmy splash over.

Jimmy's forearms hook my armpits and lift me up. Water dribbles from the hem of my coat.

"Can't take you anywhere," he says. He releases me, holding just long enough to make sure that I stand on my own in the water.

"Someone pushed me," I say. "Was it you?"

Jimmy extends his arms. "Do I look like Wilt Chamberlain?" His teeth chatter, and he starts toward the tree where their coats are hanging. "I'll get yours, Baby," he says over his shoulder.

"Thanks," Rose answers. Even in scant light I see the gooseflesh standing from her arms.

"I'm serious," I say. "I didn't fall, I was –"

"Let it go," Rose says. Her eyes tighten. "All of it, Stephen. The river wants you clean."

"Yeah, right. I suppose there's an app for that." The cold hits me, a shiver in my stomach that races to my shoulders. I turn. Anne has stepped into the stream, one shoe drenched, one pant leg wicking cold water. She's waiting for me to choose between Rose in the current and her by the shore.

"I'm coming," I say.

Rose grabs my arm and pulls me around as Jimmy drapes a coat across her shoulders and continues downstream. She cups my cheek. "You know I'm right."

A part of me does know, the part that danced with Amanda's ghost, the part that drew me to church that day and urged my disastrous walkabout. The part that slept while Mystery died on my stomach. My hand goes to the wound in my side, no more than a frowning white line after Frank's care.

I want so badly to wash away the diseases I've been running from, but it's a lie to think I can. There is no easy way out, no magic kingdom. *Breathe,* I think. *You can kill me, but I will not make it easy.* I think of a kitten on the palm of my hand, and a sob pushes up from my chest.

Rose nods at the moon. "The final phase," she says. "The letting go before rebirth." And then she's guiding me toward Anne, one arm draped across my shoulder. *Splat-splat-splat* our footsteps sound. My pant legs drag in the water.

Jimmy slaps up behind us. "Your keys." He presses a mass of rough edges into my hand. A half-moon plastic eyelet clings to the ring.

"The flash stick, where's the flash stick?"

Jimmy frowns. "Didn't see one."

I lunge for the river. Jimmy grabs my arm.

"You don't understand," I pant. "My book's on that drive."

Jimmy glances back. The river is darker than the sky. "We'll find it in the morning, okay? When there's more light. Don't you have it on your laptop?"

"No."

Jimmy squeezes my shoulder. "I have two things to say to you, Stephen. Backup." He squeezes again. "And backup."

"Jimmy ..." Rose warns.

"So, he'll write it again. I have to redo bits of my act all the time on the road. Usually they come out better."

"Fuck you, Jimmy." I shove, but he barely budges. "This isn't a joke, okay? It's my life on that disk, twelve chapters. Do you have any idea how long it took?"

"Let it go," Rose says. "Fight the battle you need to fight now."

I sigh. "All I ever wanted was to write one masterwork, something meaningful to leave behind."

"The perfect joke," Jimmy says. "I get that."

"No you don't," I say, and my stomach clenches. "No one 'gets it' Jimmy. You have Rose, you have your work, you fit in. I don't have any of that. I –"

"You have Anne," Rose says, and shame slams down like a block of ice. I look to my wife, standing forlornly by the bank.

"I didn't mean ... that didn't come out right." I remember her coming to me on the stairs when Mystery died. Have I thrown that away? What's wrong with me?

Anne's shoulders slump. She reaches out, flesh so white it all but glows. "Come," she says. I take her hand. She leads me from the river. "Believe it or not," she says while efficiently stripping the coat off my back. "I do understand you, Stephen."

Without the coat I feel even colder. I pull my arms tight as the shivering resumes. Anne opens her coat wide. For a moment, I'm confused, then I understand. I step closer, and she enfolds me. I think of our honeymoon beneath the stars, sharing a sleeping bag, her naked breasts pressed to me, want surging through my body in electric waves. I believed we would go into that bundle as separate people and emerge as one.

"Thank you," I whisper. I work my arms around Anne under her coat. She leans her forehead to mine. Life didn't work out the way we planned in retrospect, but who's to say it won't this time?

"This is what you should write about," Rose says. "You've had quite a year."

Indeed.

Families

by Gay Degani

Friday, 19th December 2014

On the creek side of the Old Road, the sun dips behind the wild growth of the arroyo and hills beyond, cooling the warm California afternoon. Jamie, sitting across from Gus German on the porch of his bungalow, stops shuffling cards, places them on the small table, and zips up her sweatshirt. She glances over at Lily and Collin, her two little kids rolling down the knoll of dirt and weeds where their bungalow used to stand before a giant oak, uprooted by 100 mile an hour winds, smashed it to matchsticks back in January.

"You gonna deal those things?" asks Gus, his dog Gracie propped on his lap. His voice is gruff, but Jamie knows he's harmless. Like so many old men who haven't lived with a woman for years, he's forgotten his softer, kinder voice. Of course, Gus may never have had that voice. He certainly doesn't have it for his son, Mars.

"Hey ho!" Sybil hollers as she emerges from her own bungalow.

Jamie twists in her seat. Laughs. "What've you got there?"

Gus mumbles under his breath and Gracie perks her head.

"Martinis! It should be egg nog, I know, but it's still too warm to break out the heavy stuff." Sybil moves carefully down her front stairs and starts across the courtyard. She's wearing one of her sarongs, its slit up the side not quite high enough to allow for anything but geisha–girl steps. Jamie scoots out her chair and hurries to help, taking the loaded tray from Sybil when she reaches her.

Arriving at Gus's bungalow, Sybil asks, "How's Mars these days?"

The old codger doesn't answer, again making Jamie wonder why he hates to be around – let alone talk about – his son. Jamie says, "He's helping Ian flip a house over on the Northside."

When Sybil's eyebrows shoot up, Jamie knows what she's asking, with whose money, and shrugs. Sybil angles her chin toward Gus, but Jamie shakes her head as she puts the tray on top of the cards.

"Hey!" grouses Gus.

"Oh, have a drink," says Sybil.

Jamie does the duty, pouring martinis from the pitcher into small juice glasses. A jar of green olives perches on the edge of the tray, but no toothpicks, so she fingers out two, drops them in, and hands the first glass to Gus, which he takes, sniffs, then sips, a "Hmmmm" of reluctant satisfaction slipping out.

"He and Ian are doing it. Maybe Ian's mom lent them the money." Jamie pours one for Sybil and offers her the chair.

"Thank you, sweetie." The older woman sits and raises her glass to Gus. He grunts, raising his own in return, frowning at the tray still covering the cards.

Jamie plops onto the porch's top step, grins at her kids who are chasing around the weedy dirt where her own bungalow used to be. "What're you going to do with that spot, Sybil?"

"Not going to rebuild, that's for sure."

"We should plant a tree there," says Jamie. "A Christmas tree, and that way we can decorate it every year, right out there on the lawn."

"Christmas trees don't look good in people's yards," mutters Gus.

"What do you have against Christmas trees?" asks Sybil.

"I don't, but it'll stick out like a sore thumb all year long. Get one of those deodars they got up there north of town. Plant something like that."

"Those are too big. Maybe just a pine. A regular pine, the kind with long thick needles. We can still string lights on it." Sybil squints as she talks, like she's trying to visualize, then says to Jamie, "There're two juice boxes on the tray for the kids."

"I saw those. Thanks," says Jamie. "Don't want to call them over just yet. They're having so much fun. So strange to be back, Sybil. Thank you for letting us move into Mrs. Renke's."

"Not a problem. Glad you got back when you did."

"Oh good God," grunts Gus.

Jamie glances at the old man, his mouth a scowl.

Collin yells, "Mom, Mars is here!"

Of course. Gus's son. She doesn't understand it. Not really. Why Gus and Mars don't get along. When she'd first met Mars, he'd made her nervous with his beseeching eyes, and Gus seemed almost proud of him. Now almost a year later, he regards the man with what amounts to disgust.

Mars lifts Collin and swings him around, then follows the boy over to the mound of weedy dirt where they both get down on hands and knees. Lily scrunches her face, arms folded tight against her chest. Bugs, thinks Jamie. Collin and his bugs.

She glances at Gus. He's staring into his juice glass of vodka. What happened between the two while she and her kids had been away? A murder, for one, a neighbor woman strangled and dumped in the arroyo across the street. The cops picked up Mars because he was an ex–con, in prison for robbery, maybe more than one, but when they couldn't find any evidence he'd had anything to do with the murder, they let him go. Maybe Gus still believes he's the one, but Jamie doesn't think that's possible. Mars is kind and patient with the kids. He likes her and she's beginning to like him, but she's careful now. One failed marriage is enough.

When Mars stands, he brushes dirt from his pants and waves. Jamie waves back. The kids race toward the porch. Gus bolts up, his face purpling, knocking over the table, tray and glasses crashing to the porch floor. With Gracie in his arms, he stumbles into his bungalow and slams the door.

Handing the kids their juice boxes, Jamie sends them back to their bugs. As soon as they're gone, she helps Sybil clean up the mess, crouching down, tossing shards of glass onto the tray, not wanting to look at Mars. He says, "I should go."

"No you shouldn't," says Sybil. She touches Jamie's head and turns to pound on Gus's front door, saying, "I'm coming in, you old coot."

Once Sybil's inside, the door closed, Jamie looks at Mars, whispers, "Has he always been this way?"

"Let's talk on your porch."

Sitting on the bottom steps, Jamie and Mars watch the kids march around the courtyard in a game of follow-the-leader, Collin matching each of his sister's hops, jumps, and arm waves.

Without looking at Mars, Jamie asks, "So why is your father so –"

"Angry with me?"

Her eyes meet his, and she realizes she wants there to be a compelling explanation.

"He blames me for my mother's death."

"Why?"

The streetlights glow up and down the Old Road as a breeze rustles through the neighbor's camphor tree. Jamie hugs her knees.

Finally he says, "I don't know. I liked to take things. Steal things. I was always in trouble. Don't really know why. Ran away from home a couple times. Didn't finish anything I started. Maybe I was ADD. I don't know."

Jamie shivers, waits. The kids lie still on the lawn, talking, giggling.

"So I was fifteen, I got this girl pregnant. You have to understand. My mother, she went to Mass every day, ran the women's league, sewed altar cloths, and she was humiliated. She locked herself in the bedroom and wouldn't come out. I ran away. I don't know which shamed her more, having a bastard in the family or a coward for a son. She took a bunch of pills. They couldn't save her. Gus. He found me, beat me up, dragged me to the funeral."

Jamie rests her hand on his arm. Squeezes. Still he doesn't look at her.

"When I was eighteen, I left and we didn't talk to each other for years. Then when he got sick, I came back and we got along for a while, but I wasn't ready to change yet. That's when I ended up in jail. That stint cured me. I think it cured me."

They sit in silence a moment or two, then the kids run up, blond hair haloed by moonlight. Jamie reaches out and gathers them close, Collin wrestling with her a little bit, but giving in. She turns to Mars. Their eyes meet again and she says, "Well, I guess we'll see, won't we?"

A stranger jogs along the Old Road, his attention drawn by the sound of voices. He slows, then stops, leaning over to rest hands on knees, breathing in and out, turning his head to stare at the family on the porch of one of four bungalows. They bunch close together as the woman points to the starry sky, the moon shining across her face. Jamie.

He smiles at the sudden hardness inside his running shorts and as he stands there, he slips his right hand inside. He won't make himself wait this time. He's waited long enough.

Feliz Navidad

by Sally–Anne Macomber

Saturday, 20th December 2014

To: Milton Flaxmill, Red Cow Publishing
From: Trudy Polaris
Date: December 20, 2014 10.19 p.m.
Re: Peek–a–boo

Øslø was a bust! How was I to know they give the *Peace Prize* in Øslø, and all the *other* Nobel Prizes in Støckhølm!? So I missed out, completely. Maybe next year will be better for me. I heard on the street and also in the corridors of the King Kristian XVII Hotel and then again on the ferry across the Øslø Fjørd to Høvedøya that they never give it to you for your first nomination anyway. Thank God I did not waste my Red Cow Publishing future expense account on that tacky ocelot dress.

And no, I didn't even check to see who won the awards I was up for, Literature and Physics, but they were probably won by someone unimportant and stupid and I am not bothered that I do not know who they might be. It matters not one whit. The future holds much brighter circumstances for me.

Some other news: my husband is in the local psychiatric hospital for tax evasion, back in the Tyrol. He's getting the best care the low Austrian schilling can give him.

I am also wondering if maybe the Himalayas (ie *Nuclear Fission in The Himalayas*) are a little ambitious for my *first* book. Maybe the sheer magnitude of those mountains turned the Nobel judges against me, you know, the new kid in town getting too big for her boots already. So a rethink on the Himalayas versus Pyrénées issue would be a good thing. *Definitely* a good thing. Something smaller and subtler would be advisable. Maybe the Pyrénées are too big too.

What do you know about the Dolomites?

I have to say Boston is so *lovely* in the lead–up to Christmas!

As the year draws to a close, I find myself reflecting on the last 12 months and I can't help but marvel at the resilience of the human spirit in the face of countless setbacks. Or continued neglect. More specifically, *my* resilience in the face of countless setbacks and continued neglect. 12 months of being ignored? In my book, that's a record!

The greatest Christmas gift you could give me would be a sign from you – maybe even a meeting.

There was no plaque on the building when I arrived at 10.00 this morning here on Mount Vernon Street, but a sixth sense told me that Red Cow Publishing is on the 6th floor. I walked in and was surprised to see the receptionist wearing white, disguised as a dental nurse.

She said Red Cow Publishing had gone bankrupt and left Boston, maybe even left the planet but I know that behind that sterile white door there's a lot of book publishing activity going on. Even on a Saturday. *Especially* on a Saturday. I could smell the printer's ink disguised as amalgam!

I told nursey I wanted an appointment to get my teeth cleaned, and sat down while she pretended to look on the computer and book me an appointment. So I just hung around for a while in the waiting room and when I knew she wasn't looking (because her white cap had disappeared behind the computer screen – I am sure she was feeding her smack habit when she thought I couldn't see her!) I snuck into the restroom (as you so quaintly call them here), hid in the storage cupboard and that's where I am now, 12 hours later.

Luckily I brought my mega–foldable camp stove with me and a blow up–sleeping bag and astronaut food pills (along with my laptop, of course!) and once I sign off this email I'll get the kinks out of my back and set up camp on the restroom floor.

I'll be here when you get in first thing Monday morning.

We may even have shaken hands by the time you open this email!

I'm easy to spot. I'll be the one waiting for you in the waiting room. With the laptop on my lap. And just in case a lot of your "patients" have laptops on their laps, I'll be the one sitting under the mistletoe with the Christmas sombrero on my head.

See you very very soon, Milton, and – oh, how I can't wait! – in full sound and 3D!

Much love,

Trudelein xx

PS: It would be best to cancel all your appointments for Monday morning, as we really do need to knock the editing of my book, whatever it's going to be called, on the head.

Cruisin' on a Sunday Afternoon

by Mandy Nicol

Sunday, 21st December 2014

My heart's racing, I'm short of breath.

I watch the clouds through the window and wish I could gulp in some fresh air. I imagine I'm walking in the bush with Peregrine who's racing around barking at startled rabbits and cockatoos and blue tongue lizards. It doesn't help.

The guy on my right keeps fidgeting and sighing and checking his watch. He's not helping either.

I didn't think I'd be like this.

I had no fear of flying.

So maybe I'm worried about something else. What if I don't like Sydney? What if I don't like bobbing around on the ocean? What if I don't like the job? What if I don't *have* a job? What if I misunderstood? What if I've made it all up? What if I am mad?

I snatch my new iPhone out of my bag, fiddle around to find the text:

Nadia when can U get here? Get passport sorted.
Want to pop U on Noumea cruise Jan. nevil wu

I *do* have a job. I make a snorty chuckling noise and the guy on my right peers at me with his nose screwed up like I'm another of his problems. If he didn't look like an angry camel I'd tell him all about my job. How I stumbled across it on the internet:

> *Expert tailor / dressmaker wanted for fitting and making alterations to show costumes for cast members on board cruise ships.*

It sounded like a career you dream about. Apparently cruise ships stage a great variety of shows these days, from Broadway plays and musicals to Aqua Theatre. I could be paid to help people dress up like pirates and princesses while cruising around the ocean visiting tropical islands.

So I sent off my portfolio to Nevil Wu Costume Designs.

And then I realised I'd have to move to Sydney.

But I convinced myself that I wouldn't get the job so I didn't need to worry about it.

And then Nevil Wu rang and raved about my work and his work and how much fun it all was working with fabric and colour and actors and theatre and how he could use me as a designer as well and we may in fact turn out to be kindred spirits and did I believe in kindred spirits and when I said yes he said see there you go I knew it and when I said I didn't know a soul in Sydney so how could I possibly move there he said pffft and gave me contacts for share houses in Lilyfield and Camperdown so I said yes I'll come as soon as I can.

When I told Mum she surprised me. She smiled and gave me a hug.

We had an early Christmas and Farewell Nadia family do.

Celeste said I was mad, leaving everything I know for God Knows What and So Far Away. Then she asked what discount I get for family.

Anthony said I'm a crazy lunatic acting like a ten–year old kid running off to join the circus. Which I sort of *am*. I think he was mostly bummed because he had me pegged as housekeeper for his newly envisioned Agri–Tourism arm of his Grand Farm Revamp.

Mum told him to stop ragging me. Told him I was obviously a creative genius – ok, she might not have said genius – and that he should be happy for me. Told him it was high time I got out and saw the world. Told him if you stay in the same spot too long you get pins and needles. Then she told him to put the kettle on.

It was at that moment that I thought I might miss her, one day.

I know I'll miss Peregrine but at least he's attached himself to Anthony so I hope he won't miss me too much.

I doubt I'll miss anyone else, which is sort of sad.

The Fasten Seatbelts sign comes on and that's what I do, I fasten my seatbelt.

The End
by Margaret Bingel

Monday, 22nd December 2014

Nadia is sleeping next to her owner, kicking her legs as she dreams.

Ned, on the other hand, is wide awake, tapping his fingers to a tense rhythm.

Tap Tap Tap. His fingers march across his chest, like little toy soldiers.

Christmas is almost here. Even though he's way too old to believe in Santa, there's something about the one–week countdown to Christmas that really unsettles Ned. He can't sleep, he can barely eat, and he worries about whether or not he has the perfect gift for his mother. This year, Ned has bought her a new set of gloves, along with a card that says, 'Warm Hands, Warm Heart'.

He takes a deep breath and closes his eyes, envisioning his mother holding her boyfriend's hand with her newly–gloved one. He hopes Dr. Stanley likes the gift certificate to Nora's favorite restaurant he put in a blank card for him: that way his mother is guaranteed a good time. Ned knows that Dr. Stanley only wants to treat his mom like a lady, and he can respect that.

Ned reaches out to pet Nadia's back, her kicks dying with each stroke. He has set up a small tree on the floor for her to sleep under, and on Christmas morning he's going to hide dog treats in the branches. He found little candy cane–shaped snacks that he can't wait to feed her. He bought her a little hat too, which he rotates with the antlers and elf ears he makes her wear on their daily walks. Ned thinks it makes Nadia look more endearing, more lovable than she already is. She is such a good dog.

Waking up, Nadia looks at him with sleepy eyes.

"Come on, Girl, time to get up and go for a walk."

While Ned ties his shoelaces, his mind wanders back to Jeffery's party last Saturday, a big holiday bash where everyone brought their dogs and something to share. Ned brought soda, but forgot ice, so they had to use snow from outside. Jeffery was a really big sport about it, even warning people to not trust "dem drinks wid da yella snow!"

Shoes and coat on, and Nadia on her leash and wearing her elf ears, Ned steps outside, greeting the crisp, early morning cold. Through hell or 20 below, he takes his dog out for a walk. Ned lets Nadia choose the direction, and she pulls him east, toward the rising sun. Ned sees the icicles, so beautiful and prismatic this morning, glittering like perfect glass in the gaining light. Nadia pulls him along, sniffing anything, losing interest, and moving on.

What Ned doesn't see is a patch of black ice ahead. An unmoving slick of destiny, this puddle froze over the same spot where Ned fell almost a year ago. But there is too much for Ned to see and Nadia to sniff and sometimes you ignore what's coming up in front of you.

Ned places one foot right before the ice slick.

And sees his dog sprawled on her stomach, her paws slapping on the black ice. Ned bends down, puts his hand under her stomach and picks his dog up. Careful to side–step the black ice himself, he chastises, "You've got to be more careful, Girl. You never know when a slip becomes a fall."

Ned places Nadia on safer ground and tightening his grip on the end of her leash, they continue walking, east, towards the warming sun.

Beautiful Day

by Darryl Price

Tuesday, 23rd December 2014

It's a beautiful day, Doc. The kind of day that makes you feel like it's great to be alive, and that's what's so sad about it, I guess. I had a lot more to say to you in the lifetime, Doc, but I guess it'll have to wait. I'm not all that good at waiting around for something to happen.

Something has happened. Something that's very kind of big. So big, Doc, that it feels like the Empire State building in a room too small for even its shadow.

I don't want to say goodbye.

Goodbye doesn't work for someone you love so much. Does that surprise you, Doc? It shouldn't. It doesn't surprise me.

You brought that part of me back to life – the part that could feel things enough to love them, to care about what happens to them. How do you start to repay that with mere words?

If I thought they'd do the trick, Doc, I'd stay here all night and pour them constantly over your grave like soothing water.

But the truth is, they are only my selfish tears. I got a lot of tears for you today, Doc. Great big gobs of buckets of little girl tears that I can't seem to control right now.

Maybe I shouldn't have to.

You were my friend.

If you were here, Doc, I'd want nothing more than to shake your hand a good long time, but I can't. You always liked my words, so that's what I'm giving you now, Doc, one last time, the one thing you seemed to like about me the best. Right now I don't see it. I can't see anything. I'm blinded by this.

Thank you, my dear, dear friend, for being kind to me.

One last story, for old time's sake, Doc, just the way you like them: there once was two little boys who were very close childhood friends. They did everything together, went fishing, watched TV, talked about girls. You name it, they did it. The only problem was one of the little fellows was beginning to fade. He'd fade a little bit more each and every day. This alarmed his dearest friend to no end, but they never really spoke about it, but it was the really big question on everyone's mind, when would all this fading stop, and if it didn't stop soon where was it going to go to exactly, and to what lengths? The fading boy was fast becoming quite transparent in spots. Still he insisted on being treated like everyone else. Then one day all that was left were his hands, his smile, and his eyes. I guess I'm out of here, he exclaimed, and in a flash he was. The other little boy thought he should follow suit, but as hard as he tried, by scrunching up his own wet eyes and screaming real loud at the air, he couldn't make one bit of himself disappear. Over time the boy grew up. He never forgot his friend, he never would, and every now and then he still scrunches himself up in a sad attempt to wink out of the picture, too. Instead he got married and started a family of his own, who turned out to be all girls.

Good-bye.

Noel

by Teresa Burns Gunther

Wednesday, 24th December 2014

Susie's late as usual. I asked her last week if she wanted me to get her a date. She laughed, more like a squeal and said, "You don't do blind dates on Christmas Eve with family!" It used to bother me the way she thought everything I said was funny, but she says making people laugh is a gift. Who knew? She tells me she's bringing her co–star.

"The *sleazy doctor*?" I tsked. She has terrible taste in men, except for Steve, but he was gay and it didn't last.

"God, Rachel," Susie said. "It's just a role."

"But he has to know the part to play it."

"Well, I play a slutty nurse."

"True …" I say. "You are not a nurse."

Susie squeaks my name in outrage then she makes these funny noises. I ask if she's okay. She's laughing. She can't stop, she's talking, gasping and snorting and all I can make out is "crazy". I tell her to hang up and put the pedal to the metal, that I hate tardiness and I have things to do.

I finish setting the table while Kevin, in my apron, makes crostini and sings along to his cowboy music that is starting to grow on me. Another surprise, just like him. I'm wearing the red cowboy boots he bought me with my mini–skirt he likes. He sent me a link to an article about men who cook being sexy. Watching him now I have to agree. He looks good in the sweater I bought him, but my ruffled apron …? I pull another present from under my tree and make him open it. *Ho ho ho* he says, and hugs me. He likes everything I give him, even the gifts Susie says are dumb. But she's right about one thing: people love presents. I never knew how much I liked them myself. He pulls out the tuxedo apron and shouts a *yippe ki yay,* and whips off my ruffly one. I tell him I want to take him into my bedroom and … he shushes me, reminding me Mrs. Franklin is there. She sure is, listening to every word and grinning like a bad elf.

The doorbell rings. Gail, my officemate, hands me homemade brownies that look like she sat on them driving over. Her husband has a handlebar mustache. And people say I'm odd. He keeps pumping my hand saying how happy he is to meet me while Gail heads right in to check out my house.

Of course my father has to make an entrance with a big bouquet of flowers. He's wearing a shirt and tie and pulls a bottle of scotch from under his arm. Very good scotch! I thank him and let him kiss me and I'm surprised that I'm happy he's come. I introduce him to Mrs. Franklin who pats the couch next to her and says she'd like a word. *Give him hell,* I tell her. Dad, I agree to call him that tonight, pours me a drink and showers Mrs. Franklin with man attention, which makes me want suddenly to kiss him back. Mrs. F's cheeks glow, she pats her hair. She's flirting with my father! I serve the hors d'oeuvres. It's my first Christmas party, my last resolution of the year.

Kevin calls me to the door saying, "Larry and Joyce are here." I say So? Invite them in, but he tells me they have a surprise. They brought their plant with them? Weird. It's a baby tree, but they say it's a present for me! In a large pot, cobalt blue, my favorite color, with a big silver bow.

"It's a cutie tree, seedless tangies, your favorite!" Larry says, chest out, beaming, his arm around Joyce. He caught me pulling cuties off their tree once. Joyce hands me a bottle of wine, kisses my cheek and wishes me a *very Merry Christmas!* I'm so surprised my eyes sting.

"Say thank you," Kevin says. I do and they all laugh.

"Please come in. Merry Christmas," I say twice before I can stop myself.

Everyone's talking and laughing and drinking. Stella is on her best behavior until she puts her head on Joyce's knee! I tell Stella *No!* but Larry says, "Its alright, Rach," and scratches behind Stella's ears which she loves. Kevin plays corny Christmas songs on his guitar and it's just too much. I look at them all, happy, in my apartment, and I can't breathe.

I slip outside to my front porch and focus on the lights, trying to breathe. I squint my eyes at the houses on my street lit up with color. Kevin helped me put white lights around my windows. Even the Jewish family down the street has lights, all blue holiday solidarity. I think back on a year ago, my miserable Christmas. Alone. What a year: 2014. So much has happened. I wonder what resolutions I'll make for 2015, but I can't imagine things getting better.

A car squeals to the curb and Susie hops out in a short, glittery red dress. The *sleazy doctor* pays the driver. She introduces us. I start to tell him he looks shorter than on TV but stop myself. Susie looks worried.

"Why aren't you in your party?" Susie asks, looking worried. I tell her I'm waiting for her. I'm getting better at lying, an important part of people skills. She takes my hand and squeezes it as I lead them in.

Mrs. Franklin's delighted to meet Susie's date. She watches *As The Sperm Turns* religiously. She slides closer to my father and signals *sleazy doctor* to sit next to her. "My neighbor is a vamp," I say, caught up in the holiday cheer. Susie hoots and hugs me, tries to pick me up, staggering in her tiny heels.

"I have missed you, you nut!" she says and kisses my shoulder because she's such a shrimp, then hurries back to perch beside her sleazy doctor.

Kevin's watching me with those eyes. He's a looker. He wraps his arms around me and nuzzles my neck. "Nice party," he whispers. And I am thinking this is happiness until I hear Stella barking then a riot of chicken noise, squawking and squealing in Larry and Joyce's garden.

"Who let my dog out?"

Morgana Malone and the Promise of 1000 Tomorrows

by Matt Potter

Thursday, 25th December 2014

"One big fantastic time we be having," Ludmilla says. Greasy grey–brown hair sticking out from under her bearskin hat, she sucks on her Christmas cigar. Clouds of eau de old–shoes–left–for–too–long–in–a–mouldy–wardrobe puff past my face.

"Christmas in July in June? No!" Now Ludmilla stomps her feet on the grey paving then throws her arms out like she's about to break into a show tune. "No no no! Christmas in December in Paris!"

Who would have thought?

Paris!

with Ludmilla!!

on Christmas Day!!!

Through my glasses, the high, wide entryway on the opposite side of the Louvre courtyard grows closer and closer with each stride.

I am not interested in why my former housemate and fortune teller is trying to be amusing. Nor am I interested in her wheezing or why she smokes celebratory cigars on Christmas Day. All I want to do is fasten the padlock on the famous Pont des Arts, then throw the key in the Seine. A photo of the padlock on the mesh railing glistening in the winter sun would be a bonus, but my camera is nestled in my suitcase back in our twin share at the Hotel d'Arabesque so I'm not counting on anything. It's just bridge, lock, throw. Anything else is a miracle.

I pick up speed, heels scuffing on the grey stones louder and louder and faster and faster.

The padlock weighs down the pocket of my puffy beige coat, banging a rhythm against my leg. And my fingertips are pink through fingerless gloves as I stride through the covered entryway, beneath hundreds of years of history (not that I'm interested in any of them), and step outside the Louvre. Ahead, I can see the famous pedestrian bridge and only metres away, catch a glimpse of the river.

"Wait!" Ludmilla calls out behind me. "Why you hurry? Bridge is falling down?"

I resist the urge to hurl a crack over my shoulder about this being Paris, not London, but western European bridge jokes are probably beyond her.

She's still yabbering on. "Stop! Why you be the bitch who stole Christmas?!"

God? fate? traffic? is with me as looking straight ahead I step off the kerb, no glance left or right, and onto the zebra crossing. My hair is short now, the leftover orange bob gone, chopped out, replaced with a brown and grey–streaked au naturel pixie cut, an early Christmas gift / holiday surprise / life–is–really–good celebration I gave myself two days ago. The puffy collar is warm against my neck as I hunker inside the coat.

And I'm charging, heels echoing on the black and white stripes and Ludmilla, who has kept me company ever since we left Adelaide at 10.35 last night, flying Emirates to Bahrain and then to Charles de Gaulle Airport, her gasps and wheezes and coughs grow fainter with each stride.

("No wondering no sheikhs are coming here," Ludmilla said as she sat beside me on the Emirates flight. "You looking like

Lebanese butcher." Then I shuddered as her hand ran up the back of my hair. "Your head is full of pricks.")

Bridge. Lock. Throw.

I will have a bruise on my thigh from the padlock bashing against it – the padlock's large and gold, though not gold just golden, maybe brass, maybe just wrapped in gold foil, I don't know but it *looks* gold and it has our names engraved on it.

Perhaps if I keep walking I can make London by sundown, or sundown tomorrow given it's winter and it gets dark by 5.00pm according to the internet.

Maybe I can escape Ludmilla.

Last night, I caught a cab to Adelaide Airport. *Meet me inside the international departure lounge,* Barry's text had said.

My armpits were sticky with the summer heat as I walked through the echoey terminal. And a grin spread across my face as all other travellers' noise faded away and I saw Barry standing outside the Customs check–in, in profile, high cheekbones on a thin face and short dark hair atop deep brown eyes.

But then he turned and it wasn't Barry, it was Grigor. His twin. Cheeks smoother than Barry's, nose finer than Barry's, forehead blander than Barry's … and he smiled when he saw me.

"Morgana," Grigor said, "it's good you could make it."

(What else was I going to do? On our two–week anniversary Barry bent down on one knee and said, deep brown eyes looking straight into mine, "Susan, you can sing carols at Christmas dinner for my homeless mates at the Whitmore Square Shelter, and I'll organise a screen for you to stand behind so you won't see their faces watching you while you sing" – which was tempting – "or we can fly to Paris on Christmas Eve and have croissants by the Seine on Christmas Day. You choose.")

"Where's Barry?" I asked. I would have fluffed my new hair except it's so short there isn't much to fluff and my hands were full holding my new puffy coat (bought just for Paris) and my carry–on luggage heavy with the three layers of winter clothes I'd packed to change into on the plane.

"In hospital," Grigor said, his deep brown eyes looking straight into mine. "Having a bit of a Christmas episode."

And then I saw Ludmilla standing behind Grigor, just as Grigor took my hand in his. Which was awkward as it was my left hand, half–buried under the puffy coat.

"Barry's fear of flying and of being trapped in confined spaces for a long time have taken their usual toll and he's having a rest on the psych ward," Grigor said. "It's a Christmas tradition. Although his fear of tinsel is new."

The puffy coat slid off my arm. "Barry flies to Paris every Christmas?" I looked down at the coat, pooled at my feet.

Grigor nodded. "He attempts to, yes. Barry's trip to Paris is a work in progress."

My hand slipped out of Grigor's clasp, just as Ludmilla peeked over his shoulder. "Barry ask me to Paris to go for him," she said.

"But I was with Barry this morning. We picked up my new passport together."

Grigor patted my hand. "Barry knows how to manage his illness. He knew weeks ago this would happen. And you can't fault his psychotherapy training, he recognises the signs."

"Barry give this for you," Ludmilla added, and handed me the padlock and key. The padlock was engraved with *Barry and Susan 25.12.14*, inside a heart. "He say, Tell Susan, Go! So I think you be this Susan."

I bent down to pick up the puffy coat. As I grabbed it, I saw a shiny new red and yellow overnight bag on the floor beside Ludmilla's feet. I stood up. "So this was all planned?"

"Go," Grigor said. "Don't even question it Morgana, just go." And then he added, "What other plans do you have for Christmas anyway?"

I did not expect to share my first visit to the most romantic city on Earth with Ludmilla. But maybe, while we were having our Christmas croissants by the Seine, I thought, I could give her the slip. Maybe push her in the river.

I opened my carry–on bag, took out my boarding pass and passport, and snapped it shut. I stepped around Ludmilla.

"I noticed your hair is no longer the colour of my favourite vegetable," Grigor said behind me.

I shuffled into the queue for Customs.

"It looks very attractive," Grigor said, "and not that masculine when you become used it."

Smiling at the woman in blue, I handed her my passport and boarding pass.

Thousands of padlocks glimmer in the muted sun.

Bridge. Lock. Throw.

My footsteps slow as I walk the Pont des Arts, wooden planks scuffing beneath my feet as I search the mesh railings for a spot for the padlock. The padlock in my coat pocket, banging against my leg and creating a bruise. The padlock Barry gave to Ludmilla, because he fears flying and cramped spaces and Christmas tinsel – haven't seen any tinsel in Paris so far, though I've really been too angry to look – to make the trip he'd planned for us both.

Bridge. Lock. Throw.

I thrust my hand inside the coat pocket. The padlock, key inside it, is cold against my fingertips. My eyes dart around the bridge, around the other pedestrians, searching searching searching the railings for a spot.

Bridge, lock, throw.

I spot a spot big enough to manoeuvre the lock into. Stepping up to the rail, I look over my shoulder towards the Louvre. Ludmilla, breasts bobbing, is heaving towards me.

This was supposed to be my moment with Barry.

bridge–lock–throw

And I don't want to share any more of this moment with Ludmilla.

bridgelockthrow

I'm standing on the bridge.

Bridge.

I pull the padlock out of my pocket, gold key still wedged inside it.

Lock.

The padlock is open so I snap it shut. I pull out the key. I see *Barry and Susan 25.12.14*, surrounded by the engraved heart.

Throw.

I swing my arm back and throw the padlock over the rail.

Throw.

I throw the padlock off the bridge.

Throw.

I throw the padlock off the bridge and into the river.

Throw.

I don't even hear the faintest plop as the padlock hits the water.

I look down. The key glimmers in my hand.

My head snaps back towards the Louvre. Ludmilla has stopped walking. Her mouth is open. Perhaps she is dribbling, or perhaps it is too cold to dribble. Either way, she is not saying anything and she is standing stock still, fur boots nailed to the wooden planks of the Pont des Arts.

My mouth is open too. But the insides of my cheeks are dry and my tongue is cold, so I close my lips and wait, arms by my sides. I think I might be pouting.

Burrowing into the neck of my coat again, I pull my bottom lip over my top lip and breathe out, my mouth a funnel, fogging up my glasses.

I can't see through the fog.

In Telluride

by Gary Percesepe

Friday, 26th December 2014

Gabrielle decided to meet me for Christmas back in Telluride, with Anna in tow. My ski partner and former college roommate Henry joined us, bringing his girlfriend Kate, thinking this was too good to miss. We booked a room in Mountain Village and settled in for the week. Christmas was weird, alternative and swell. Presents all around. The next day Gabrielle wants to ski backcountry, so we leave Anna to ski with Henry and Kate, and head out. We're an hour from Telluride when my phone rings. It's Henry.

"Gary, Frankie's here. She got in early this morning. I picked her up from the airport. Where in the goddamn hell are you? It's the fucking day after Christmas and you kidnapped the kid's mother? Are you fucking kidding me?"

"What the fuck! What is she doing there?"

"How the fuck should I know, man!"

Henry lowers his voice, and whispers, "She's your wife, remember? Where are you guys?"

"We're getting close to Ouray. Is she there next to you?" I ask.

"What do you think?"

"Put her on," I say.

Gabrielle glances over at me from behind the wheel. She accelerates smartly into a curve, pushing my shoulder into the car door. I grab the handle above the window and drop the phone.

I pick the phone off the floor. Its silver skin is nicked from a hundred drops. The small screen is smudged with fingerprints.

"Frankie," I say.

"Gary?"

"Yes."

"Did you drop the phone?"

"Yes. I'm sorry. We hit a curve."

"Is Gabrielle driving?"

"Yes."

Silence on the line. "Listen," she says. "Is it OK if I stay in the hotel suite with you all tonight?"

I hesitate a second too long. I register the mistake, but hesitate some more, compounding the error. Then say, enthusiastically, "Of course." Which sounds idiotic.

Gabrielle pokes me in the ribs. I frown and cover the mouthpiece. "What," I say to her.

"What?" says Frankie.

"Nothing. Sorry. Sure, it's OK. It's not a problem at all. I want you to."

"Good," Frankie says. "Because there are no rooms in Telluride over the holiday. You guys are the local Hilton."

Gabrielle pokes me again. "What's she saying?" she asks.

I cover the mouthpiece again. "We're the Hilton," I say.

"No fucking kidding," Gabrielle says.

Gabrielle arches an immaculate blonde eyebrow.

"Ask her where she's going to sleep," Gabrielle says to me.

I make a quizzical face, and then cover the phone up again.

"Jesus! Gary. We don't want a No Room At The Inn scenario, do we. Which room does she want? There's not enough room for everyone to have their own room, duh. Does she expect to sleep with you or what? How does she feel about the couch?"

I shake my head, no. As in, there is no way I am asking that question on this phone.

Silence again on the other end.

Gabrielle takes the phone. She checks the Motorola's bars for reception, and then quietly kills the call with one manicured finger. But she goes on talking into the mouthpiece.

"Hi, Frankie, this is Gabrielle Marceau. I've kidnapped your husband but I'm returning him in a few hours, intact for the most part. Do you still want him?"

She snaps the phone shut and drops it in my lap. Then she steers the Range Rover into the lighted island of a Conoco station.

"Do we need gas?"

When that gets no response I say I'm sorry.

"Yes. Never the fucking less, we got us a housing situation here," Gabrielle says. She ticks the ash from her cigarette.

I am officially rethinking my lose–your–life–in–someone–else–for–a–while theory.

We pull into Telluride, opting to take the stairs up to the suite. I slip the key card into the slot, and push the heavy door open. It's quiet inside, and there is no one to greet us. It smells like vanilla. A single candle burns on the coffee table. We walk into the kitchen. Frankie stands at the stove. She's wearing a boyfriend blazer over a sequined T–shirt, black jeans and boots, stirring a saucepan with a whisk. She wipes her hands on her jeans, and then holds one out for Gabrielle to shake. "Hi, I'm Frankie," she says. She pecks me on the cheek.

"What are you cooking?" Gabrielle asks.

"Baked ziti, garlic bread," Frankie says. "Something simple. Tossed salad. A bottle of good Chianti."

"You've been busy," Gabrielle says.

"There's a great market in town. Henry and the others are still out skiing. I thought it would be fun to eat in tonight, instead of going into town. Did you guys eat?"

"We had some lunch on the road, thanks."

There's a saucepan simmering on the stove. "What's this?" I ask.

Frankie's pan is filled with white cream. She's got a carton of eggs on the counter, flour, salt, some oranges, and a box of chocolate. There's an open bottle of single malt scotch next to the stove. Her blazer is a gray pinstripe with narrow lapels.

"It looks like an orange and chocolate soufflé you've got going," Gabrielle says.

"That's my favorite," I say.

"I know this one," Gabrielle says. "I have it in a book somewhere at home in Greenwich. Here, let me help you."

Gabrielle takes the carton of eggs. She opens two or three cabinet doors and finds a mixing bowl. She starts separating the eggs. The yolks slide from their cool white shells into the clear Pyrex bowl.

Frankie uncaps the scotch. She opens the refrigerator and takes out a tray of ice. Then she shakes her head, and puts the ice back. She grabs three tall glasses and places them in turn under the refrigerator's ice maker. The ice clinks into the glasses in a satisfying way. She asks the two of us if we want water with our scotch. We both shake our heads.

"Salut!" I say.

We tap glasses.

A few minutes later we tap again with new ice, then repeat.

Frankie laughs at something. She begins to whip the egg yolks. She has a Cameron Diaz laugh, filled with mischief and surprise. I stare at her ass in the black jeans. I am pretty sure they are new jeans. Ditto the boyfriend blazer. The boots I recognize. Around her neck and in her ears are diamonds I gave her from previous Christmases.

Next to her, Gabrielle whips the egg whites. I refresh our drinks. We work as a team. The cream bubbles to the top of the saucepan. Frankie lifts it off the gas burner. Gabrielle adds the eggs. Frankie pours in cognac, and then bends low to smell. "Mmmm," she says.

Gabrielle shreds the rind of an orange while I melt bittersweet and semisweet chocolate in a small saucepan. Frankie comes up and dips her finger in the pan and puts her finger to her mouth. The tips of her fingernails are pure white, a French manicure.

The egg whites are foamy. Frankie adds sugar, beating the mixture until it is stiff. She folds the whites into the chocolate mixture. Gabrielle dips two orangey fingers into the chocolate. Frankie grabs her hand and pulls the chocolate finger to her lips. Then she turns to me and says, "What a charming family you've found, Gary. *La jeune fille et sa belle mere.*"

Which for some reason cracks Gabrielle up. She goes into fits of laughter, braying loudly, bent at the waist. Her blonde hair scrapes the saucepan, dipping the ends brown. Which makes us all laugh harder. Frankie reaches in and smears Gabrielle's cover girl face with chocolate. Gabrielle hand wrestles her, their chocolate fingers laced together, and backs her down over the counter. She's got three inches on Frankie, a longer reach, and, I'd guess, ten pounds. I shake my head and pour a fourth glass of scotch.

There's an old Woody Allen line, where he says, "I was always better in my art than I was in my life." In my California filmmaking days I used to think about that line. I watch these two women's performance, if that's what it is, and think about shooting them, in this kitchen light, my head a whirring camera. But the light's not right and I'm starting to lose my buzz. They're just playing, but I don't feel part of the game.

I know I'll immediately regret it but I ask anyway. "So Frankie, how was the bag boy?"

Frankie looks past Gabrielle's shoulder, at me. Gabrielle starts to pull away but Frankie keeps hold of her hands, and pulls her back in. "He wasn't bad, actually, but I'd rather kiss her." Then she does.

This time I laugh. And then I do shoot them in that light, a medium two shot, until they release. It's a stage kiss, but it's effective. I pour us all another drink.

De–Cloned

by Nathaniel Tower

Saturday, 27th December 2014

Samford is lying in a comfortable bed, a woman's arm draped over his chest. He wakes up stiff, unaccustomed to sleeping on his back. He glances at the woman and smiles to himself. Gently, he removes her arm from his chest and scoots himself off the bed, trying not to wake her. Clothes and used condoms are scattered all over the floor. Samford tiptoes around the room like he is maneuvering through a mine field.

"What are you doing?" the woman asks just as he steps into the master bathroom.

Samford stops in the doorway and glances back at her. "I'm taking a leak," he says. "But I'll be back for whatever you want in a second."

"Hurry up. I need a lot." She blows him a kiss. "In fact, I need it all."

Samford laughs and turns in a hurry, not wanting her to see his sudden erection even though she's obviously had it inside her plenty. He closes the bathroom door and struggles through a boner piss, the urine spraying in an uneven stream he can barely control. His dark yellow pee squirts onto the white porcelain, making him aware of his severe dehydration. He doesn't bother flushing or shaking off the drips.

Samford steps to the sink, his boner starting to shrink back to its small flaccid counterpart. Instead of washing his hands, he reaches for a pickle jar sitting next to the soap dispenser. He holds the jar up in the light, staring at the long metal chip inside. His lips mouth the long string of numbers.

Still holding the jar, he peeks out of the bathroom. The woman is uncovered, a hand gently caressing her crotch. Samford watches her until she notices.

"Knock it off, you perv." She doesn't stop touching herself.

"Want something bigger in there?" he asks from the doorway.

"Come give me everything you've got."

Samford drops the jar on the carpeted floor. As he bounds to the bed, his asshole seems to wink goodbye at the strange chip trapped in the jar. In a matter of seconds, his boner has returned to its full force. For the first time in his life, Samford knows exactly what to do with himself.

Gifts

by Kimberlee Smith

Sunday, 28th December 2014

In the kitchen, Mum has a tangled bunch of limp snakes in her hands. Taipan, Western Rattlers, and Death Adders. She shakes them loose into a cardboard box that has 'MASTER BEDROOM' written across it in square black letters, then looks at Etheline, who toddles toward her. Mum's expression – pinched brow, pursed lips – says *Don't come near. This is grandmum's work.* Etheline stretches out her arm, cups her hand as if it's cradling something precious, and then blows at her palm while she looks at her grandmum. Her eyes are pure golden amber; the sun shining into their kitchen has contracted her pupils to slits as thin as papercuts. She purses her lips and blows a kiss at Mum, and Mum raises her hands in front of her mouth, catches the kiss, and mimes gobbling it up. Then she turns back to the terrariums and collects two more handfuls of dead snakes. Those are the last.

Etheline stands one foot away from the meter–wide telly screen; so close her hair is full of static from the electricity. She has gone back to watching *The Wiggles*. It is a daylong marathon, interrupted only by having her diaper changed, her bottle filled with cordial, or plucking a Tim Tam from the box on the floor of the family room, which is peppered with crumbs. She is transfixed while Mum continues with the unpleasantries of this day, none of which includes properly cleaning the house. There is a nearly–empty bottle of gin on the kitchen table and a pot in the sink with spaghetti sauce crusted on it. Two plates with wormlike noodles glued to them sit on the draining board.

Dorothy the Dinosaur is dancing up a storm: kicking her foot as high as it will go, which means the actor's cumbersome costume only allows it to go straight at the knee and no higher. She and the Wiggle in the purple shirt have their arms locked and are imitating dancers at the Moulin Rouge doing the can–can. The pirate jumps across the stage and plucks two large red feathers from his hat and hands one to each of them. They wave them around, apparently working hard to look silly, but it seems as if they're actually having fun. But they are actors, acting.

Etheline swings the belt from her bathrobe above her head like a cowboy lassoing. She shakes her other wrist, and the bracelet her daddy made for her from real snake rattles ticks, fast and noisy, like live snakes rattling. In the other room, Mum hears it over the cacophony blasting from the telly. She's unnerved by the sound of rattles these days. She's physically shaking when she hears it. And her eye twitches. She clenches her teeth. But she says nothing and lets the bub carry on, playing with the only friends she has, the ones on the television she's been watching, day in, day out, for weeks.

It's been just that long since she and Etheline returned from their road trip to find Brother Tom, using up a 36–pack of adult diapers, only stopping for petrol and to feed and change the bub. She kept herself going on caffeine pills. She didn't stop to sleep.

Now she's crippling herself with booze and alienation.

Mum's been in a catatonic state ever since she encountered Brother Tom's new family, helping deliver his wife Alice's newborn son and bury its stillborn twin, Jacaranda, my new baby here in the afterworld. I'm not sure she'll ever come out of it. She moves around like she's had a lobotomy. A botched one. She doesn't think or feel any more, other than yammering to herself and shooting poisonous looks at Etheline. Resentment.

Disappointment. Jealousy. She's accepting the minimum to get by: minimum sleep, minimum air, food, and substituting liquor for water. Always.

I try to reach out to her but she's not listening.

The bub often cries a little too long. She simmers in acidic diapers for hours, her tiny pink throat becoming swollen and pimply. Dry and angry. Her eyes don't spend tears. She cries now. And her eyes stay dry. She is sunburned. And what makes me crazy more than anything else, is that she has discovered fear. She acknowledges she is alone in her world.

What I want Mum to know is that we all have been renewed through a death. Even though I'm gone from the living world, and Brother Tom is gone from her life, Mum is no exception. Etheline can replace me, the daughter she lost. I've received the greatest gift I've ever known by way of the greatest tragedy of someone else's life. Jacaranda is not just my half-sister, she's my daughter. I wish there were a way for me to save Mum. And thank Alice.

I'm here for the long haul, looking over them all.

Lots of Ways to Die

by Vanessa Weibler Paris

Monday, 29th December 2014

There are lots of ways to die.

You can die of embarrassment. Seeing a woman in a doctor's waiting room, just the two of you there. Words are exchanged, with little sense and less connection, but you imagine yourself telling the story later on. To parents, friends, eventually children. "I was watching her read her magazine. I didn't even mean to say it out loud. I'm pretty sure she thought I was nuts!" Meet cute made meet–cuter by counterpoint. "I didn't even notice him; I really didn't. And then he suddenly burst out with – what was it? Something about January? I still don't really get it. But yes, nuts. I kind of thought he was."

Instead, the reality: she looks at you not just like you're nuts, but like you're a creep. Like you disgust her, with your bony body. You see her take a quick step back, nearly stumbling, and her head jolt back on its neck as though it's the latest dance move. You imagine dancing with her, high–school style, your hands faux–lding her waist while her arms circle your neck. 'Stairway to Heaven' is playing, and it's eight minutes long, long. But she looks at you, magazine forgotten, pupils pinpointing, heeled feet shuffling backwards, no story writing for friends, family, eventually children, and there, you die of embarrassment.

You can die of virginity. Can you? You turn pragmatic, looking for statistics to normalize you. "WELL," you imagine tossing off in a not–quite–condescending tone, "According to the Centers for Disease Control and Prevention, the average age Americans lose their virginities, defined here as vaginal sexual intercourse, is 17.1 for both men and women." You take a sip of your water, small so as not to choke, swallow and add, "The CDC also reports that virgins make up 12.3 percent of females and 14.3 percent of males aged 20 to 24."

"Your father and I saved ourselves," your mother whispers as you wish you were anywhere else but here hearing anything else but this, "we saved ourselves for marriage, for our wedding night, so special it was so special because we waited." But they were 22, your parents, you're nearly 30, none of this helps, and so you die of virginity.

You can die of diet, not that you ever would because you've spent your life trying to gain, but when your only work friends are women decades older who spend every day every week every month every year trying to lose that last five ten fifteen fifty pounds, you hear the angst fourfold. *If I have to eat another iceberg lettuce salad today, I will DIE.* Dead of diet. *If I don't lose at least half a pound after eating nothing but celery and poached skinless boneless chicken breasts all week, I will DIE.* Diet, die.

You can die of not aging. You can die young. You find yourself born on February 29, and then you don't have a birthday and don't have a birthday and don't have a birthday and then finally have a birthday, and then it starts all over again, for the rest of your life. You're nearly legal to drink but not quite qualified for kindergarten.

You can't die of being ugly on the inside, rupturing and infecting like sepsis. If you could, Iris would be long gone.

You can't die of being full of holes, nostrils and navels and marrow and pores. If you could, we'd all be dead.

You can die of water intoxication.

(You can.)

You can die of loss, of regret, of sadness.

(Can you?)

You can starve to death. Not accidentally, not circumstantially: *purposefully*. In the name of art. As a creative exercise. As a debt owed Iris. As a *favor*.

You can reverse things spectacularly, guzzling and binging, to show that you won't be an experiment, an exhibit, a pièce de résistance. You can Prader–Willi your way out, drown in a bottle of Dasani. A cure for curation.

Or .... you can just die.

Rewind the year that changed everything. Regain a bit of hope, not too much. Find your family. Find your friends. Make amends for what you gave up with her, for her.

Go back to being Slim Jim. Iris–free. Go back to that life.

Have beers with your buddies, when they can escape from their wives.

Crunch salad with the work ladies, and tell them they look thinner even when they don't.

Tend Dougie's grave, and apologize for not being there at the end, knowing you're already forgiven.

Eat cake on your birthday, every four years.

Blow out the candles, smiling faces flickering around you, wishing for nothing more or less than you already have.

All these thoughts float through your head as you sink back onto the white sheet, and the white pillow, and watch the white ceiling blur in and blur out, and your breathing slows ... and slows ...... and .... slows .... and your lungs rattle ....

And then you, eventually, uneventfully ..... die.

Endings and Beginnings

by Joanne Jagoda

Tuesday, 30th December 2014

"Hey Cass. Aren't you done? We should be at Denise's soon. She wants to leave by 2 so we make it to Tahoe before dark."

"Yeah, I'm almost finished."

"You're bringing way too much stuff."

"I know Rob, but I can't decide what to take."

"Why are you in such a crappy mood?"

"I'm uh, not in a crappy mood."

"Yeah, you are. You've been so quiet the last couple of days. I know you, and you can't fool me. Stop with the packing and you're picking your cuticles."

Cassie blurts out, "I did something sneaky ... behind Mom's back."

"Ooo ... this sounds too good. You, Cassie, the Perfect Donaldson Daughter??? Come on Cass, *what* did you do?"

"Rob, I'm serious. Mom got a letter and I hid it from her."

"Go on."

Cass digs under a pile of clothing in her top dresser drawer. "Here … it came a week ago. I was curious when I saw the envelope."

Robin picks it up and notices the postmark from Scotland. "I don't get it. Mom doesn't know anyone in Scotland."

"Yeah, she does. Read it. "

Dear Annie,

I never regretted anything in my life but meeting you. I've lived one lie after another and never cared. The time I spent with you I saw what a real relationship could be. You trusted me, but I used you in the worst way.

I'm living in a tiny village near Dundee in Scotland. It's green and peaceful. I hike every day. It's not the Napa Valley but the countryside is lovely. You might be surprised that I'm working in a pub, minding my own business. For the first time in a long time I'm staying in one place. I have a small flat not fancy, but I don't mind it. I just wish I didn't have to be looking over my shoulder. I hope my former employers will grow tired of looking for me.

Annie, come to see me. I want you to meet the real me. I'm still discovering that person every day. I have sent you an open ticket. Write back to me. Give us a chance to start all over.

Yours, D

Robin raises her voice. "Shit Cass. He wants her to come to Scotland? What did you do with the ticket? That bastard!"

"I hid it in my drawer. I didn't want her to see it."

"Would she go to be with him? Leave us?"

"I don't know, Rob. I know she loves Sandy but … part of her thinks about Damon. One night she didn't see me but I found her looking at the pictures they took on their Napa Valley trip. She was crying hard, this sad silent cry."

"Do you think she cares about him? How could she after what he did to her?"

"I don't know, but I suppose he was exciting and not at all like Dad or Sandy. Rob, I didn't want her to get … uh … confused or tempted. I was afraid she might do it … go to him, leave us. I guess that's crazy."

"Cassie, you did the right thing. He was a sneaky, ruthless asshole. He would have hurt you or worse to get Grandpa's plans for the ransom. Now, you got him back good. Mom doesn't need to know about the letter and the ticket. It's our secret. Give me the ticket. Let me tear it up."

"Here it is. I feel so much better since I told you, sis."

"And I have a secret too, Cass."

"What Rob? You've got a huge grin on your face. Tell me right now."

"I wasn't supposed to but what the hell. Sandy and I went shopping for Mom last week. We picked out a gorgeous sapphire and diamond ring. He's going to propose on New Year's Eve, tomorrow night.

"Rob, I knew it. I knew it! Let's jump on the bed. Yahoo. There's your cell, Rob. It's Mom."

"Shhh, Cass. Don't say anything to Mom."

"Alo–HA, Mom. How's Maui?"

"Hi Rob. Ummm, this resort is luxurious … palm trees everywhere, atrium in the lobby, parrots in cages and white sand beaches. We have an ocean view suite and are sitting on our balcony now. I'm being very spoiled by Sandy. Going down for brunch in a minute, then we are having massages. When are you leaving for Tahoe?"

"Soon. Cassie has to finish packing."

"Promise me you won't be driving around tomorrow night. New Year's Eve is crazy in Tahoe … and the roads are slick and people drink and …"

"Mom, you've told us a hundred times. Bye, chill, have a good time. Say hi to Sandy."

"Bye Hon. 2015 will be a better year for all of us, I know it for sure. Love you guys."

Both girls yell into the phone, "HAPPY NEW YEAR!!"

§

It's 9PM in a little village in Scotland. It is raining hard. Damon Southeby is about to leave for his shift at the pub. He opens his mailbox at the end of the lane for the fourth time today, looking for a letter from Anne Donaldson. The mailbox is empty. He curses and slams the mailbox shut then takes out a disposable cell phone and dials a number.

"Yeah, it's me. I'll take the job. I'm ready to get back to it in 2015. Tell me the details."

A Road Through the Desert

by h. l. nelson

Wednesday, 31st December 2014

Dear Diary,

Right now, I'm in a car, hurtling through a hot desert. Temple sometimes smiles at me like she's the Louise to my Thelma. But we're not alone.

We've been driving this way for what seems like forever. But I know that can't be so. I remember Anne's party as if we were still there. The Christmas tree aflame, the ice sculpture melting in the blaze, and bodies writhing everywhere.

But let me rewind a bit so I can tell the story.

To take my mind off Brandon and the kids, Robin, Julie, and I helped Anne every week in November and December until the party. We were good little helpers to Anne's face, but took every opportunity we could to undermine Winter Wondersnatch. Without alcohol, Robin was even funnier, giving the caterer and designer the incorrect address, moving the specially–placed poinsettias and topiaries of mistletoe to the wrong places, then we'd watch Anne blow her top. I even hid her $400 cold cream. It has roe in it, for god's sake.

Besides that little incident, Anne thought we were so nice and helpful. It was all a ruse. We felt sure there was no helping Anne, and that she was going to get exactly what she needed.

Finally the big day arrived, and all of us showed up early to help get the tables set up, supervise the caterers (Yes, she ended up hiring multiples, "in case one of them screwed up"), and to lug the ice sculptures into their proper places. The centerpiece was a seven–foot installation, a huge chunk of ice that Anne had insisted the sculptor chisel into a family of swans. I'd handled that call myself. It was to remain curtained until the "Big Reveal," and I'd assured Anne that I checked it myself, that it was just beautiful and perfect for the party. She'd beamed, and continued barking orders at the caterers and florist, while the designer fumed. Many of them looked like they wished she was dead. I wished then that they could be there for the party, thought how bright their smiles would be after.

We also helped dump all the pounds of Swiss chocolate into the "chocolate mountain" that Anne had bought for the occasion. Most people just rent these things, but not Anne. I may have had quite a bit of the sticky, sweet stuff, shh. We had to turn the thing on several hours before the party even started, because it all had to melt in "cascading rivulets" down the "rocks" like Anne wanted.

Oh, and we spent hours putting together little waterproof votive candles, because Anne wanted to float them in the pool. Even though no one would be using the pool. It was December, for god's sake. Anyway, an hour before everyone was to arrive, we had to manually light each candle and set them afloat. I asked her why the staff couldn't help, and she said she didn't "trust those morons to do anything correctly." I wondered why the hell she hadn't fired them yet.

I'd handled the invitations. Or, rather, I stole several of the extras, then took them to the bar where I'd met Temple. Lo and behold, she was already there. And, of course, she said she knew I'd be coming. Nothing surprised me anymore where Temple was concerned. She said with a wink that she'd make sure her friends were invited.

Winter Wonderbread was looking like it'd be quite a good time.

Guests finally started arriving around 6 p.m., and Anne was still upstairs dressing. I let them in, showed them to the refreshments, and made sure the 12–piece string orchestra began their set. I poured the contents of a small thermos, secured from Temple the day prior, into the Waterford punch bowl while everyone else was occupied.

Julie stayed near the bar and refreshments, making sure guests were getting a large helping of the punch, which she was hawking as "Anne's own special recipe" and Robin near the large ice sculpture. It would not be unveiled until Anne had made her grand entrance, around 7 p.m. She'd given us explicit instructions.

A few things happened right about the time Anne descended like a queen down the massive staircase and through the French doors, trailed by a Korean lady–in–waiting, who held Anne's drinks, fetched her tiny bites of food, fixed her taped–up tits, and any other small whim Anne wanted fulfilled. The orchestra had begun 'The Swan' by Saint–Saens. So Anne was posing there, in a fur–trimmed (faux, but very real–looking, so real that she may have just *said* it was faux) short, deep–red jacket with beadwork, over a luxurious silver silk gown. She had on custom Cinderella slippers. Pretty, yes, but ridiculous. When she was there in front of the French doors, Temple and her friends came pouring out of the great room. Temple said, "Nice gown, Mama," grinned, and hip–bumped her way to me.

Anne's and the other guests' jaws dropped as the parade of what appeared to be prostitutes, druggies, and other unsavory types descended on the gathering. For a moment, no one knew what to do. Temple enveloped me in a big hug, smelling like wet earth and spices, and said, "*Now* it's about to be a party up in here." She smiled and turned away, but then turned back and, holding up a small black device, added, "Oh, and this little thing'll cut their cell reception so we can really party." Then she sashayed her tight–clothed ass away from me, to the beat of the cello and violin ensemble.

I saw Anne trying to escape inside, probably to find her cell or use her alarm system to ring the police, so I fast–walked after her, convinced her I would take care of it, then ushered her back outside to sit in the chair of honor next to the large ice sculpture. Temple and a thin woman in a leopard–print mini and a blonde wig were waltzing together with very serious faces, then they cracked up and gyrated instead.

I fixed a glass of punch, grabbed the mic from the orchestra, finger–motioned them to finish up their song, and strolled over to the sculpture, where Robin and Julie jittered, both smiling nervously, ready to pull the curtain aside.

Anne, in the seat of honor by the covered sculpture, leaned toward me and whispered fiercely, "Are the police on the way?" I nodded yes. "Thank GOD. I don't know how these people found out about Winter Wonderland, but this is the WORST."

"I know, it's terrible. Here, a drink to take the edge off. I put something special in it for you." I handed her a glass of punch and winked. She looked down at it, then up at me, so I smiled warmly at her. I'm pretty sure she figured I'd popped in a Xanax or two, because she downed the entire glass. For the tiniest moment, I felt bad for the spiked punch and for Anne, with her rich, but empty life. I saw Temple across the pool, standing tall and majestic near the chocolate mountain, her eyes closed and lips moving. I turned my attention back to Anne, and in that moment, I think I really saw her. Watching her scared face, in a flash of insight, I realized how very much Anne and I had in common. I didn't want to unveil the sculpture anymore. I knew then that Anne was already suffering, that I was suffering, and I no longer wanted to contribute to our shared pain.

That's when Robin gave the signal, and she and Julie pulled back the curtain. There stood, at seven feet tall, an incredible likeness of Anne, completely naked and looking back over her shoulder, a perfectly pink—colored circle of ice around her cold bleached anus.

There was complete silence for maybe ten seconds. Then someone vomited right into the chocolate mountain, and every person except the four of us ladies and the one who puked burst into uproarious laughter. Anne's mouth was almost big enough for me to crawl into, she was so aghast. She turned her incredulous expression toward me. By now, there were multiple guests puking. Some in the pool, others on each other, on the lawn and topiaries. It was the drug, coming out full force. "You," she said. "You did this." She looked like she would kill me.

I said nothing, just waited.

With that, Anne punched me in the nose so hard I fell on the sculpture. Right onto Ice Anne's back thighs, breaking her frigid legs, her freezing torso falling on me, knocking the breath out of my lungs as it shattered against my body and the lawn. The ice shards cut into my scalp and back as Anne jumped on top of me, slapping and punching me while screaming. Through Anne's thrashing arms, I saw Robin and Julie running to my rescue, but I managed to wave them off. They stopped and took in the improbable scene.

I had become the epitome of everything I'd always hated. I wasn't mad at Anne. I realized all of this while she was beating my face and chest with her fists. My blood spattered her silk dress and faux fur jacket and I started laughing. It was so ludicrous, all of it.

Anne stopped hitting me and I sat up. We both breathed in ragged gasps. The freezing air gave me clarity. I looked to her and, smiling, leaned over and gave her a big hug. She softened against me and hugged me in return. Then we both started laughing hysterically. Flat—out, no holds barred, belly—grabbing laughter. In the midst of it, she stopped and threw up all over her gown.

"Let's jump in," I said, nodding toward the pool. "Come on, ladies!" I yelled at Robin and Julie as I tugged my dress over my head while running toward the pool.

I cannonballed in, hit bottom, and surged back to the top. Robin, Julie, and Anne plunged in, in that order. We'd disturbed some of the floating votives, but others were still flickering, bobbing on the concussive waves. Beyond the pool, all around us, people were silent with big eyes, yelling, or vomiting. Many were curled into fetal positions on the lawn. Some of the unsavories were roving around, asking the guests if they were okay.

"I accept! I accept!" Anne yelled in the pool, and I knew her trip had begun.

"Are you okay?" Robin asked me, dog-paddling nearby.

I thought for a moment, feeling my swiftly-closing right eye and throbbing nose and jaw. "Yes. Absolutely." She and Julie looked relieved, and we watched the pandemonium as a group of the guests stripped off their gowns and tuxes and ran across the lawn and jumped over the fire pit. One of the naked men picked up a potted Christmas tree, lugged it to the bonfire, and tossed it in. The tinsel went up in sparks and sent plumes of black smoke toward the open sky. It was then that I saw Temple, backlit by the roaring tree, her arms spread wide and teeth gleaming in the night. Then she was leaning over the side of the pool, handing the three of us glasses filled with the pure drug mixture. She stroked my hair, her pupils reflecting the tiny votive flames. Robin, Julie, and I clinked our glasses together. I said, "To friends."

Temple, Robin, Julie, Anne, and I have been in this car, in the desert, ever since. We've all changed, in our own ways. Robin is so funny and vibrant, no longer angry. Julie has more gumption, speaks her mind like she never did before. They're both strong, fierce. Anne and I, we paint together. We create like twin artists, playing off each other. Not to be too hippy-dippy about it, but now she is like the other half of my soul. I guess hippy–dippy is okay sometimes, because I have seen many things over the last year, and I know there really is no going back. Not in the way you might think.

Dear diary, I don't need you anymore. I am complete now. But, I am completing you with this entry. I couldn't leave you hanging.

What I want to tell you is that us women will drive through this steaming desert forever, leaving a billow of dust behind. The road will stretch ahead, always, stretching us out beyond ourselves, and circling us back. That is not what is in question. What is in question is if we can make it through the heat and sand, tired and lost, until we find our way home.

Pedal to the metal,

Joan Colderman

Authors

Rachel Ambrose

is a twenty–something fiction writer from Connecticut. Her favorite season is winter, she enjoys well–made Manhattans, and she loves Southern fiction. Her work has appeared in *Crack the Spine*, *Exiles Literary Magazine*, and *The Colton Review*. She is currently at work on her second novel and she blogs at http://victorywhiskeyjuliet.tumblr.com.

Lynn Beighley

is a fiction writer stuck in a technical book writer's body. Her stories often involve deeply flawed characters and the unsatisfying meshing of the virtual and actual world. She has an MFA in Creative Writing and currently has 16 books published.

Margaret Bingel

is just a writer, living in Manchester, New Hampshire. She spends her time working at her father's beer store, art modeling, and writing (when she can). She doesn't have a website or a blog yet, but who knows, maybe she'll have one in the future.

Guilie Castillo Oriard

is a Mexican writer currently exiled in the island of Curaçao. She misses Mexican food and Mexican *amabilidad*, but the laissez-faire attitude and the beaches of the Caribbean are fair exchange. Plus, the bounty of cultural diversity inspires great culture-clash fiction. Guilie is currently revising and editing her first novel. Her short stories have appeared in *Fiction 365*, *Lady Ink Magazine* and *Pure Slush*. She blogs at http://guilie-castillo-oriard.blogspot.com.

John Wentworth Chapin

lives and writes in Baltimore, where he is too frequently starting Project B before finishing Project A. John writes non-fiction as well as fiction. Find him at http://johnwentworthchapin.com.

James Claffey

hails from County Westmeath, Ireland, and lives on an avocado ranch in Carpinteria, CA with his family. He is the author of a collection of short fiction, *Blood a Cold Blue*. His website can be found at http://jamesclaffey.com.

Gay Degani

has published online and in print including *The Best of Every Day Fiction* editions and her own collection, *Pomegranate Stories*. She is the founder-editor emeritus of EDF's *Flash Fiction Chronicles*, a staff editor at *Smokelong Quarterly*, and blogs at http://wordsinplace.blogspot.com where a list of her work can be found. She's had two stories nominated for Pushcart consideration and won the eleventh Annual Glass Woman Prize for her flash piece, *Something about L.A.*

Michelle Elvy

is an editor and writer who has meandered from the shores of the Chesapeake to New Zealand's Bay of Islands. Michelle has published poetry, short stories and non–fiction about travel, faraway places, food, motorcycling, slow travel, the kindness of strangers and raising children in unusual places for numerous literary journals and magazines in the US, Canada, Australasia, the UK and Europe. She edits at *Flash Frontier: An Adventure in Short Fiction* and *Blue Five Notebook*. She can also be found regularly at *Awkword Paper Cut*. More about manuscript assessment and Michelle's take on editing and writing can be found at http://michelleelvy.com.

Gloria Garfunkel

is a psychologist and writer with a Ph.D. from Harvard University in Psychology and Social Relations. A former psychotherapist, she has published many stories in literary journals and anthologies.

Teresa Burns Gunther

has had fiction and non–fiction appear in numerous literary journals and most recently in *Northwind Magazine*, *Bookslut* and *Best New Writing 2012*. Teresa is the Editor of *The Lakeside*, an online literary magazine, and she founded Lakeshore Writers Workshop in Oakland, California where she leads creative writing workshops and classes and works one–on–one with writers. You can find more information and links to her work at http://www.teresaburnsgunther.com/.

Gill Hoffs

lives with her family and an ever–dwindling supply of Nutella in the North of England. Find Gill on Facebook or as @gillhoffs on twitter, email her a dirty joke at gillhoffs@hotmail.co.uk, or leave a clean comment at http://gillhoffs.wordpress.com/. *Wild: a collection* was published by *Pure Slush Books* in 2012. Her non–fiction book *The Sinking of RMS Tayleur: the Lost Story of the Victorian Titanic* is out now from *Pen & Sword.* Feel free to send her chocolate.

Joanne Jagoda

of Oakland, California, took an inspiring writing workshop after retiring in 2009, and launched on a long–postponed creative writing journey. Since discovering her passion for writing, she has worked non–stop on short stories, poetry and non–fiction. Her work has appeared in a number of e–zines and print anthologies, including *Pure Slush* and *Idea Gems Magazine*, and she was a poet of the month for a Jewish news weekly in Northern California. When not taking writing and poetry classes, Joanne enjoys being a writer–coach for ninth graders, Zumba, and visiting her three grandchildren in Jerusalem.

Len Kuntz

is a writer from Washington State and an editor at the (currently on hiatus) online literary magazine *Metazen.* His work appears widely in print and online, and you can find more of his work at http://lenkuntz.blogspot.com.

Sally–Anne Macomber

was born and raised in Toronto, Canada, and studied journalism at Concordia University in Montreal. Her work on high fashion and the demise of haute couture has appeared in various online and print publications in both Europe and North America. She turned to writing flash fiction in 2010, and hasn't looked back.

Jessica McHugh

is an author of speculative fiction that spans the genre from horror and alternate history to epic fantasy. A member of the Horror Writers Association and a 2013 Pulp Ark nominee, she has devoted herself to novels, short stories, poetry, and playwriting. Jessica has had thirteen books published in five years, including the bestselling *Rabbits in the Garden*, *The Sky: The World* and the gritty coming-of-age thriller, *PINS*. More info on her speculations and publications can be found at http://www.jessicamchughbooks.com.

Gwendolyn Joyce Mintz

is a fiction writer and aspiring photographer. Her work has appeared in various online and print publications. In other incarnations, Mintz is a writing instructor, a teddy bear maker and somebody's grandmother.

h. l. nelson

is Founding Editor/Executive Director of *Cease, Cows* lit mag and a former sidewalk mannequin. Pub credits: *PANK, Hobart, Connotation Press, Metazen, Drunk Monkeys, Red Fez, Bartleby Snopes*. She's also editing an anthology which includes stories by Aimee Bender, Roxane Gay, Lindsay Hunter and other fierce women writers. Her MFA is currently kicking her ass. Tell her what you're wearing: heather@hlnelson.com.

Mandy Nicol

grew up in Melbourne, Australia and made a tree change to country Victoria in the mid-nineties – the decade, not her age. She has various animals including a flockette of pet sheep that are thankful for her vegaquarian habits. She writes short stories and loves flash fiction. *Pure Slush* is the first venue to publish her work.

Derek Osborne

lives in eastern Pennsylvania. His work has appeared in *Boston Literary Magazine*, *Bartleby Snopes*, *Literary Orphans*, *The Linnet's Wings*, *Pure Slush* and many others. To read more visit http://gertrudesflat.blogspot.com, or you can email him at derekosborne1@gmail.com.

Vanessa Weibler Paris

lives in Erie, Pa., with a guy, a girl, a boy, a bunny rabbit and a dog. She writes things both real (for work) and pretend (for fun). Her favorite things include hot peppers, bad puns, small-world stories, and tales with a twist at the end.

Gary Percesepe

is Associate Editor at *New World Writing* (formerly *Mississippi Review*) and a Contributor at *The Nervous Breakdown*. Author of four books in philosophy, Percesepe's poetry, fiction, essays, and interviews have appeared in *Story Quarterly*, *N + 1*, *Salon*, *Mississippi Review*, *The Millions*, *Brevity*, *PANK*, *Metazen*, *The Brooklyner*, and other places. His collection of short stories, *Why I Did the Grocery Girl*, is forthcoming from Aqueous Books. His poetry collection *falling* and his flash fiction collection *itch* were published by *Pure Slush Books* in late 2013. He has taught at Saint Louis University, Wittenberg University, and University of Dayton. He lives in Buffalo, New York.

Matt Potter

is an Australian-born writer who keeps a part of his psyche in Berlin. Matt has been published in various places online, and he is, rather amazingly, also the founding editor of *Pure Slush*. You can find more of his work at http://mattcpotter.webs.com/.

Darryl Price

was born in Kentucky and educated at Thomas More College. A founding member of L. Jack Roth's Yellow Pages Poets, he has published dozens of chapbooks, and his poems have appeared in many journals. He currently edits *Olentangy Review* with his wife Melissa.

Stephen V. Ramey

is an American author from New Castle, Pennsylvania. His work has appeared in many places, including *The Doctor TJ Eckleburg Review, The Journal of Compressed Creative Arts,* and *A Capella Zoo. Glass Animals,* his first collection of (very) short fiction is available from *Pure Slush Books.* Find him and more of his work at his website: http://www.stephenvramey.com.

Shane Simmons

is a self–confessed coffee shop writer who believes that regardless of quality, each paragraph penned should be rewarded with sweet treats (cake, muffins, Belgian waffles, etc). London–born, he ran away to Glasgow ten years ago. Since then he has expanded his waistline and he now blogs at http://scribblingsimmons.wordpress.com/.

Kimberlee Smith

is a writer whose poetry, essays, fiction, and creative non–fiction have been published in numerous literary journals and anthologies. She was awarded a residency to the Jentel Arts Program in 2013. She received her MA in English from the University of Sydney, a certificate in the Creative Writing Program through UCLA, and her BA in Journalism from the University of Southern California. She can do a headstand on a trampoline, kill a chook, and make hard cider from the apples in her orchard.

Andrew Stancek

was born in Bratislava and saw Russian tanks occupying his homeland. His dreams of circuses and ice cream, flying and lion-taming, miracle and romance have appeared in print in *LA Review, Windsor Review* and *New Sun Rising: Stories for Japan*. Among the many online publications featuring his work are *Every Day Fiction, Gemini Magazine* (Flash Fiction Contest Grand Prize Winner), *fwriction, r.kv.r.y. quarterly literary journal, Tin House, Flash Fiction Chronicles, The Linnet's Wings, Connotation Press, THIS Literary Magazine, LA Review, Windsor Review, Thrice Fiction Magazine, New Sun Rising,* and *Pure Slush*.

Susan Tepper

is the author of four published books of fiction and a chapbook of poetry. Her most recent title *The Merrill Diaries* (*Pure Slush Books*, July 2013) is a Novel in Stories that follow a young woman's adventures in love and lust on two continents, spanning a decade. Tepper has received nine Pushcart nominations, and one for the Pulitzer Prize in fiction. You can visit her website here: http://www.susantepper.com.

Nathaniel Tower

lives in the Twin Cities with his wife and daughter. After teaching high school English for nine years, he decided to pursue a career in writing / publishing / editing. His fiction has appeared in over two hundred online and print journals. His first collection of fiction, *Nagging Wives, Foolish Husbands*, was released in 2014 through *Martian Lit*. Nathaniel is the founding and managing editor of *Bartleby Snopes Literary Magazine and Press*. You can find out more about Nathaniel at http://nathanieltower.wordpress.com.

Townsend Walker

lives in San Francisco. His stories have been published in over fifty literary journals and included in seven anthologies. One story won the SLO NightWriters story contest. Two were nominated for the PEN / O. Henry Award. Four were performed at the New Short Fiction Series in Hollywood. He is associate editor at *Grey Sparrow Journal.* During a career in finance he published three books, on foreign exchange, derivatives and portfolio management. Educated at Georgetown, NYU and Stanford, you can find his website at http://www.townsendwalker.com.

Michael Webb

is continually surprised anyone is interested in what he has to say. He blogs at http://innocentsaccidentshints.blogspot.com.

Other 2014 compendiums from Pure Slush

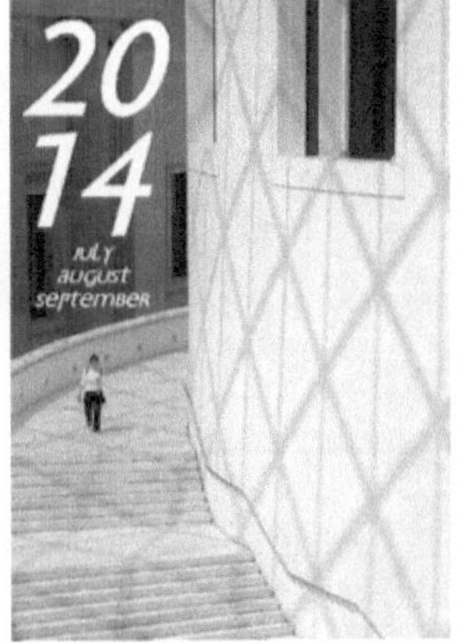

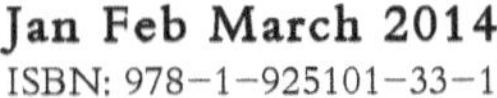

Jan Feb March 2014
ISBN: 978-1-925101-33-1

April May June 2014
ISBN: 978-1-925101-46-1

July Aug Sept 2014
ISBN: 978-1-925101-47-8

For the complete catalogue of
fiction and non-fiction
print books and eBooks
visit the Pure Slush Store at
http://pureslush.webs.com/store.htm

www.ingramcontent.com/pod-product-compliance
Lightning Source LLC
Chambersburg PA
CBHW030352030726
47497CB00002B/297

* 9 7 8 1 9 2 5 1 0 1 4 8 5 *